C000063081

1/4/13

ESTEBAN'S GOLD

by

Leslie H. Allan

**Grosvenor House
Publishing Limited**

This book is published by
Grosvenor House Publishing Ltd
28-30 High Street, Guildford, Surrey, GU1 3EL.
www.grosvenorhousepublishing.co.uk

A CIP record for this book
is available from the British Library

ISBN 978-1-78148-592-7

This book is dedicated to the memory of Edward (Eddie) Ingram

Acknowledgements

To Heather, my love and thanks for her wholehearted support in the production of this book

My grateful thanks to the 'Family Greaves' foursome for their inspiration

Sincere thanks to my fishing friend Peter Lloyd for the excellent cover design of this book

To all at the Caledonian St Andrew Angling Club, my appreciation for the friendship and fellowship that this great club generates

Preface

Flickering candles cast a dim light in the bed chamber of the newly-wed Senora Maria Cortez. The moving shadows settled on the figure of Father Tomas, the family priest, who stood against the wall nearest to the door. Crucifix in hand, and in a low voice, he quietly implored his God to bless the union between the elderly bridegroom Don Philippe Cortez and his young bride. Father Tomas was fully aware of the circumstances that had brought about this marriage, for he had taken the Confession of both. Maria was with child and her young lover, Esteban Santara, had fled the country with a price on his head, the bounty offered by a vengeful Senor Valdez, Maria's father.

The priest was a simple man who had total belief that the Almighty heard every prayer and would answer. It did not matter how important or insignificant the troubled persons might be, God would show the way. The marriage of Don Philippe Cortez and Maria was such a situation. The Don had recently lost his wife whom he had loved dearly, but who had been unable to produce an heir to carry on the family name and thereby inherit the considerable family estates.

Maria, a young woman of sixteen, was in the early stages of pregnancy. Her reputation and that of her family were in danger of ridicule and shame, in a society where honour was everything. The solution was therefore simple. The marriage would provide an heir for Don Philippe, hopefully a male, and for Maria a husband of considerable wealth and standing in the community. Father Tomas smiled inwardly with content. His God did indeed work in mysterious ways his miracles to perform. The priest's presence in the room was to provide a reliable witness to the consummation of the marriage. Once this had taken place he would sign a document to this effect. Any gossip that might arise from a 'premature' birth would be quickly quashed by the production of the document. It would also provide legal confirmation that the child was the true and undisputed heir to Don Philippe Cortez

Maria lay on the bridal bed. She had been washed and dressed by two maids earlier and now awaited the arrival of her husband. Her thoughts were confused and she was apprehensive of what was to come. Her father's angry words were never to be forgotten. She had sinned against God and shamed her family, and she must do whatever was necessary to undo the great damage her weakness had caused. She must undertake that which was required of her, with no regard to her own well-being. Her happiness was of no consequence. The safeguarding of the family reputation was the only consideration.

The minutes passed, and Maria was grateful for the draught one of her maids had pressed to her lips and urged her to drink before leaving the room. The maid's whispered words assured her that the potion would help Maria to relax.

In her half drugged state Maria was taken aback to find that Don Philippe had arrived in the bedroom unheard, and now stood by her bedside. He did not speak, but lowered himself upon her and in a surprisingly gentle way entered her. The act was over quickly and he rose and left the chambers, accompanied by Father Tomas. She was barely aware of the tears that ran down her face. A great tiredness overwhelmed her and she surrendered gratefully to the darkness and escape of a deep sleep.

The maid who had earlier provided the draught for Maria quietly entered the room. She tenderly covered the sleeping figure on the bed with a warming blanket and extinguished the candles, then without a backward glance left the chambers. Today had been an eventful one, but household matters were awaiting her attention, and she must complete these before she too could enjoy the warmth and comfort of her bed.

CHAPTER ONE

Senora Maria Cortez was dressed in black, confirming her status as that of a widow after fifteen years of marriage. It was late afternoon on a typical summer's day and her room overlooked the main plaza of the city. Maria observed the children playing, their voices faintly invading the chambers she had retired to since the death of her late husband, Don Philippe, three months previously. Further in the distance the Castell de Montjuic towered majestically above the surrounding area that was Barcelona.

Maria's thoughts however were on other matters. She turned to her solicitor, Senor Pedro Palacio, a friend and confidant of many years standing.

"So Pedro, I am a wealthy woman, and relatively independent. My son Hernando has become of age and inherited his father's title and property." Maria toyed with her rosary before she continued. "He is fifteen years of age and a stranger to me. It is clear that he has no regard or concern for my welfare. My time is now my own and this will enable me to give my attention to other matters that are dear to my heart. You know of what I speak my friend, for I have enjoyed your confidence since I was a little girl." She smiled wistfully and rose, moving gracefully nearer to Senor Palacio.

"I must find him, or learn what has become of him or I will never know peace," she stated with a voice intense with emotion. "You must know this," she implored her old friend.

Pedro Palacio knew only too well to what Maria referred, for it was he who had brokered the marriage of the pregnant young girl to Don Philippe Cortez, a man of sixty two. The Don had endured a childless marriage to his beloved wife who had died some years earlier as the result of a fall whilst out riding. Desperate for an heir, he agreed to marry the young Maria, subject to the utmost secrecy being observed regarding the true circumstances of Maria's pregnancy. The child, and any subsequent children, would belong to Don Cortez and be brought up accordingly.

Maria took no part in the discussions regarding her future, but had reluctantly agreed to the arrangements reached, having succumbed to remorseless pressure from her father, Senor Roberto Valdez. It was he who had placed a bounty on the head of young Esteban Santara who was Maria's lover and father of her child.

Despite his best efforts over the years, Pedro Palacio had been unable to uncover any information on either the well-being or whereabouts of Esteban. The youth was known to have narrowly avoided capture and death after landing in the southern Americas port of New Orleans, before fleeing northwards, his pursuers close behind. Maria had never given up hope of being re-united with her lover and lived for the day when they would be together once more. In the meantime she had faithfully kept her part of the marriage arrangements, and had undertaken the obligations of a dutiful wife to the best of her ability. Don Philippe Cortez was indifferent to Maria and regarded her as a means of providing the male heir he so desperately wanted. That the child might be a girl was never a consideration.

To the great delight of Don Philippe, Maria gave birth to a son. He was named Hernando and, all too quickly, his mother was denied access to her son. Maria was treated with courtesy but had no influence in the boy's upbringing. Hernando wanted for nothing, and by the time he was fifteen he had become a spoiled, arrogant and selfish youth, whose narrow views were imposed on those companions whose shallow existence depended on his beneficence. Maria was heartbroken but helpless to intervene, as any attempt to do so was ignored by Don Cortez.

Senor Palacio sighed deeply. He loved Maria as if she was his own daughter. It was his opinion that she was still young enough, and indeed beautiful enough to attract a potential husband. A pale smooth skin that highlighted her full red lips to best advantage matched her dark brown eyes and hair. Maria had remained as slim of waist as she had been in her teens.

Pedro stroked his grey goatee beard. He had already silently acknowledged that she would pursue her goal with or without his help. What could an old man do in these circumstances? He shook his head in surrender, for he knew that he would do whatever he could if there was the slightest chance that Esteban could be found.

"I can deny you nothing Maria," the old man said, "even although the chances of finding Esteban alive are extremely unlikely." He dared not say that if Esteban was still alive he might have made a new life for himself that included a family. Such a possibility was not an option that Maria would consider, so sure was she of Esteban's love for her.

During the years of her marriage to her late husband, Maria had planned for the time when she could openly attempt to trace Esteban's movements and ultimately discover where he was living. To be re-united with him was her sole purpose in life. She had for some years received regular tuition in English, as well as a good grounding in business skills, from a Scottish merchant, Mister Peter Lloyd. Together they had slowly and patiently built up joint business interests in the New World. Apart from a few minor failures their venture had flourished over the years and Peter was planning a journey to the Americas to consolidate their commercial position. Maria was adamant that this was the opportunity she had waited so long for, and that she too would travel with Peter to begin the search for Esteban.

"Please arrange for Senor Peter to receive me at his offices tomorrow. I would be grateful if you would accompany me." She smiled as she spoke, for the excitement of what she was planning was like a heady wine, and she was enjoying the moment.

—☠—

It was early afternoon on the following day when Maria and Senor Palacio were ushered into the cool offices of Lloyd Shipping Merchants. The building was situated a short distance away from the edge of La Ribera district, half of which had been cleared some fifty years previously to make way for an imposing fortress, El Cuitadella. The nearby port serving Barcelona was a surprisingly small one. The City Fathers had on numerous occasions discussed plans to extend the harbour areas, but despite this little expansion had taken place.

Senora Consuella Lloyd entered the comfortable room that was set aside for receiving special guests and greeted the two visitors warmly.

"Maria my dear, you are looking quite radiant. There is a sparkle in your eyes that I have not seen in a long time." Turning towards Senor Palacio she continued, "You sir are always most welcome here."

The old gentleman bowed deeply, a broad smile on his face.

"Thank you Senora, your beauty makes me wish I was much younger, and I would steal you away from the Scotsman you call your husband." All three laughed for they shared a deep friendship that had developed over the years that they had come to know one another.

At this point Peter Lloyd entered the room, and taking Maria's hand kissed her on both cheeks. Turning to Senor Palacio he shook his hand vigorously.

"Welcome my friends, it is always a pleasure for Consuella and me to have you visit us, even if Pedro tries to charm my wife away from me," he laughed.

The Lloyds made a striking couple. Peter was tall and only the slightest touch of grey in his hair hinted that he might be older than he first appeared to be. He was dressed smartly and moved in the relaxed manner of a man confident in his own ability. Consuella was a tall dark eyed beauty who looked ten years younger than her husband. Her slim figure was clad in a simple dress. The jewels she wore were kept to the minimum, which helped to show her loveliness to great effect.

When all four friends were seated with a chilled glass of finest Madeira wine to hand, Maria spoke.

"It is time for me to be totally open on matters that have been kept secret by a few who have sworn never to reveal what I am about to tell you. It is regarding my son Hernando." She paused and eyed Consuella for a moment, a slight smile playing on her lips. "You were never convinced that I conceived my son as quickly as was stated, or that he was born prematurely." Consuella nodded her affirmation and smiled back at her friend who continued.

"Esteban Santara is the father of my son and is, and always will be, the one true love of my life." There was a silence before she continued. "Esteban evaded the men who were sent by my father to kill him, and escaped to New Orleans. It is known that he then travelled northwards, still pursued by those who wanted to claim the bounty placed on his head by my father. Some of those men never returned and the bounty has never been claimed. He is still alive and it is my intention to travel to Boston and begin my search for him from there!" She turned to face Peter.

"You have already convinced me of the need for you to go there in connection with our business activities in the Americas. Would it be too much to ask that I be permitted to accompany you and Consuella, and indeed use your contacts on our arrival there?"

At this point Senor Palacio spoke, his face reflecting his concern.

"There is one thing I have learned in the years I have known Maria, and that is when she has made her mind up on a course of action, she will not change it." He sipped his wine then continued. "I will stay here and look after Maria's affairs until her return. Hernando has been placed under the guardianship of his uncle Don Juan Cortez. He is an honourable and capable man who will guide and educate his nephew on the management and responsibilities of his title and wealth. If Maria insists on this dangerous course of action then now is the best opportunity for her to do so. I would consider it a great service Peter if you will agree to allow Maria to travel with you. It would give me much comfort to know that she would be with loyal friends to help her in her quest."

The discussion that followed was heated but brief. Consuella was delighted that Maria would accompany both she and Peter to Boston, and firmly rejected her husband's objections to Maria's request. Maria trembled with excitement. At last her long awaited search for Esteban could begin.

—◊◊◊—

The weeks that followed were frantic, the final preparations taking far too long for an impatient Maria. There were so many details to be dealt with, including the vital selection of suitable clothing. Finance had to be made available and a plethora of other matters that caused further delays. She felt she could scream with frustration at the time taken to deal with the various, but necessary, matters that had to be resolved prior to her departure on her quest.

The Lloyds and Maria would be accompanied by two serving maids and a trusted manservant, Manuel Jamon, who had been in the employ of the Lloyds for many years, and was well versed in looking after the welfare of his master and mistress. Using his many contacts, Peter had previously obtained travel documents from both the British embassy in London, and the American authorities located in Boston. The Spanish Government had sided with France in the recent war against the

British, and these papers would prove invaluable in safeguarding their ship against seizure by either the Royal Navy or the Americans. Although the ship they were to sail in would be Spanish, she would do so under the protection of the British flag.

The merchant ship 'Santa Maria' had been commissioned by Peter for the long journey that lay ahead. He regarded the vessel as the swiftest of the merchant ships available for the voyage, and had total confidence in the ship's Master, Capitan Alonso Reina. The 'Santa Maria' became a hive of activity as she was made ready, every last detail being checked and re checked under the watchful eyes of her Master. It would be a dangerous voyage due to the perils presented by pirate ships, allied with Mother Nature's insistence on producing weather both foul and ever changing. The 'Santa Maria' was regarded as the fastest in her class, and there was confidence in those who knew her that she could outrun any pirate vessels encountered on the way. That was the common belief, and most accepted this although the assumption was accompanied by a few whispered prayers, just to be certain!

Finally, the 'Santa Maria' weighed anchor and set sail for Boston on 24th May 1764. Hernando had not seen fit to visit his mother prior to her departure, and Maria's requests to meet with him before her leaving had received no response.

The 'Santa Maria' would initially sail to the island of Lanzarote where further water and fresh provisions would be taken on board, before again setting sail on the longer and more dangerous final leg across the mighty Atlantic Ocean to Boston. The Atlantic crossing in this age of sail would depend very much on the trade winds being in the travellers' favour and the avoidance of storms. Given the blessing of the Weather Gods the voyage could be completed in just short of two months.

Maria refused to contemplate anything less than success in her venture. To fail to find Esteban alive and well was not an option. Peter and she repeatedly debated how best to organize the resources available to them if they were to succeed in finding Esteban. Oh how she wished that the 'Santa Maria' could grow wings and speed them to their destination! She must not however waste a moment of her time dreaming, but must plan and seek to improve upon these plans until every possible avenue that might lead to the whereabouts of her lover had been exhausted.

Chapter Two

The initial part of the voyage took the 'Santa Maria' beyond the towering cliffs of Gibraltar and into the Atlantic Ocean. Not a moment was wasted as Capitan Reina grasped every opportunity to drill his crew to the peak of efficiency. There was no doubt in his mind that their safe passage would rely heavily on his sailors' ability to meet the challenges that lay ahead. The passengers were not exempt from training in the ship's responses to heavy weather or attack by pirates. Drinking water and food were valuable commodities not to be wasted. Equipment and weaponry were to be maintained to the highest standards, for the lives of everyone on board the ship may well depend on this being so.

On the evening before landing at the port of Arrecife, Capitan Reina entertained his dinner guests with information about the island. He explained that Lanzarote was part of an archipelago called The Canaries. Although a population of wild canaries did exist on most of the islands there were no birds of this kind on Lanzarote. The popular theory as to how the name came into being was due to early settlers being impressed by the size of the hunting dogs found there. The title of Canaries was derived from Canus, latin for dogs.

The island was not without its share of romantic history. The Capitan took great delight in telling of the former mistress of King Ferdinand of Spain, Beatrix de Bobodilla, who resided on the neighbouring island of La Gomera in the late 15th century. Christopher Columbus had visited the island four times and on the first three occasions had allegedly had a romantic dalliance with the lady. By his fourth visit Beatrix had married Alonso Fernandez de Lugo, one of the most powerful men on the islands. Columbus cut his last visit short and sailed off to explore elsewhere!

The following morning the 'Santa Maria' anchored in the compact harbour of Arrecife that was overlooked by the Castillo de San Gabriel and the nearby Castillo de San Jose. Capitan Reina had arranged for Peter and his two lady companions to be driven in a small wagon to the Governor's residence which was situated inland at Teguise. There they would meet Father Andres Lorenzo Curbelo who had maintained a written daily record of the volcanic eruptions that had taken place on the island from 1730 to 1736.

The journey took the group around the fields of lava that had been created by the recent eruptions. Huge crusts of what had been molten rock gave the area an appearance unlike anywhere else seen by the travellers. Jagged outcrops towered above smooth clusters of outpourings that the inferno had created in temperatures hotter than could be imagined. The visual effect was a creation by an awesome and malignant power, so strong that words were of no consequence. To see the legacy of the eruptions was confirmation of the power of nature when unleashed upon the earth.

Father Curbelo proved to be a most articulate and knowledgeable host who told of the terror that the six years of eruptions had inflicted on the inhabitants of the island. It was a blessed miracle from above that during all this time no lives were lost to the boiling lava that daily encroached on the dwellings and farmland of the people. The island Governor had ordered the building of the Fortalego de Hombre (the Human Fortress) as the people were starving. The work provided both work and money which helped to alleviate their hardship. Indeed, plans were under discussion to introduce vines to the island to encourage the production of wine. Further research was required but the climate and soil were thought compatible for such an industry to thrive.

It took three full days of back breaking work to replenish the ship's stores and replace faulty equipment. Every last detail had to be carried out to Capitan Reina's high standards. Many of the repairs undertaken were to rectify problems that had come to light during the various drills carried out prior to their arrival in Arrecife. At last, much to Maria's delight, the 'Santa Maria' finally weighed anchor and eased her path clear of the port area. As the ship slowly headed for deeper waters another vessel passed astern. An unimaginable noxious stench emanated from the craft that did not abate until she was some distance away. Capitan Reina, noting the curiosity created by the passing ship amongst those aboard the 'Santa Maria', spoke with anger in his voice.

"The ship is 'The Hannibal' from the port of Bristol in England. She is a slave ship, no doubt with a cargo of poor souls from Guinea which is south of here on the west coast of Africa. The unfortunate wretches are shackled and stacked like books on a bookcase. They must endure unspeakable squalor in the gloomy and fetid holds. The life expectancy is poor, as one in eight will perish on the voyage. They are chained in cramped spaces and are infected by the human waste in which they must lie. Most who die succumb to the flux, the symptoms being a tortuous mixture of severe vomiting and diarrhoea. A more painful or dreadful death for anyone would be hard to imagine."

The ship's Master slammed his fist on the guardrail.

"It is a damnable trade that many of the European nations, including Spain, are content to take part in. Profits are high and consciences low." He grimaced before continuing. "It is ironic that many of the slaves are captured by local traders and tribal chiefs, who are equally to blame for this foul trade in human misery in which their own people are victims." The Capitan paused for a short moment, then excused himself and made his way towards an unfortunate sailor who had failed in the performance of some task that had not escaped the sharp and unforgiving eyes of the ship's Master.

Once clear of coastal waters the 'Santa Maria' sped onwards under full sail towards her destination of Boston. Hopes were high for a safe and swift journey for all on board. There would be hardship ahead and disappointment for some, but at this time failure was a word not to be spoken. The distant shores that promise so much are out of reach for many, who do not realize that they will never attain the paradise they seek. Even those who achieve such fulfillment must recognize that whatever a land may freely offer, it may also demand a remuneration of courage and strength.

CHAPTER THREE

Bright spring sunlight flooded the valley and the surrounding hills. The crisp clean air gently shook the young leaves of the cottonwoods into movement. A hawk soared overhead, wings spread wide to fully utilize the rising breezes, his sharp eyes seeking any sign below that might indicate potential prey. The bird veered to one side to avoid passing over the Indian encampment that lay ahead. Smoke arose from the tops of the fourteen or so tepees that nestled between a stand of aspen and a nearby river.

James McDonald, known to his Indian friends as Shouts Plenty, watched the hawk's progress until it was no longer visible. He sat outside the entrance to his tepee and was in a contemplative frame of mind. He watched his wife, Little Bird, as she busily prepared the midday meal. Aware that her husband's eyes were upon her she looked up and smiled in his direction. James returned her smile. He adored his wife who had shared his life for sixteen summers and given him two children, Shining Star and her younger brother White Eagle.

James and his family had lived with the Nez Perce tribe for the last ten years. They were a peaceful group who were skilled in the art of farming and produced a variety of crops that were much sought after by other Indian tribes. Most of all, they were highly regarded for the superb quality of horses that they bred and trained. The tribe was one of the first to appreciate the value of the horse and had taken every opportunity to select only the best for breeding purposes. Their knowledge of equine matters improved with the passing years, and the reputation of the supreme quality of Nez Perce horses was well known throughout the Indian tribes. They bartered often with passing nomadic bands that followed the herds of migrating buffalo. Such a lifestyle was of little appeal to the Nez Perce who preferred to move only short distances from where they reared their horses, and grew the food that both fed them and provided a valuable commodity for trade. All things considered it was a good existence, and one that James and his family had embraced with enthusiasm.

The tribe, although of peaceful intent, was still more than capable of defending itself against marauders and James was regarded as a man who could be relied on in times of possible trouble. Most Indian tribes regarded the theft of horses and desirable items, such as the food grown by the Nez Perce, as opportunities for warriors to show how skillful they were at stealing. A successful thief was seen as someone who had the guile to properly provide and protect his family and their property.

The daily existence of the Indian was a precarious one. James was aware that it was a way of life that was under threat from the white man. It might yet be years before the flood of settlers would invade the vast areas of unspoiled land, but they would come and they would shape the plains and forests to suit their needs. The advancement of civilization would ultimately sound the death knell for the Red Indian tribes unless they could adapt their present lifestyle accordingly.

"Damn," he cursed, for he privately admitted to himself that he should have earlier confronted the need to make a decision regarding the future of his family. If they were to journey eastwards to the lands already settled by the whites, they would have to accept that there would be considerable difficulties for a family of mixed blood. On the other hand to stay as they were would deny his children the opportunity to integrate into a changing world that could offer a better way of life, despite the problems that they would have to overcome along the way. Some years before, and much to the amusement of his family, he had given each of them a name in English. His wife became Janet, their daughter Shining Star was Fiona and his son Douglas. Whenever they practiced this language, they would use these names.

He swore again. In his hand was a two year old newspaper he had traded from an old mountain man called Mad Tom who had ridden into camp a year previously. James smiled at the memory, for Tom may well have been daft in the head, but he had struck a hard bargain. He had chuckled gleefully as James had reluctantly parted with his spare pistol in exchange for the newspaper, some powder for his musket and some coloured beads and trinkets for Little Bird and Shining Star.

Mad Tom was the first white person that James had seen or spoken to in over ten years. The old mountain man was considered to be touched by the Gods and the Indians never harmed him. He would seek shelter during the winter months with whichever tribe encampment was nearest and welcoming, until the weather had improved enough for him to continue his 'yondering' and living out his lonely existence.

A few days after his arrival in camp, Mad Tom left, with no words of farewell. James never saw or heard of him again.

The newspaper had been read so many times by James that he almost knew large parts of it by heart. It was this information that had brought about much discussion amongst all four members of the family.

CHAPTER FOUR

The newspaper told of the continuing war between Britain and France, both empires competing to extend their influence over the emerging Colonies that would one day unite and become a nation. The importance of the struggle between these two great powers was not so much control of the land, but sea power, without which neither side could sustain their vast empires. One article referred to fierce naval battles that had taken place during the summer of 1759. The Royal Navy had struck a massive blow in August of that year by attacking and severely damaging four French warships off the coast of Portugal. The action took the enemy by surprise and the remaining ships were then blockaded in Cadiz. A second naval encounter leading to the destruction of the French Atlantic fleet took place in November in the dangerous Quiberon Bay on the Brittany coast

Spain had entered into war, siding with France against Britain in 1761. Two years later a peace treaty was signed in Paris resulting in the Spanish loss of the Florida Keys to Britain. This gain, coupled with the withdrawal by the French in North America, left the British in possession of the lands from Nova Scotia and the Great Lakes, down through the Ohio Valley and southwards to the recently acquired Florida Keys.

The implications of the reports contained in the newspaper were not lost on James. These events had been forecast years before by his friend Seth Parker, who had also warned of a backlash if the Colonists were denied a voice in the passing of legislation that affected them by a distant Parliament, be it in London or indeed Paris. James was fully aware that the information he read was out of date, but it was sufficiently clear that major changes were taking place that would dictate how this new Colony would develop and grow. It was a time of great debate and change, and he was in no doubt that he and his family should be a part of the process.

There was one crucial factor amongst many that had to be overcome. This was the arrest warrant against him for the murder of Captain Antonio Marana. It was eighteen years since the escape by James and his four companions from Marana's ship 'The Mermaid.' It had involved a fight between James and the Captain that resulted in Marana's death. There would need to be some prior contact between James and one or more of his friends who had escaped with him, before he dared return openly. Douglas McDonald, a close friend of James since childhood had based himself in Georgetown where they had set up a freight business. William Porter, a surgeon from Edinburgh, and his widowed sister Moira Smith had opened a much needed medical practice that was also based in Georgetown. Moira's daughter Isabel formed the third partner in this venture. Advance warning that an arrest warrant had been issued led to the hurried departure of James and Seth from the town. At that time both businesses were proving to be highly regarded, and the services available were in great demand.

It had been some sixteen years since James had managed to send a letter to Douglas, along with two packhorses loaded with prime pelts. There had been no further contact between them since. The correspondence and furs had been delivered by a Captain Robert Campbell, whose life Seth and James had saved when he had been attacked by some Pawnees on the warpath. James sighed. He wondered how Douglas was and if he had married the lovely Isabel. Her uncle, William Porter, was an outstanding man of great vision who had become highly regarded by those who knew him. It would be no surprise if he had entered into the field of politics, for he had the gift of speaking clearly to audiences of different backgrounds in a way that showed an understanding of the issues under debate. Moira meantime had been courted by Hugh Mercer a surgeon from Aberdeen. Had they too become wed?

A pang of nostalgia stabbed through James. He had fled from Georgetown when advance warning of the arrest warrant reached him. How were his friends? Did they remember him? Were they still alive? He shook away the questions. He must deal with one thing at a time. Decisions had to be taken, and each member of his family would have the opportunity to express his or her views about where their future lay.

There were some positives in the equation, for all of them could speak and write in English, something James had insisted they learn. He also repeatedly spoke of the way of life he had left behind him, and how the white man and his ways were not sympathetic to the Indian culture which differed greatly. He imparted as much information he could to his family in the belief that they be as well informed as possible for the time when they must choose how to live their lives.

"As there are different tribes such as the Sioux, Comanche, Nez Perce and the Crow (he spat as he spoke the name of that hated tribe), so does the white man have different tribes with their own beliefs and some even of a different colour of skin. These peoples are like us in some ways, for they have good and bad amongst them, leaders of peaceful interests and those who worship war."

CHAPTER FIVE

We sat in our tepee, my wife and my two children. The cover to the entrance had been closed as an indication that no visitors were welcome. Indian etiquette required that any caller would come in only if the cover was not in place. The evening meal had passed, eaten in silence, for the time for talking was yet to come. What would become of us? As a family of four we had to discuss and decide what was best for our future existence, our togetherness, and indeed how to prepare ourselves, both as a group and as individuals. I closed my eyes in thought. What would become of the Indians? There was little doubt in my mind that it would be similar to that which had happened in other places across the world. Some would go further and further back into the hills until they could retreat no more. Some would fall by the way, but a good many would move out into this New World and they would do well. If they succeeded they would be accepted. What would eventually happen here had taken place across the world since time began. The migration out of Central Asia into Europe had displaced and absorbed other peoples. History showed time and again that whenever two cultures collided the more efficient way of life was that which would survive and flourish.

My family waited in silence for me to speak. My wife Little Bird, whom I called Janet in our private moments, watched through eyes that could read my mind as though I spoke aloud. She knew of my concerns, although she could not fully understand my urgency to consider such drastic action as leaving the place where we had found much happiness these past few years. To depart to the uncertainty of a life amongst the distrusted white man, of whom she had little knowledge, was something she feared greatly. That she would follow me to the ends of the world as she knew it, was as certain as the morning sunrise, for her love of me knew no bounds. I was indeed a fortunate man.

My daughter Shining Star was a special person in my life. She was a tall dark haired, brown eyed beauty who moved with the grace of an antelope. I had tired of the number of young hopeful bucks who had turned up at our tepee with horses and numerous other gifts in exchange for my approval for her agreement to marriage, Indian style. Many an evening was spent listening to the magic flute playing, reading of poetry, and singing of some young male suitor. These flutes were highly valued in assisting in winning the heart of a young maiden and were made by the local medicine man at considerable cost to the young love-sick hopefuls. Some of those rejected young men came back time and again, but the answer was always the same. She was not interested and the inevitable response was a resounding rebuff, much to the dismay of the young buck concerned. I had also given my daughter another name, Fiona, after a much beloved aunt of mine from my previous life in Scotland. She could debate with the best and was competent with all manner of weapons. It was of concern to me that she, above all of us, should be able to dictate where she saw her future. The average Indian maiden was married at twelve or thirteen and Fiona was a number of summers beyond that age.

My son, White Eagle, was much darker skinned than his sister and was proving to be a useful addition to the well-being of our encampment. He was an intelligent young man with the enthusiasm for sporting activities that only a youth of thirteen years can have. He excelled at games, and although unusual for one his age, also cared deeply for the knowledge of horses and the growing of the crops that sustained our group. There was a touch of magic in his nurturing of the variety of plants that he tended, but most of all was his ability to communicate with the Indian ponies. The local chief, Talks to Horses, took my son under his wing almost from the first day we had arrived in the Nez Perce camp.

"White Eagle has been given a great gift from the Gods, for he can think as the horses think and he is regarded by them as a brother." The old warrior shook his head to emphasize his words. "He has things yet to learn, but I will teach him."

So my son White Eagle, whom I called Douglas in memory of my best friend, became a pupil of Talks to Horses. There were moments when he reminded me of my old companion, as he had the same stocky build and a determination that would not let him quit, even when exhausted.

I shook away the memories and addressed the matter in hand. All eyes were upon me as I spoke.

"For too long I have allowed the stability and security of our present circumstances to cloud my judgement. Our family is well fed and clothed this day and we are content with our lot. There are provisions that will enable us to cope with the hardships that the changing seasons might impose upon us." I paused to emphasize my next words. "We have all read the reports in the newspaper that Mad Tom brought here. Events may well be taking place even as I speak, that will greatly impact upon our future. The white man will one day come to these lands in great numbers and they will bring their 'civilization' with them. It is their custom to impose their manner of living upon those that they meet along the way. These things I have told you many times." I was aware that all eyes were on me as I continued.

"Most white men do not understand the Indian, and do not think it important to try. They will regard the Indian as an obstacle to settlement of the land, which they regard as something to own. Their way is to build houses and fence off the surrounding areas. The young Indian who would win honour among his people can only do so through hunting or war. He has no other avenue. The old Indians who fought their wars counted coup, taking scalps and stealing enough horses to make them rich and gain status within the Indian community. How is the young Indian to do this? If the old warrior wishes to accept the incomers and make peace, the young Indian will wish to make war. He cannot get a wife until he has proved himself as a man, as a warrior, so he must steal horses to trade for his bride. She will want the things the white man has, as will he, and the only way he can get them is by trade or stealing. He has little to trade, so he will steal. The white man's laws will punish such actions severely." A lengthy silence followed my words.

"You speak with the knowledge of one who has seen and experienced the way of the whites," my wife said in a soft voice, choosing her words with care. "The rest of us have to decide the way forward without these memories. You have told us in the past that amongst the white man we would face suspicion and even ill-will because we have Indian blood. It is a difficult thing to choose. We have no experience on how we should compare our present existence with what could be a life unlike the way we live now. I do remember the reasons why we had to leave my own people, the Sioux, for although you were one of them you were still a Waschitou, a white man, therefore never fully accepted by some. I believe it would be the same for us in the white man's world."

I nodded with respect, for the comments were well spoken. I then summarized the advantages and disadvantages, as I understood them, if the decision was to go east. There were friends there, I believed, who would help us. I was hopeful that the money invested with Douglas in a freighting company before my hasty departure would provide some source of income for my family. There were also the gold nuggets that had come into my possession from the dying young Spaniard Esteban Santara, whose life Seth and I had tried to save. The young man had come upon our winter cabin sorely wounded, and despite our best efforts had not survived. I still had Esteban's diary which contained a map showing the location of where the gold had been found. The diary was in Spanish, but Seth was fluent in that language. The location of the mine, including identifying landmarks, had been translated into English and remained in my possession. It was my intention that we should risk trying to find this place. If we were unable to make contact with, and gain the help of my friends, extra gold would prove invaluable to us.

The arrest warrant against me for the murder of Marana was the major problem. I could only hope that there was some way this could be dealt with that would allow me to retain my freedom. Even if this was possible, it did not mean that my family would be able to adjust into the new and potentially hostile environment in which they would find themselves.

"We will talk no more tonight, but you must think about what has been said. A decision must be made soon." I gave a half smile as I said those words, for I could only guess at the confusion that existed in the minds of my wife and two children. There would doubtless be little sleep taken tonight as they sought to come to terms with the discussion that had taken place.

CHAPTER SIX

Shining Star was restless. Her father's words had stayed with her throughout the night. Sleep would not come and she was aware that her brother who lay nearby was also awake. There had been many times when there had been talk of a life different from the Indian way, the one that she knew so well. Never, until last night, had her father spoken so seriously about the need to consider what must be done to secure their futures. For the first time ever she had seen uncertainty in his eyes, or was it fear of the consequences of what might lie ahead? That, more than anything that had been said, gave her a cold feeling in the pit of her stomach. She began to realize that it was her mother who was the strong one in the family. It was she who had left behind everything and everyone she had ever cared about for the love of her husband. Shining Star was a baby when they had fled from the Sioux encampment where they had lived, to escape the dangerous and rising resentment against them that had become more life threatening by the day.

There was a part of her that had no wish to live as other Indian women. A daily existence of back breaking toil that aged them all too quickly. Even her own mother was showing signs of slowing down as the demands upon her diminished only slightly, as her daughter became more able to share her workload. It could be many summers before the influence of the invading whites became a reality. Could they not wait until that time to change their way of life? As she asked herself this question she knew that to stay was not an option.

The thought of an alternative way of life excited her, despite her father's warnings that there would be difficulties to be overcome, or at least recognized and accepted, as part of the price that would have to be paid. She had always listened eagerly to the stories of how her father had grown up, about his family and friends and the events leading to where they, as a family, were today. There was a whole new world out there, and yes, with many dangers to be faced, but life is full of challenges. Father had said that their existence was governed to a much greater extent than they knew, by events over which they had little or no control. They must navigate the rivers of change while doing what they could to avoid the rapids and whirlpools that awaited the unwary.

The wise words her mother had spoken last night were not forgotten. Only father had been to the places that the decision to go eastwards, if agreed, might yet take them. A well intentioned parent, or the silver tongued storyteller, can give an honest description of places and events that will whet the appetite for more. It is only when the individual visits, sees and experiences these things, can they truly comprehend the reality of the situation.

Chapter Seven

My wife and I stood beside the river bank and breathed deeply of the crisp morning air. The view was a fine one, and as I looked upon it I enjoyed both the quietness and the beauty of the gentle hills that lay before me. It reminded me of my own Highland glen and of those I had left behind.

The decision had been taken some five days before, after much talk and soul searching. My family would move eastwards once all the necessary arrangements had been made. There were still major concerns by all involved and these had been aired openly and honestly. There was no point saying one thing while thinking another, for such situations can only lead later to disharmony and bitterness.

One of my last formal duties before our departure had been to thank Talks to Horses for the kindness shown to my family and me. The Nez Perce had been quick to welcome us and each member of our small group would leave with warm memories of our stay amongst our hosts. The Chief and I had talked well into the early morning on many occasions, our words exchanged with honesty and a desire to understand each other's opinions. We disagreed on numerous subjects, but he never ridiculed my views, strange as they may have seemed to him.

This was to be our last meeting, and when I entered his tepee I was aware that he had donned his finest attire in honour of my visit. I skirted behind those present to the opposite side of the tepee facing my point of entry. I took care not to come between any of those present and the fire, for this would be seen as very bad manners. A nod from the Chief signified that I should be seated, crossed leg as was the way of the men. Any women present at such events were required to kneel.

The group consisted of Talks to Horses, his wife, and two senior warriors. Nothing was said as the old chief went through the formalities of lighting a pipe. He puffed noisily and made a mumbled prayer to his gods. The pipe then passed to each of the two warriors before it came to me. I recited the Lord's Prayer, in English, and added some pleas, in their dialect, asking for prosperity to all who dwelt here. This was acknowledged by my host. Nothing further was said until Talks to Horses laid his pipe to one side. It was time for me to leave. As I arose the Chief's wife opened the flap covering the exit from the tepee. I stopped and nodded to each of the men. Each nodded in return. This done, I left the tepee. The meeting was over. We would now begin our journey.

The way would be long and not without its dangers, especially the time we would spend seeking to find the source of Esteban's gold. However there was a positive feeling among our small band that we were doing the right thing. There was an excitement in our hearts as we waved a final farewell to our friends in the Nez Perce encampment. Whatever difficulties lay ahead, they would be met by a family strong and united in its belief and determination to succeed.

—◊◊◊—

The sharp eyed eagle watched from high in the skies, searching for potential prey. He tended to follow the same daily aerial pathway as he had done for some years now. He noted the small group on horseback as they made their way from the cluster of tepees that lay below. It had been a good day for hunting and he had taken two hares back to his nest during the course of the morning. The never ending fight for life over death continued as the great bird veered away and sought out his next victim, whose carcass would provide him and his offspring with the strength to compete in nature's eternal quest for survival.

CHAPTER EIGHT

It was a hot, bright, Boston morning and a smattering of white clouds hung in the sky. The busy port was jammed tight with vessels of all shapes and sizes, their masts competing to determine which were the tallest amongst the ships present. The view across the harbour made it appear that a multi-legged insect was lying on its back, struggling to right itself.

To one side of the main jetty lay a series of buildings that housed the various offices of the Port authorities. One structure in particular was host to a group of about thirty men who were engaged in heated debate. One man was trying hard to make himself heard over the babble from those around him.

"Hear me gentlemen, let me speak if you will," he pleaded, "if we are to make any progress we must behave in a manner conducive to honest and fruitful debate." The noise abated in response to his urgings, and a number of those present nodded their agreement that he should continue free from interruption.

"There are those amongst you who do not know me. I am Douglas McDonald, a Scotsman who loves this land, and who wishes to play his part in helping and watching it grow. Unlike my former homeland there are fewer taxes, although they are growing more plentiful by the day." There was a chorus of agreement before he continued. "Neither are there any titled proud lords to dictate over those of us of more humble circumstances. Here men are valued in proportion to their abilities, their actions and the honest way in which they conduct themselves."

There was a further murmur of approval for the words of the tall, dark haired speaker who stood before them. His hands were placed on his hips and his eyes searched the faces of those present, almost daring anyone to interrupt him.

"Like most of you I fought against the French in the belief that it was right to do so, and that our Colonies would become entitled to constitutional rights, a voice in the Parliament in London. This is being denied us." He paused and lowered his voice as he continued, as though he was speaking personally to each man in the room. "I am unique in one way. I have fought against the English and lost. I have fought with the British against the French and won. I have no wish to fight against the British again, despite the views of many of you in this room that we should do so." There was an angry swell of disagreement at his words.

"Revolution is not the answer my friends," Douglas continued, "The thirteen Colonies must meet and agree the way forward, speaking with one voice. Only if we achieve this will we be regarded as people deserving of the ear of those in power in London. We must negotiate, apply political pressure on Parliament, and argue our case in a civilized and reasoned manner if we wish to be taken seriously." Douglas extended his arm to identify the person he was about to refer to.

"My friend, William Porter, whom all of you know, would speak to you. He too has experienced the barbarity of war. Think carefully gentlemen, I beseech you. To destroy is easy, but to build is much more difficult." Douglas turned on one of the group who had jeered at his words. "To scoff is also easy, but to continue in the face of ridicule, to do what is right, is the way of an honourable man."

There was a muted response to Douglas' words and a few derisory comments as Porter rose to speak. "Gentlemen, Sons of Liberty, if there is one thing war has taught me, it is that God takes a neutral stance on those who take to the field in battle. He who is better trained, armed and equipped is the likely victor. Courage alone is not enough to win the day. As a surgeon of some years experience I have seen many, aye, too many lives given to causes that could have reached peaceful conclusion if dialogue had taken place beforehand. My friend Douglas speaks wisely. We must unite the Colonies, difficult as it might prove to be, for there are many differences to be resolved."

An outbreak of booing and shouts of derision arose in response to William's words. The crescendo of noise made it impossible for him to continue. He sat down feeling angry and disappointed, his slight frame bent forward while he fought to control his feelings.

Afterwards the two friends agreed that the likelihood of conflict between Britain and the Colonies was ever nearer.

"There is a deep mistrust of every action the London Parliament takes," said Douglas, "and this latest Stamp Duty, another form of taxation imposed on the Colonies, is seen by many here as the final insult." Porter was saddened but resolute. "If it comes to war Douglas, and I pray that it will not, I must be true to the Colonies." He smiled ruefully.

"There are those who see conspiracy in every corner and under every bed. It encompasses trade, religion, taxation and politics. The much beloved British Constitution is in tatters and is failing all those who believed and fought for her against the French. I fear that Briton against Briton, father against son and family against family will result. This will be a tragedy, as most people want only to be left in control of their own destinies." Both men sat in silence for some minutes before Douglas spoke. When he did, it was to sadly agree with his friend's assessment that it was unlikely that the Colonists were of a mind to attempt a united political policy amongst themselves. After a light shared meal they parted, Douglas back to his hotel and William to a further meeting with political acquaintances.

Douglas felt depressed as he walked the short distance to his hotel. At least he had earlier that day concluded a good piece of business for his freight company, and tomorrow he would be returning to his wife, Isabel, and their two children, James and Anne.

It had been a long tiring day, and after a last drink at the bar Douglas retired to bed. As his eyes closed he wondered how he had changed over the twenty plus years since he and his friend James had fled from Scotland. Where was James now? Was he even alive? Sleep denied him a reply.

—⁂—

William Manson had listened with great interest to the debate that had taken place earlier that evening at the port. In particular the words of Douglas MacDonald had been absorbed and could have been recited almost word for word if he had wished to do so. He was of nondescript appearance, of average height and weight with no distinguishing marks. His manner and voice were readily forgotten by those who came into limited contact with him. He came and went about his business leaving no impression on those he met in his passing. Manson was ideally suited to his profession as an assassin, his speciality being the murder of the political and religious opponents of his faceless paymasters. Tonight was to be the last in the life of Douglas MacDonald.

The outside window of the room where Douglas slept opened easily and without noise. Manson had tested it earlier that day when the accommodation had lain unoccupied. He had memorized the layout of the room carefully and planned how he would approach his intended victim. The only light was provided by a crescent moon that was partially hidden by heavy black clouds. Manson drew his knife, a favourite weapon for such moments when stealth and quiet were needed. The shape of the body that lay on the bed was barely discernable in the darkness. The killer took two steps nearer and paused. The sleeping man's steady breathing continued unabated. A further step and Manson was ready to strike. He poised above his victim, knife tightly held and ready to deliver.

Without warning the prone figure kicked out, catching Manson in the side, causing him to stop his intended attack long enough for Douglas to grab the wrist of the arm holding the knife. The two grappled, knocking a chair and a bedside table aside in their struggle. Douglas swung a punch with his free arm that caught Manson on the top of his head. The killer gasped and staggered backwards before launching a kick that landed painfully below the right knee, causing Douglas to release his grip on the attacker's knife hand. Manson was no fool. He had lost the advantage of surprise, and the shouts from the adjoining room told that the sounds of the struggle had been heard. Without delay he dived through the open window and was gone into the darkness.

Douglas rubbed his knee as he unlocked the door to allow the curious occupants of the room next to his to enter. His life had been saved by his years of living during dangerous times. Sleep was taken in snatches and the body would subconsciously respond to the slightest of noises or changes that could prove to be life threatening. He gratefully acknowledged this fact to himself. He had been very lucky for his assassin had been good, too good by far. Another split second and it would have been all over. The commotion had ruined any further thought of sleep and Douglas promised the apologetic hotel night manager that he would speak with the town sheriff before his departure.

Who wanted him dead? There was little chance that it had been a case of mistaken identity. This was an unwanted additional concern over and above the political unrest and the looming threat of war. Douglas had spoken publicly against any conflict, except as a last resort when any chance of peace had gone. This had not been well received in certain quarters, although he had made it clear that he would fight for his adopted country if called upon to do so.

He would speak to William before he left Boston, for his friend may also be in danger.

CHAPTER NINE

The British man o' war ordered the 'Santa Maria' to heave to and to make ready to be boarded. 'The Albion' was a magnificent ship, and even Capitan Alonso Reina grudgingly acknowledged this as the experienced boarding party was smoothly transported onto the decks of the Spanish craft. A smartly turned out Royal Navy Lieutenant saluted Capitan Reina before bowing deeply towards the ladies who had come on deck to watch the proceedings.

"Sir," the officer said, "do I have the honour of addressing Capitan Alonso Reina, Master of this ship, the 'Santa Maria' out of Barcelona?" The young speaker failed to hide a smile as his words caused some surprise amongst those within hearing distance.

Recovering his composure quickly, the Spaniard responded formally confirming his status as ship's Master.

"That you are aware of our existence is clear, and suggests that you will also know that we possess travel authority from your embassy to be permitted to sail under the British flag, and to enjoy the protection this entitles us to. You will also no doubt be aware that Mister Peter Lloyd and his family and companions are on board. Please accompany me to my cabin in order that all the necessary checks of our credentials can be carried out."

The process was quickly and efficiently completed, enabling a glass of chilled Madeira wine to be gratefully quaffed before the return of the boarding party to 'The Albion'. Prior to his departure the Lieutenant confirmed that the arrival of the 'Santa Maria' had been expected following word from the Admiralty in London. Mister Lloyd clearly had friends in high places. Boston was less than two days sailing away and a berth had been reserved for them in advance.

Excitement amongst those on board rose at the positive turn of events. The relief at the safe crossing, coupled with the knowledge that their arrival was expected raised the spirits. Tomorrow they should be safely at anchor in Boston harbour.

"So far, so good," Peter whispered in his wife's ear. "Let us see what awaits us."

—〰—

Alexander McDougall was a small wiry man who, at the age of six, had come to the New World with his father from the Scottish island of Islay. Now, 26 years later, he was a successful sea captain and prosperous merchant based in New York. He had come to the harbour to greet the arrival of the 'Santa Maria' and to meet Peter Lloyd for the first time.

Since contact had been established between the two men some years earlier, it had become a fruitful business partnership for both parties involved. Now that the seven year war between the British and French was over, there were opportunities for further expansion, and of course increased profits.

McDougall waited impatiently for the final docking of the Spanish craft to be completed before he could board her. As the Master of two British warships during the recent conflict against the French, he acknowledged that the ship before him gave every impression of being a well built and speedy craft. The war at sea had been a great opportunity for McDougall and others like him, for ostensibly these were British warships fighting the French, but that was an excuse to be privateers, robbing ships of many nations and trading in slaves, molasses, tea and rum.

There were those who objected to the activities of the privateers and the financial gain they made in the war against the French. The harbour contained a variety of captured craft of French, or occasionally Spanish, origin, but now the property of the privateers and not of the British or their allies. All manner of these ships and their contents were sold openly on the various markets in Boston and New York. The finance generated by these activities provided a very healthy income for those such as McDougall who had no qualms about their actions. War was war, and if the opportunity arose to make a profit whilst serving one's country, then why not? The fact that some regarded the privateers as pirates mattered little in the eyes of McDougall and those like him.

At last a gangway was in place and he strode onto the ship's deck. Peter Lloyd was waiting to extend a welcoming hand that was accompanied by a huge smile.

"So Alexander, we meet at last. There is much to discuss." Turning to one side he introduced Capitan Reina, Consuella and Maria.

McDougall bowed deeply to each of the ladies in turn, giving an admiring look of appreciation in their direction before he spoke.

"Welcome, your beauty has brought the sun to these shores. Are all Spanish ladies so very attractive as those before me? If this is indeed the case then I must amend my travel plans to include Spain." Both Consuella and Maria smiled their amusement at McDougall's flattery, before Capitan Reina invited him to join them in his cabin for a glass of wine. This would enable some initial discussions to take place regarding the various arrangements for accommodation in Boston and meetings with some of McDougall's business contacts. There was also the important matter of the unloading of the cargo of trade goods that Peter had selected as very attractive items for the Boston and New York markets.

Peter had no doubt, based on his dealings with his business associate, that the preparations made on their behalf would be meticulously planned. This proved to be the case. The party would spend the first week at The Grand Hotel, Boston's finest hostelry. During this time there were four properties for renting that could be viewed before a decision was taken on which was the preferred choice. There would also be a full day of sightseeing, as well as a number of social events to which key business contacts had been invited. Time had also been set aside for a visit to the theatre.

McDougall rose from his chair and drained the last few remnants of wine from his glass.

"You will find a carriage outside on the docks in about one half hour. This is to transport you all to your hotel. A second carriage will arrive shortly afterwards for your staff and your baggage and any other belongings you may wish to bring. Nearby rooms have been provided for your staff. On your arrival at the hotel a light lunch has been arranged. I will call round later this evening to ensure that everything is to your satisfaction and to provide you with suggestions for the disposal of your ship's cargo." With a bow he turned and departed the ship.

It had been a good start and Peter and the ladies were pleased that the early impressions were so positive. Maria had been sorely tempted to broach the subject of Esteban and his whereabouts, but had refrained from doing so. There would be time to do so soon, Peter had advised her, and she had agreed.

Peter spoke with his manservant, Manuel Jamon, and explained what arrangements had been made on their behalf by Alexander McDougall. Manuel would organize the transfer of the luggage and other bits and pieces to the hotel, as well as ensuring that the two maids, Ania and Simone would be suitably catered for.

Peter checked his watch. Time was moving on and the carriage would soon arrive to take them to the hotel. The next few days, weeks and months, could prove challenging in so many ways. There were numerous business opportunities to be assessed and he was looking forward to testing himself against some of the sharpest minds in Boston commerce. He had not forgotten Maria and her quest to find Esteban. That was an issue high on his list of priorities and the matter would be raised at the earliest and appropriate time.

CHAPTER TEN

The first grey light of early sunrise was fighting to gain a foothold in the sky as the lone rider made his way homewards.

Douglas McDonald rode cautiously, alert to any indication that might suggest the risk of ambush. He felt reassured that his sixth sense, honed during his years of travelling over dangerous terrain, had not diminished. The inborn ability of his subconscious to register and respond to the slightest hint of danger had proved, not for the first time in his life, to be in good working order.

Before leaving Boston he had spoken with his friend William Porter about the attempt on his life at the hotel. After a lengthy discussion however, neither was any closer to the reason for the attack, although both dismissed the possibility that it had been a case of mistaken identity. William's final words of warning came to mind.

"There are many different beliefs on how the Colonies should move forward. Most are related to political views, some of which are extreme. It is perhaps the views you have publicly expressed that have brought you to the attention of such a group, who now regard you as a threat to their ambitions. Take great care Douglas, for if this is indeed the situation there will be further attempts on your life."

Douglas stopped to allow his horse to take a breather. The trees of aspen and spruce dominated the hillsides. Was he being watched by hidden eyes? Who would want him dead? He lightly touched his heels to his horse who had been happily cropping a lush patch of grass. There were three or four more hours riding to complete before they would reach their destination, and there was no reason to delay the journey any longer than necessary.

There are few better opportunities than when riding, to think about matters of the mind. Thoughts can be dissected, reassessed, then discarded or stored as worthy of further consideration at a later date. Douglas did just this, although his alertness never faltered. The seed of concern increased as his horse covered the miles towards home. Who were these people who wanted him dead? Why should this be? Who would gain by his death? Douglas conceded that these were questions for which he had no answers.

He was a man who in his earlier years had dedicated himself to the life of a soldier and protector of his friend James McDonald who, due to politics, had forfeited the right to become the next Chieftan of the Clan McDonald of Clanranald. The experience gained during these years had enabled him to take a detached view when danger existed, and to assess the strengths and weaknesses of the factions involved. He was quick to realize that he was vulnerable, and in fact there were few positives to be found in his present position. He had enemies who wanted him dead, although he did not know why. His freight business required him to travel a great deal, often alone. Most worrying of all, his wife Isabel and their two children, Anne and James, lived on their ranch which was in a fairly remote area. There were of course loyal and trusted ranch hands that worked for them and were on call, but the safety of his family could not be guaranteed.

The cold fingers of fear stirred in the pit of his stomach. Was he over reacting? An inner voice told him otherwise. Douglas delayed no longer and kicked his horse into a gallop. His place was with his loved ones at this moment and he would waste no more time.

The heat of the mid-day sun was warm on his back as Douglas topped the rise that opened up a panoramic view of the valley that lay before him. On one side, next to a narrow but deep river, there nestled a highly functional saw mill. Beside this was a small dam that provided the water that turned the mill wheel. The construction provided cut timber for all manner of use, including the building of new homes, the provision of fencing and the repair of the wagons used to transport the freight to various destinations. A blacksmith's forge was housed nearby. The river also provided clear and fresh water for the animals grazing in the valley. These included the many horses and mules essential to his freighting business, as well as the cattle Douglas was keen to establish as a source of quality beef.

In the centre of the valley, some five or so miles ahead, were the ranch buildings. Great care had been taken in the positioning of the main house which could not be approached from any direction unseen. There were three corrals set apart to one side, and a number of well tended vegetable patches promised provision of a plentiful source of fresh food for the dinner table.

All this Douglas took in at first glance. Mercifully there were no signs of trouble. As he rode closer he could identify some of his workers going about their business. As he drew nearer to the house one of them approached him on horseback, waving a greeting as he did so. Douglas recognized him as David Wilson, a Scotsman who had worked on the ranch for a number of years and who was a steady and reliable ranch hand.

"Afternoon Mister McDonald, you seem to be in a hurry," he commented having noted that his employer's horse had been hard ridden. "Where's the fire?" he half jokingly asked. The lack of a response warned that Douglas was not in the mood to exchange any light hearted banter.

"Have there been any strangers around here recently, or any unusual incidents during my absence? Think David, it is important." The ranch hand paused before he replied.

"There have been the usual folks passing through on their ways to somewhere else, and the regular people who had business with the freight line. I can't think of anyone out of the ordinary though and I haven't strayed too far from the ranch while you've been away." He awaited a response but none was forthcoming.

Douglas frowned and nodded in the general direction of the ranch buildings. He did not speak for a few moments before he finally responded to Wilson's earlier feedback.

"There are rumours of some band of robbers heading in this direction and it would do us no harm to be on the lookout for any strangers passing by. Give the word to all the hands to keep their eyes open."

Douglas lightly kicked his horse into a trot and headed towards the familiar buildings, where his mount would receive a well earned nosebag of oats. It had been a hard ride for both horse and rider, and Douglas was relieved to be home.

As he drew nearer to the ranch he spied a petite figure on the porch. It was his wife Isabel who was shading her eyes against the sun. She waved as he rode closer and he responded in kind. Douglas smiled a greeting as he stopped and dismounted. Isabel came to him and they embraced before he kissed her and held her close for a few moments. He stepped back and looked admiringly at his woman for a few seconds more before he spoke.

"Someone told me that there was a pretty lonesome young lady living here who was looking for a man. Wouldn't be you by any chance now, would it?"

Isabel, keeping a straight face, walked back towards the door, then halted, turned towards Douglas and beckoned him with a finger.

"Come on in so I can look you over." She laughed and stepped inside and he followed.

As he entered the cool of the ranch house he was met by a chorus of welcome from his two teenage children. His younger offspring was Anne who gave him a peck on his cheek. She was a pretty redhead girl just like her mother, who, being surrounded by so many men, had become a bit of a tomboy. Her attire consisted of jeans and a checked shirt, and Douglas could not recall when he had last seen her in a dress. His son James was the elder of the children and at eighteen had grown up at ease around all kinds of livestock. He could ride and shoot straight, but his reading and writing skills had also been developed to the extent that he had a good grasp of the running of the freighting business. Anyone looking at James would have no doubts about who his father was. Unlike his sister, James had the same solid dark looks and sturdy build as Douglas. It was often stated by Isabel that her son also had the same stubborn streak as her husband.

James poured his father a glass of cool water. The contents were gratefully emptied with a sigh of satisfaction, before Isabel suggested that Douglas had just enough time to enable him to have a wash up before they had lunch. This said, she disappeared into the kitchen to speak with their cook Nan, an Irish lady who over the years had become almost like a member of the family. There would be time enough to catch up on the news during the mealtime. Meantime Douglas obeyed his wife's 'suggestion' that he clean up before eating, and made his way to the washroom.

After they had eaten and Douglas had listened to the reports from James on freighting matters, he took his wife to one side. When he was sure that they could not be overheard he told of the attempt on his life to a shocked Isabel. He went on to relate his discussions with William and of his warning about further attempts to kill him. Isabel listened in silence, her face pale as Douglas spoke.

"It is a complete mystery to me for I cannot think who would have cause to wish me dead. However what is of more concern is the safety of you and the children. It will be impossible to live a normal life if we must forever be on the lookout for possible attack. We must therefore make our family and friends aware that we need to remain alert whilst carrying out our business as usual." There was a moment of silence as each stared grim faced at the other. Isabel spoke first, nodding her agreement of her husband's words as she did so.

"We must not delay. James and Anne need to be told at once, and then our ranch hands. The more people who are made aware of the threat against us, the less chance there is of any attack succeeding. Of course both James and you will need to curtail your journeys outside the ranch boundary." Isabel raised her hand to quell any protest from Douglas. "At the very least you cannot travel alone. Either James or David Wilson must accompany you in any future journey that takes you away from the ranch."

James and Anne were summoned and listened in silence as their father informed them of the situation, and stressed the need for caution by all concerned. He studied his children as he spoke, and was reassured to note that both were treating the threat as serious. With this task done, Douglas called the ranch workforce together and outlined the situation to them. There was an angry murmur at his words, for those who worked for him had a high regard for the McDonald family. Any attack on Douglas or his family would be seen as an attack on them. The evening meal was a quiet affair, for each present at the table had their own thoughts on what had taken place earlier. It brought home to all of them that the security and protection that the ranch offered should never be taken for granted. Sometimes the good things in life are regarded as a right and under-valued. It is only when these things are threatened that we value them much more than before.

The night closed in as a gentle breeze followed the contours of the higher ground. The silvery moon cast a soft glimmer onto the leaves as they rustled on the wooded slopes overlooking the ranch. There was a further stirring amongst the trees as the soft wind withdrew, then stillness descended everywhere.

CHAPTER ELEVEN

They had travelled for many weeks without seeming to get closer to the area where any of the landmarks shown on Esteban's map could be identified. The journey had not been rushed, as great care was needed if they were to avoid being spotted. Eight horses and four strangers, two of whom were women, would be a great temptation to any unfriendly Indians, and would certainly invite attack. Nerves were taut and a gnawing nervousness lay within the group, weighing heavily upon them all. James acknowledged to himself that rest in a safe place was needed, a temporary haven where they could take refuge away from prying eyes. There would be less chance of being seen if they stayed in one place than if they moved onwards.

A mountain lion picked up the faint scent of men and horses. He paused and sniffed the air again. Some early memory stirred inside him, alerting him of possible danger. His experience cautioned him to take heed of this inner voice. A growl rose in his throat and he warily turned towards his lair amongst the nearby rocks where he would wait in safety.

The weary group negotiated a steep climb following what appeared to be a faint track barely wide enough for them to pass through. This led to an uneven plateau that provided a sweeping view of the surrounding hills, canyons and lakes. Small patches of meadow nestled amongst the various stands of trees, fertile spots for the wildlife that existed in the area. As they continued onwards across the plateau the sullen towering cliffs created an unwelcoming greeting, and there was no sound except that of the horses' hooves. It was James, on looking backwards to check their trail, who spotted the opening to a cave that had been concealed from them in the direction they were travelling. He pointed it out to the others.

"That looks a likely place to rest up for a while." As he spoke he nudged his horse towards the cave and was pleased to confirm that his choice was a good one. Within a short time there was a small fire going, tucked away to the rear of the cave. The chances of it being spotted were very slight indeed and the warmth it spread inside the cave was most welcome. A hot meal was provided and in no time at all spirits had risen.

Their horses were tethered outside in an area of lush grass, and a small stream nearby provided both animals and humans with the welcoming treat of cool fresh water. It was an opportunity to relax but not to be less aware of the potential dangers that might be nearby. James would take the first watch and each of the others would follow in turn. It was a chance to take stock of their situation and to carry out minor repairs to clothing and other items.

Later, James sat in a corner of their temporary shelter and viewed his family in turn. His wife, Small Bird, smiled in his direction and he was comforted to know that he still had her support in how their journey had fared so far. Shining Star lay asleep in another corner, while her brother was outside on watch. This was a good place and James decided that it would make sense to make full use of it for at least two or three days before moving on.

It was on the morning that they had agreed to move that they stood and studied the land that lay ahead. Nothing was said as they observed the vista which spread before them. From their earliest years they had been taught to see and register in their minds any landmarks that could provide some future guidance for themselves and others who might follow the same path. There was beauty out there, even in the chilling desolate mountains that lay in the valleys between. James was holding the map in his hand when White Eagle excitedly grasped his father's wrist and pointed to his right.

"Look father, that column next to the double rock fingers, is that not on the map?" Even as he spoke the youth also identified another feature that was clearly shown on Esteban's drawing. There was no doubt. They were within reach of the gold, a tantalizing bonanza that could provide them with a foothold in the new world. Without the gold there would be a less certain future awaiting them.

The next part of their journey would be more dangerous than that to date. They must find a base nearer to the features identified on Esteban's map, and from there carry out a search for the location of the source of the gold. This approach had already been discussed at length prior to their departure from the Nez Perce encampment. James and one other would together venture out daily on foot while the others would remain behind to tend to the horses and keep watch for hostiles.

It was hoped that by keeping the area to be searched clear of horse tracks there would be less chance of being discovered. It would take longer to explore the region on foot, but the safety of the group was the priority.

The sun was low in the sky, barely visible above the jagged peaks of the mountains, before they found a suitable place to set up their camp at the mouth of a small steep sided canyon. There was a deep overhang that provided shelter and kept them out of sight. The horses were picketed further into the canyon where there was a supply of water and a limited amount of poor quality grass which would be augmented by the feed they had brought with them. After a cold meal they prepared for sleep, each due to take a turn on watch until morning. Tomorrow the search for the gold would begin.

The following day they arose to a brief cooling shower of rain. The horses were checked before a cold meal was taken. James studied the map once more, although he could picture it clearly in his mind. He would divide the most likely places into some priority, and then search each of them in turn for the markers that Esteban had left to enable the source of the gold to be found. These markers would be small and hard to find, as obvious ones might have attracted the attention of a casual passersby. The searches would have to be painfully slow to avoid overlooking these crucial clues to the location they sought. At the same time they must remain watchful for any danger from hostiles.

James and Small Bird set out together, stopping at regular intervals along the way to scan the surrounding area for any sign of possible threat. It was a laborious way of moving but necessary for their safety. A landmark had been identified in advance, and each took a turn at leading towards this whilst the other attempted to cover any sign of their passing. James was all too quickly coming to realize the enormity of the task he had set his family. The chances of being discovered were high. Now that they had started seeking out the signs that might lead them to the gold, the risks would increase greatly. It was not a position he wanted to be in, and he decided they would have four days then leave, regardless of whether or not the source of the gold was discovered.

The morning passed slowly. It was a very tiring procedure that required both of them to seek out any of Esteban's markings, yet also stay alert to danger. It was hot and they rested for a short while. Small Bird had brought some dried meat and James some water. They ate in silence, each continuing to survey the surrounding area, each deep in their own thoughts. The midday heat had brought out the flies in their hordes and even the liberal application of bear grease that they had put on earlier did little to alleviate the constant bites inflicted.

"We are as well continuing our search as lying here providing food for the flies"' said James through gritted teeth. His wife needed no encouragement and they both rose to resume their search.

Above them and only a short distance away, Lone Wolf, a warrior of the Hunkpapa Sioux, viewed them with interest as the couple below stood up then started forward. He took care not to stare directly at them for any length of time but focused slightly to one side. Experience had taught him that people who faced dangers every day could develop a sense of awareness that would warn of being watched. Lone Wolf was puzzled why they, and the two others in their party, had halted and set up camp for a stay clearly longer than an overnight stop. He had followed their trail for three days as he had been curious who the travellers may be. Once he had caught up with the group he was pleased that he had stalked them. Here was a rich prize indeed! Eight horses and two women, the younger female one of great beauty. He said a silent prayer to his gods as he inched backwards and away from any prying eyes. His pony was in a safe place about three miles away and he took care to leave no sign of his passing as he made his way there.

Lone Wolf was highly regarded amongst his people as a hunter, for he had sharp eyes and the ability to follow even the faintest sign left by either man or beast. The other members of his hunting party were only a half day ride away and he mounted his pony and headed in their direction. He was pleased for he would be hailed as a great tracker by his friends. They would join him in returning to attack the travellers he had just left behind. It was a good day and he quietly sang to his pony as he rode away.

My horse be swift in flight; Even like a bird
My horse be swift in flight; Bear me now in safety
Far from the enemy's arrows,
And you shall be rewarded, with streamers and
ribbons red

When he reached camp he would tell his story and ask his brothers to join with him in returning to the camp of those he had watched these past few days. The leader of the hunting party was Potaka, a warrior of note who was absent from their camp but due to return shortly. Lone Wolf would ensure that two of the younger bucks would stay behind to tell Potaka of the planned attack, and perhaps join in the victory celebrations that would follow. Lone Wolf wanted the young woman for himself and he intended that the camp be overrun and scalps and horses taken before the leader's return. As the one who had discovered the camp, Lone Wolf would have the right to claim the young woman as his own. He smiled at the thought.

CHAPTER TWELVE

Peter Lloyd was pleased. Alexander McDougall had exceeded himself in arranging a ball. The great and good people of Boston, New York and other centres involved in the wheeling and dealing of trade and commerce were present. He took a tiny sip of his wine, always aware that he would need to keep his wits about him for the verbal sparring that undoubtedly lay ahead. He would be carefully scrutinized by those sharp business minds in attendance that evening. Although McDougall had opened the door of opportunity, Peter alone could plant the seeds that could grow into a very lucrative business for all concerned. Most of all, he admitted to himself, it could prove to be a fruitful bonanza for the Lloyd trading enterprise.

Across the ballroom he noticed Consuella laughing at McDougall's best efforts to amuse her. She was most adept at flattery, without giving any signs of encouragement that could lead to future misunderstanding. Peter trusted his wife completely but also knew that a pretty face and kind words could often soften the most hardened businessman's heart. She looked particularly beautiful this evening. A dark ankle length gown showed her smooth shoulders to best effect. At her neck was a small choker style necklace, the centerpiece a single stone supported by a velvet ribbon that matched her gown. Nearby Maria shared the company of Capitan Reina who looked quite splendid in his naval uniform. Maria however was the honey trap, and the number of male bees surrounding her was evidence that her beauty, and single status, had not gone unobserved by those present. Peter smiled to himself in contentment. Everything was going according to plan. The ladies had made a huge impact upon those present this evening, including the female guests who flocked to enquire about the fine materials worn by the visitors. A woman's word in the ear of her husband would often carry a great deal of influence in most households, as Peter himself knew from experience.

A deep voice interrupted his thoughts, and he turned to find himself facing a man standing well over six feet in height. His ruddy cheeks and high forehead were surrounded by a shock of striking auburn hair. He had narrow shoulders and broad hips, and his powdered hair was tied at the back with a velvet ribbon. His blue piercing eyes viewed Peter with a hint of challenge, and he paused before speaking.

"Mister Peter Lloyd I presume," he smiled and bowed slightly. "May I introduce myself?" He paused again. "I am George Washington, at your service." Peter acknowledged the greeting and extended his hand.

"It is a pleasure to make your acquaintance sir, for I have heard much about you and had intended seeking you out this evening." Peter paused as he recalled the detailed reports on influential guests which Alexander McDougall had provided him with a few days earlier. Washington had been near the top of the list.

"My understanding is that you have given valuable service to The Crown during the recent war against the French, and have been vocal in your support for the retention of a union with Britain." As he spoke Peter already knew that his companion had recently begun to publicly challenge the legislation being passed by the Westminster parliament in London. His response would be very informative.

His companion smiled knowingly.

"Come Mister Lloyd, I am certain that Alexander has also told you of my reservations about such a union. The British seek to levy a range of taxes upon the Colonies that will help towards the cost of the recent conflict against the French. This would not be unreasonable if we had an official voice in Parliament and a major say in our destiny. At present this is not the case and the feeling on these shores is an increasing sense of resentment." For a moment Washington watched the dancing couples twirling to a lively jig on the dance floor before continuing. "I am greatly curious about you. It is clear to me that you are a man of considerable influence, at least with the Admiralty in England, for it is not often that one of His Majesty's flagships is ordered to arrange an escort for a trading vessel from Spain."

Peter began to feel uncomfortable under Washington's steady gaze. This man was no fool and had clearly taken time to make enquiries about him and his existing business interests in the Colonies. It was Consuella who broke the silence when she appeared at Peter's side and linked an arm through his. She smiled at both men.

"I fear I might be interrupting some grand business scheme that you two are discussing, but my husband has been neglecting me and I must claim him for a dance before the music stops." Washington bowed in response and with a slight smile on his face watched the couple head for the dance floor. There was more to Mister Lloyd than the sharp mind of a successful business man, much more. He made a mental note to make further enquiries. The priority now however was to seek out his wife for a dance. There were many important matters that required his attention, however he would put these to one side. Washington had earlier made a promise to his wife that he would devote the bulk of the evening to dancing with her. He was many things to many people, but was never considered by anyone to be a fool.

It was on the afternoon following the ball that a formal gathering of eight businessmen met at the Boston offices of Alexander McDougall. In addition to the host, those present included Peter Lloyd, Douglas McDonald, Capitan Alonso Reina, George Washington and Benjamin Franklin, who ran a very successful publishing business. The remaining two present were local merchants representing the interests of a group of small commercial traders. The meeting had gone well as the various goods brought in on the 'Santa Maria' had been quickly purchased by the resident businessmen. The swords and knives from the Spanish forges of Toledo, just south of Madrid, were of the finest steel and they had proved to be extremely popular. Almost as much in demand were the fine materials and wines from the countries around the Mediterranean Sea. These would be given priority on the future cargo listings of merchant ships sailing on Lloyd's vessels from Spanish ports to the Colonies.

Capitan Reina had confirmed the details of the cargo that had been loaded on his ship in preparation for the return journey to Barcelona. The departure was due two days hence. The 'Santa Maria' had been given a thorough series of checks and, after some minor repairs, she was declared fully seaworthy by her Master. He had also sought, through the agencies of those present, written guarantees of safe passage and protection issued by both the Colonists and the British naval authorities. It was after all in the best interests of those parties present to help in ensuring that the 'Santa Maria' and other trading ships could ply their trade in relative safety. With these issues and other discussion points finally agreed, the group retired to a nearby room for a glass or two of wine. Peter found himself forming part of a trio with Washington and Franklin. Talk was light hearted to begin with, but soon became serious, with disquiet being voiced by the two Colonists about the issue of the imposition of taxation on the Colonies by the British government.

"It is damnable sir," said Franklin angrily. "Where is the justice in their thinking? We fought the French alongside the British, the vast majority of our people are of British stock and yet we are denied a voice by those who wish to govern us." He beckoned to a waiter for a refill of his wine glass. "What do you say in this matter Mister Lloyd?" Peter took the opportunity to ask the waiter attending to Franklin to also top up his glass, gaining a little time to think before framing a reply.

"As a native of Scotland I have seen families divided, fathers and sons becoming bitter enemies and too many weeping womenfolk. Conflict can be started easily and yet is very difficult to stop. Most conflicts are for the benefit of the few at the expense of the many. My answer sir is to negotiate, and if this fails then negotiate again, and again. War is rarely the answer." There was a short silence before Franklin spoke.

"You are either a very well informed gentleman, Mister Lloyd, or have identified my own feelings exactly regarding possible conflict between families whose beliefs are at odds with one another." He looked away for a moment as though composing himself. "My own son William is a staunch supporter of the Crown, and he has declared openly that he would take up arms against the Colonies if such a situation came to pass. I fully support your view that dialogue must take place between London and here. I only hope if it does it will be meaningful and honest with no hidden agenda."

Peter sighed inwardly with relief. He had no wish to become embroiled in politics, but self interest declared that his business ventures could be very much put at risk if hostilities were to break out between the British and the Colonies. It was his intention to stay as neutral as possible, for he also had trade links with England which were of considerable value to his company. He would be reluctant to jeopardize either business outlet.

The afternoon finished on a lighter note and further small talk took place before the meeting broke up. Before this happened Peter took time to speak with Douglas about how the McDonald freighting line could be utilized to the benefit of both parties. He also wanted to ask Douglas for advice on a personal matter concerning Maria. A meeting was arranged for the following morning at the rented house now being occupied by the Lloyds and Maria Cortez. Peter thanked Alexander McDougall for his excellent arrangements for the meeting then took his leave.

CHAPTER THIRTEEN

The chilly morning air was surrendering to the warmth of the rising sun as Douglas, accompanied by David Wilson, rode through the wooded outskirts of Boston. They were only a few miles away from the Lloyds' residence and the directions given to them had been easy to follow. The early autumn colours were showing in the trees and it was a time of year that both men enjoyed. The tinges of brown and gold were displayed boldly amongst the green leaves which were reluctantly bowing to the demands of nature as one season made way for another. A man could always find time to stop and breathe in the beauty of his surroundings at moments like this.

Both riders reined in their horses and silently enjoyed the view of the wooded slopes that gently rose towards the sky. No words were spoken, nor were they needed. They lingered there for a few minutes before Douglas urged his mount into movement. Wilson followed closely behind and the two headed off towards the Lloyd residence where the meeting would take place on their arrival.

It was less than half an hour later when they pulled up in front of a wooden mansion house that was surrounded by a wide ground floor balcony. They were met by a servant, who took their horses and invited David to follow him to where some hot food awaited. Peter had been made aware of the appearance of the two riders and came out to greet Douglas and usher him indoors where Maria and Consuella waited. It was Peter's intention that the initial discussions would concern the services that could be offered by the freight line. Once this had taken place advice would then be sought about finding Esteban. He had not however taken into account an impatient Maria, who as soon as greetings were exchanged began to divulge to Douglas the details of her quest, and to beg him for his help and advice on how Esteban could be found.

She blurted out her story, fighting back her tears as she did so. She did not spare herself in the telling and made no attempt to do so.

"Senor Douglas, you may think me a foolish woman with no pride who asks you to help in this matter, but I have lived much of my adult life in hope that someday I would find out what has become of him." Her shoulders shook as she sobbed, beseeching Douglas to understand how desperate she was. He was aware that all eyes in the room were upon him as he searched for the best way to respond to Maria's pleading.

"Senora Maria, I will do all I can to help you in this matter and will do so with the utmost discretion. My first responsibility however, is to advise that you should not place too much hope in ever finding Esteban. The Colonies cover a huge area, much of it as yet relatively unexplored." His eyes held Maria's tearful gaze for a few moments before he continued. "My freighters carry out our business as far south as Savannah in Georgia. It would be possible to convey word that information is being sought on Esteban's whereabouts, and that a reward will be paid for such information. From what you have told me it is possible, but unlikely, that the bounty hunters chasing him are still trying to find and kill him. We must plan our course of action very carefully, and I will seek advice from my contacts on how we should proceed. In the meantime every scrap of information you can provide me with would be of help."

Maria fought back her tears and forced a smile. "Thank you Senor Douglas, I am very grateful. Regardless of whether Esteban is found or not, I will be forever in your debt."

Peter called a halt to proceedings at this point and invited Douglas to join them for lunch. It had been an eventful morning and there was much to think about.

It was nearly two weeks later that a detailed hand-out was finally approved by Maria, before being passed to Benjamin Franklin's publishing company for many hundreds of leaflets to be printed. The handbills gave as detailed a description of Esteban as was possible under the circumstances, and offered a substantial reward for information as to his whereabouts. Maximum distribution would best be achieved by using the McDonald freight collection and delivery points, where copies could be given out and taken further afield by the company's customers. In addition, other copies would be sent to businesses that employed travelling salesmen, with a request that they arrange for the notices to be displayed in some prominent position in the places visited by their staff. Franklin also arranged for advertisements to be placed in various newspapers and repeated at monthly intervals. Maria insisted that all the costs of these arrangements be met from her own resources. In her view it was money well spent, and she would continue to spend while there was any hope of fulfilling her dream. She was pleased at the plan and hopeful that some information about Esteban would be forthcoming.

Douglas was at great pains to caution her against raising her hopes too high and reminded her constantly how the odds were against success. The distribution of the leaflets began, a process that would take many months before the bulk of them were delivered. They must now wait.

Meantime Peter became increasingly involved in meetings, with a view to forming partnerships that would not only receive the goods brought into the Colonies, but would identify goods for export. He was greatly excited by the challenge and did his best to involve Maria as much as possible, for apart from being a junior partner in the company she had a sharp mind and a ready way with figures.

George Washington had interests in numerous businesses and was a leading member of the very powerful Ohio Company, a group of speculators. Peter found himself spending more and more of his time in the Virginian landowner's presence. A wary respect rather than friendship developed between them and Peter was invited to meet with some of Washington's friends from time to time. The main topic of conversation was always the widening gap between the Colonists and the British Parliament, although there were some who openly supported the latter and remained hopeful that common sense would prevail. Peter rarely expressed an opinion except when encouraged to do so, but listened, watched and learned much.

Chapter Fourteen

Shortly before the fingers of morning light crept over the horizon Lone Wolf had selected a safe place that would enable him to observe any movement at the cave mouth. He lay in a small hollow at the edge of the rocky rim that overlooked the plateau below. He had insisted to the twelve warriors who had come with him that he should observe the intended victims one last time before any attack. His companions now waited in a small gully nearby for his return. Caution and patience were admirable traits in any warrior, and he wished to ensure that there had been no changes either in numbers or routine of those below. He did not have long to wait before the tall man and the young woman emerged from the cave. After a careful look around the pair set off on foot heading in the same direction that they had done on previous occasions. Lone Wolf waited unmoving, his sharp eyes seeking for some sign of the other two members of the group. His restraint was rewarded when the young brave appeared and made his way into the small nearby canyon where the ponies were tethered. Still Lone Wolf waited. There was no need to rush. He wanted some sign of the presence of the older woman before he would return to his band to tell them the plan for attack. Movement below caught his attention. The older woman now stood at the entrance to the cave.

Lone Wolf gave a start. She was looking directly at where he lay! She did not move but stood motionless, staring, for what seemed forever. The warrior was unnerved for he had seen the power of the medicine women of his tribe and their ability to see things that others could not. He shook away his fears. This was a day when he would become known as a warrior and leader, scalps would be taken and the young woman would be his. He left quietly, careful to leave no evidence of his having been there. He would delay the attack no longer.

Small Bird could see no sign of anyone watching them but she felt a presence. Her instincts had seldom let her down and somehow she knew danger, great danger, was about to descend upon her family. She forced herself to stay calm. James and Shining Star were some distance away, but near enough to hear a gun shot. Her husband and daughter would be better placed to defend themselves if attacked out in the open, and she determined that she would fire a shot if White Eagle and she were set upon by hostiles.

White Eagle gently rubbed the muzzle of his pony with one hand and stroked the beast's ears with the other.

"You can feel that we are being watched my brave one," he whispered, "we have stayed here too long and unfriendly eyes are upon us." Even as he spoke the youth continued to carefully examine the surrounding area for any sign of intruders. His unease was picked up by the horses and they showed their restlessness, for they too wanted to leave this place. Earlier that morning his father and sister had left to continue the search for the markings that might lead to the gold. This was to be the last day spent here, whether or not the source of Esteban's nuggets was found. White Eagle made his way the short distance back to the mouth of the cave where his mother had been packing in preparation for their leaving later that day.

As her son drew near Small Bird nervously put her hand on the handle of her knife at the sound of his approach. She heard him whisper her name as he came closer to her. She was angry at herself for failing to hide her fear from her son, but his expression confirmed to her that he too was aware that danger and a threat to their lives lurked nearby.

She shaded her eyes with a raised hand and searched the area for any sign of her husband and daughter. Time was moving much too slowly, and she wished them back with her so that they could all ride away from this place. She could not see any movement, so turned and made a pretence of continuing with her packing. Her eyes met with those of White Eagle. She knew her son well and although he tried to convey an air of calmness, she was aware that he also was apprehensive. The feeling of danger almost overwhelmed her and it was with great difficulty that she fought against the panic rising in her throat! She reached a hand towards her son, her heart pounding as she touched his shoulder.

"My son, you have made me so very proud of you, and if we have to die together then I die knowing you were with me at the end." She stepped back and drew her knife. In her other hand she had a pistol, primed and ready to fire. The sound would alert James and Shining Star of the impending attack. She was a woman of the Sioux and she would not die easily. White Eagle smiled at his mother casting his fear to one side. He stepped forward to be nearer to her.

"It is a good day to die mother. Let us show those who would kill us that we do not fear death!"

Ten minutes earlier and less than a mile away James had at last found a marker, a stone with the letter 'E' carved into it. The middle prong had an arrow head that pointed towards a large boulder that stood close by beside a small stream. They had passed within a few yards of the spot yesterday but had missed the marker.

"At last daughter, we have finally found the place we seek." James moved closer to the rock and immediately saw the glitter from a number of bean sized gold nuggets lying in the shallow water. Within a few short moments he had filled one small sack and was halfway to filling another when the faint sound of a shot reached them. They had been discovered and the camp was under attack! Both father and daughter rose as one and sprinted back towards the cave. As they drew nearer they could see and hear the screeching of a number of warriors grouped around Little Bird and White Eagle, who lay on the ground, motionless and covered in blood. James screamed his clan battle cry with as much breath that he could muster. It would alert the attackers but might also draw them away from Small Bird. His hope was in vain. As he came within a short distance of the camp he saw a warrior wielding a war club land a fatal crushing blow to Small Bird's head. A red mist descended over him and he lashed out in all directions cutting and stabbing whenever his blade struck flesh. He was vaguely aware that Shining Star was also in the thick of things, slashing and stabbing, screaming her hatred at those who had taken the precious lives of her mother and brother. The fight was a hopeless one for they were outnumbered.

A blow to the head from behind laid James low, leaving his daughter, knife in hand, to face the encircling ring of attackers. She positioned herself by her father's prone body, defiant to the end. Lone Wolf licked his lips in anticipation, for this woman had cut his shoulder open with her blade and he would make her pay! By the time he finished with her she would be begging for death. The warriors drew closer like a band of rabid wolves ready for the kill.

"Hold!" a voice cried from the edge of the group. "Enough. Step back and put your weapons away." The warriors, recognizing the voice of their leader Potaka did as ordered and moved away from the young woman and her unconscious father.

The warrior studied the chaotic scene before him. Three of his followers lay dead and another four were wounded. The anger in his voice as he spoke was frightening in its intensity.

"You are an impatient fool Lone Wolf, with the brains of a rabbit. If you had taken time to learn more about those you were so anxious to attack, you would have recognized that they carried the markings of our People, the Sioux. Your great leadership has left us with three dead and most of the remainder with wounds of some kind. This great victory of yours has been achieved against one man, two women and a boy." He dismounted as he spoke and approached Shining Star until he was close to her. He looked into her eyes, and after a pause asked her who she was and where the party had been headed.

Holding her head up high the young woman proudly indicated her fallen mother and brother in turn. "She was my mother and he was my brother. They died bravely against this pack of dogs. My father Shouts Plenty lies at my feet, a warrior of great repute. He is not yet ready to give his scalp to this group of coyote droppings." A murmur of protest arose from the angry band of warriors at her words. A silence descended as Potaka reached down and sliced open the shirt of the figure lying before him with a quick movement of his blade. He nodded in confirmation of what he had not thought possible. This was indeed Shouts Plenty, who was once a friend of Potaka before circumstances had forced him and his wife and child to leave the camp of the People.

The leader turned slowly to face the warriors gathered before him. Taking time to coldly gaze at each of them in turn he spoke, his voice dripping with contempt.

"Look you fools and see the marks on his body, for this is a warrior who has undertaken the ritual of the Sun Dance. His courage is greater than all of you put together. This is bad medicine. A day of great shame has been brought upon The People." Turning to the young woman he spoke softly so that only she could hear his words.

"We will arrange for the burial platforms to be built then leave you and your father to share your grief. Potaka salutes both of you with the great respect befitting those who are Sioux, The People." He turned and issued precise instructions before mounting his horse and riding away without a backward glance.

The burial platforms were quickly erected and the humiliated warriors collected their dead then rode away, knowing that they would face the ridicule of their friends and families once Potaka had reported this day of bad medicine to the tribe elders.

Father and daughter sat by the bodies of Small Bird and White Eagle for three days and nights. The searing heat of the day burned them throughout the daylight hours and the chill of the night added ice to their bones. Neither spoke during this time. Finally, at the end of the third day James rose and, with his daughter's help, placed the two bodies onto the burial platforms. They gathered their belongings together, including the two small bags of gold nuggets that had proved to be so very costly, before mounting up and continuing their journey eastwards.

At the end of the first days travel James turned to his daughter, his face drawn with the pain of their loss.

"They will be forever in our hearts, but I no longer have any regard for the Indian way of life. From this day forth you will be known as Fiona, daughter of James McDonald. We will exist as whites within their community. We will live as they live and die as they die."

The following morning they ate before mounting up. James pointed his horse and the packhorses eastwards towards the rising sun, and his daughter Fiona followed.

CHAPTER FIFTEEN

Sitting in a darkened corner of his New York hotel room Henri Chirac awaited the arrival of William Manson. He was impatient for news of what progress the hired killer had made with those he had been ordered to eliminate. The Frenchman was a man popular with people who knew him socially, although few were aware of his undercover activities. He sipped a glass of wine as he waited, his head filled with memories of the conflict against the British during the Seven Years War that had ended in the defeat of his country in 1763.

He swore and hurled his glass against the wall. Chirac had been a young Lieutenant whose first taste of action had been the humiliating defeat at Quebec, when the French held fortress was taken by the British forces led by General James Wolfe. The bitter memory of that day, and the shame of further defeats that followed burned deep within his soul, feeding the hatred he had for the English. He poured another glass of wine with shaking hands. Revenge would be his if there was any justice in the world. His eyes gleamed with the fervour of a fanatic, for Henri Chirac was a man with a mission, a mission that, if successful, would drive the English out of the Colonies forever. He smiled to himself, for the plan was so simple and was achievable largely due to the arrogance of the London Parliament. A recent example was the stamp

duty levied on a whole range of public documents including newspapers, contracts, wills and mortgages, that had
created great anger in the Colonies. It was Chirac's
intention to spawn further discord when opportunities
such as this arose. He did so by bribing some of those in
key public positions to stoke up the resentment further.
As with most cities, Boston experienced spasmodic bouts
of mob violence. Chirac paid some of the local leaders of
the opposition to the stamp duty levy to incite the city
mobs, supply them with free drink, and attack premises
housing representatives of the British Government.

William Manson's role was to kill those selected
by Chirac and his agents. Those targeted were men of
influence who publicly objected to any move towards
independence from Britain. In addition, the Frenchman
had for some time been cultivating the friendship of
certain other Colonists who were determined that rule by
London should be ended at any cost. Relations between
those on this side of the Atlantic and Britain were
deteriorating daily, and it was the hope of the French that
this would escalate into rebellion. At that moment
France would offer itself as an ally of the Colonists and
provide military aid to fight the British. When initially
approached by his masters in Paris, Chirac had little
enthusiasm for the plan. The muddled policies passed
by the British Government, however, had soon led to
a change of heart by Chirac, for it was clear that little
regard was being given to the views and demands of
the Colonists. It would take time for the plan to reach
fruition, but time was a thing Chirac had plenty of.

A sharp rap on his door brought the Frenchman back
to the present. It was Manson, who warily entered the
room. He had previous experience of Chirac's vile

temper when roused, and he had no wish for a repeat performance. It was therefore something of a pleasant surprise to be invited to take a seat and a glass of wine poured by his employer. Manson felt a little bit more at ease, although he had yet to make his report. He took a large swallow from his glass then began.

"I got to Simpson and made sure that it looked like an accident. There were no witnesses and no suspicion about his death." He paused and took a deep breath before he continued. "I got close to McDonald but he woke just before I was going to stick him. I'll get him next time. I promise." Chirac's eyes narrowed at this news and he glared angrily at Manson before slamming his fist on the table. Both glasses and the opened bottle of wine fell to the floor. Neither man moved to pick them up.

"You were hired because you claim to be the best. We pay top wages for your services and we demand only success. Failure to carry out our wishes will not be tolerated. Do I make myself clear Mister Manson?" Both men sat across the table from one another, eyes locked. Finally the hired killer nodded his head in acknowledgement of Chirac's question. No further words were exchanged and the visitor rose and left the room. The situation was crystal clear. Douglas McDonald must die, and the sooner the better.

CHAPTER SIXTEEN

Peter Lloyd had been busy most of the day completing a number of reports that would be taken back to Spain by Capitan Reina. The 'Santa Maria' was due to sail on tomorrow's noon tide. He had finished the first one to his old friend Senor Pedro Palacio, who was in charge of Maria's financial affairs as well as overseeing the Lloyds businesses during their absence abroad. A second report was nearing completion, and this would also be sent to Senor Palacio with a request that it be forwarded to the Spanish government department that dealt with foreign affairs. Prior to his departure to Boston Peter had received a visit from a government official. He had requested that a report on both the political situation and possible openings for trade in the Colonies, please be provided by Peter. The information would be of great interest to the Spanish authorities who would, of course, be grateful to Senor Lloyd for his efforts. The request was in reality an order, and Peter had no intention of failing to submit his report. To have done so would have resulted in all manner of petty delays in the provision of documents and permits that were issued by the local authorities. Without these papers normal business would prove to be virtually impossible.

The final assessment being drawn up was by far the longest, and contained as much detail on the political scene that Peter felt sufficiently informed to pass comment on. He also gave honest opinions on high profile individuals, as well as an overall review of the resentment that was building up against the British due to the legislation introduced for raising taxes. The Colonists' basic principle was that there could be no taxation without representation. His final comment was one that he could not substantiate, but he believed that outside influences were at work. There had been a growth in the level of unrest within the towns and cities, and he considered that the increasingly violent protests were not spontaneous, but organized by an outside group. He put down his pen, for he had finished his report.

Peter sat unmoving for some minutes before he rose and placed the two that were bound for Spain in a locked cabinet. Even if they were to fall into the wrong hands there was little that could be challenged as inaccurate or mischief making, for the bulk of these two documents was related to trading matters. The third document was not quite so innocent. He would leave shortly, in the company of his trusted servant Manuel Jamon and two others, to deliver the package to Admiral Sir John McLean aboard his flagship, 'The Albion'. The ship was due to leave for Portsmouth tomorrow on the same noon tide as the 'Santa Maria'. The admiral himself would ensure the safe delivery of the report to The Right Honourable Edmund Burke MP, a lifelong friend and someone Peter trusted totally.

It was time to be off, and within ten minutes he was sat in his coach being driven to his meeting on board 'The Albion'. The package weighed heavy in his pocket for he had, at first, had reservations about providing the information that Burke had asked for. His friend had pleaded his case with all the skill of the practiced public speaker.

"I ask you to do this for one purpose alone, and that is to enable me to attempt reconciliation between the Colonists and ourselves. There are other politicians who share my views. It would be madness to deny that our ancestors have turned a savage wilderness into a glorious empire. We must think big and be generous, for is it not true that a great empire and little minds go ill together?" Peter smiled to himself at the memory, for his friend was a skilled orator and was known to have swayed even the most hardened politicians to change their minds.

"We are here Senor Lloyd." Manuel's words interrupted his master's thoughts "Do you wish me to come aboard with you?" he enquired. Peter shook his head in response.

"No thank you, my business will take but a few minutes then we can be on our way." Peter stepped down from the coach, which had stopped only a few yards from the gangway where a young officer waited to escort the visitor to the Admiral's quarters. In no time at all he was being greeted by Sir John who poured a glass of wine for his guest and indicated to the young escort that he was dismissed.

"So Mister Lloyd, we are alone. You have something for me I believe?" Sir John looked slightly uncomfortable as he spoke. "I confess that this spying business is a distasteful affair and one I do not do by choice. It does not seem to me to be an activity that gentlemen should be involved in." Peter placed his sealed package on the table before he spoke, his voice tight with anger.

"I am here because I firmly believe that the contents of this," he pointed to the small parcel he had delivered, his voice rising, "this small package may save the lives of thousands of people, perhaps even yours Admiral." He sank back in his seat, embarrassed at his outburst. The Admiral shuffled uncomfortably and took a sip of wine before speaking.

"My apologies sir, I did not mean to cause offence. As a humble seaman of some fifty years I tend to think of honour and courage as attributes restricted to those on the battlefields or warfare at sea. Your rebuke was well intended and I wish for no ill feeling to exist between us." Peter smiled, rose from his seat, and extended his hand.

"God keep you, your ship and crew from danger always Sir John. May your journey home be swift and safe. Goodbye." He left the ship and climbed into his coach. His sigh expressed a mixture of relief and tiredness. His task was done. It was up to others now to achieve the peace or face the possible consequences of a rebellion

Later that evening the Lloyds hosted a small party for Capitan Reina and the ship's officers of the Santa Maria. Amongst those invited was George Washington. Peter had spoken with the ship's Master in the privacy of his study and had handed over the two packages to be delivered to Senor Pedro Palacio. Peter had grown to like and respect Alonso Reina and had no hesitation in asking him to consider working for the Lloyds' company again. The seaman was pleased and promised that he would be happy to do so whenever possible.

Later, when most of the guests had taken their leave, Washington and Peter sat together on the porch, a glass in hand, with smoke from their cheroots rising upwards in a swirling dance into the evening sky. The stars shone through the few clouds like a million diamonds, and the two men watched the heavens in silent companionship before the Virginian broke the silence.

"Well my friend, what messages have you sent back to Spain? Nothing too bad about us I hope?" He puffed on his cheroot before he continued. "What information I wonder does Sir John McLean take to England with him tomorrow?" Both men were silent for a moment before Peter answered.

"No more than you perhaps convey and receive in your correspondence with your cousin in Yorkshire. There is surely no harm in an exchange that keeps both parties better informed as to how each regards their situation. How else can we exchange open dialogue, if it is not based on honesty regarding our disquiet about thoughts and actions that can lead to misunderstanding and ultimately conflict?" Washington smiled, but made no attempt to respond. Peter was irritated and decided to continue their exchange further.

"My correspondence is of a nature that is of assistance to fair minded people in England who wish to reach an honourable contract between those who live here and the parliament in London. They seek a vote for the Colonies in all matters that concern them, for the alternative is unthinkable. I believe that rebellion is a distinct possibility if agreement is not reached that is acceptable to both parties."

Washington continued to sip his wine, but made no comment. Finally he stubbed out the remnants of his cheroot and rose. For the very first time since they had met he called his host by his Christian name.

"Thank you for your hospitality Peter. I only wish that the British parliament, aye, and some of my own people, could speak with such honesty. I bid you goodnight."

Later in bed Peter shared his thoughts with his wife. After a lengthy discussion they were no nearer an understanding of what would happen next in the days and months that were yet to come. The one thing they agreed on was that turbulent times lay ahead.

CHAPTER SEVENTEEN

Douglas awoke early. Taking care to avoid any movement or noise that might waken Isabel he made his way to the kitchen for a coffee. Nan was already up and about, and within a short space of time Douglas was seated facing a breakfast of bacon and eggs. Nan could tell that he was not in the mood for chatter and carried out her normal morning chores in silence.

He yawned, picked up his coffee cup, and made his way to his work desk. Isabel had been in Georgetown most of yesterday and had brought back an assortment of papers that would require his attention. Some years ago his wife had been determined that she would open a school in the town for all children, and any adults who wanted to learn how to read and write. It had been a success from the first day. This was largely due to the dedication of the schoolmistress Joan Taylor, an Irish teacher whose husband Norman ran a hardware store next door to the school building. Yesterday had been a very busy but productive day. Due to the increase in pupils attending lessons, interviews had been held for the appointment of an additional teacher. The position had been offered to Mistress Rosemary Raeburn, wife of one of the doctors whose practice was in Georgetown. Already a supporter of the school, and someone whose own two daughters were receiving tuition there, Mistress Raeburn was delighted to accept. A bill for some minor repairs to the school building was one of the notes Douglas identified. He nodded in approval. A town without a school would not produce the level of education required if Georgetown was to continue to grow and prosper.

With a deep sigh he began to scrutinize the paperwork that lay before him. One letter in particular caught his attention. It was fairly bulky and had been carefully sealed to protect the contents. Douglas opened the small package, his curiosity increasing by the second. He was astounded to find that it had been sent from Scotland, and was from Ewan McDonald, younger brother of James. Reading quickly he learned that the brothers' father, the clan chief of the McDonalds had died. Ewan had inherited the title and was anxious to trace his brother. The only news that the family in Scotland had received regarding James' whereabouts had been provided by Captain Robert Campbell, whose life James and Seth had saved when the officer was attacked by a band of Pawnees. On his return home to Scotland, the Captain had told the McDonald family his news on the wellbeing of both James and Douglas. James' father, however, had refused to allow any attempt to be made to make contact with his exiled son. As clan chief he did not want to risk being seen offering support to James, a Jacobite, whom he had previously disowned.

Now that he was no longer prevented from doing so, Ewan had written to Douglas at the address provided by Campbell. He implored his help in providing any information available regarding the whereabouts of his brother, and expressed his delight that Douglas had married and was prospering in the new Colonies. Ewan's son, Cameron Allan McDonald, now a 2nd Lieutenant in the Highland Division, was due to be posted to the garrison in Boston and would arrive in three months time. A quick check of the date of the letter showed that the young officer would arrive in six weeks. Douglas reread the communication with mixed feelings. He had strong ties with the McDonalds and had somehow felt a responsibility for the terrible penalty that James had incurred in safeguarding the clan lands and titles. He chided himself, for there was no point in dwelling on what might have been. He ran upstairs and disturbed his wife's rest by jumping on the bed and thrusting Ewan's letter into her hand. He gave Isabel no chance to begin to read before he spoke, words flowing out of him like a waterfall. "We have a visitor from Scotland arriving here in six weeks or so." He paused for breath. "It is the son of James' brother Ewan who is now clan chief." He looked expectantly at his wife, who put her hand over her husband's mouth.

"Hush dear, let me read. In the meantime make yourself useful and ask Nan if she could please bring me a coffee."

Isabel read the letter twice. She was disappointed, for there was no great change in the existing circumstances. James was somewhere out there in the wilderness, hopefully still alive. Even if he returned he could not go back to Scotland as he was a wanted fugitive there with a price on his head. He had been pardoned for his involvement in the death of Captain Marano, but where was James? Over the years since James and Seth had fled from arrest their friends had tried every possible way to find or make contact with the two fugitives, but to no avail. The arrival of the young British officer could prove to be awkward for Douglas and his family given the current political unrest. It had to be recognized that the appearance of the young McDonald was an additional distraction at a time when more important issues required Douglas' full attention, including the possibility of a further attempt on his life.

Once the initial excitement had died down it was decided that the help of the officer commanding the Boston Garrison would be sought. Confirmation of what ship Cameron McDonald sailed on, and when she was expected in Boston was obtained and preparations made for his arrival. The Garrison Commander was pleased for the young Lieutenant to be released from his duties for a fortnight, but only once he had been in post for a short settling in period. Nevertheless it was an expectant group of Douglas, Isabel, young James and his sister Anne, who waited on the quayside as His Majesty's Ship 'Protector' drew alongside for docking. The Royal Marines, at attention in their splendid red uniforms, were lined up in impressive lines as the whistles from the watch sailors blew their salute. Eight officers were also on deck, swords drawn, in blue Royal Navy or red Army attire. They stood rigidly to attention as the ship and her crew paid formal compliments to the Admiralty flagship at anchorage in Boston harbour.

"Oh look mother," gasped Anne excitedly, "there are four young officers on deck. Which one is Cameron? Is he tall or short, dark or fair?" She waved her handkerchief as she spoke, quite caught up in the excitement of the moment. It was nearly twenty impatient minutes before the crew, including the officers, began to disembark from the ship. Two of the younger officers stepped onto the quay. One was heard to say to the other,

"I say Jack, is this place what all the fuss is about? By God a few shots of grapeshot would have them scurrying don't you think?" Both laughed and passed near the waiting group. Anne and the others were appalled at what they had overheard. Was one of the officers Cameron? It was a few minutes later that a voice, coming from close to where they stood, asked if they were the McDonald party. He was Cameron Allan McDonald and he hoped that his father's letter would have reached them in time to advise them that he was coming.

The young man who stood before them was a credit to the British Army. His uniform fitted his trim form perfectly. His brown curly hair peeped from beneath his officer's cap, that was angled sufficiently to satisfy Army dress regulations but tilted just enough to show a touch of individuality. There was a twinkle in his dark brown eyes as he bowed to the ladies, saluted Douglas then nodded at James before he spoke again.

"Sir I have the honour to present myself. I am Lieutenant Cameron McDonald at your service." Douglas responded in kind.

"You very much remind me of your father, who was a great friend to me before your uncle James and I had to leave Scotland rather urgently. Welcome to Boston. Allow me to introduce my wife Isabel, my son James and his sister Anne." The young Lieutenant smiled in response before replying.

"It is extremely kind of you all to take the trouble to meet me here. I have only just received my written orders and am delighted to note that I am soon to be granted two weeks leave to enable me to enjoy your hospitality."

"We were coming to Boston anyway and it seemed a good opportunity to meet with you," said Isabel. "News from Scotland would be most welcome, and we are very much looking forward to your stay with us." Further dialogue was interrupted by a drum roll from the naval vessel. Cameron grinned at the welcoming McDonald quartet. "Forgive me, for I must report to the Garrison Commander. It would do my fledgling career no good at all to be late." His eyes lingered a little longer on Anne than was obligatory before he saluted, turned, then made his way to join the assembled troops who were waiting to be transported to the barracks. Douglas led his family to their coach and no one spoke until they were some distance away from the harbour.

"I am glad that he was not one of those foolish young men we overheard earlier," said Douglas, "in fact I am very impressed by him and look forward to his stay with us."

"So do I father," whispered Anne, blushing in the darkness of the coach "so do I."

CHAPTER EIGHTEEN

James stood on watch while Fiona slept fitfully under the protection of some bushy shrubbery. He rose and draped his blanket over her. They had come far and were in need of rest. The traumas of the last two months were still fresh in his mind, for there was no escape from the constant torment of having witnessed his beloved wife being battered to death. He eyed the surrounding pine ridges. Distant thunder rumbled its warning of rain to come, the echoes penetrating the far canyons. When it rained at this time of year it could last from dawn until well into the blackness of night.

He made further preparations in anticipation of the downpour to come. His thoughts were dark and he felt the cloak of hopelessness wrap a weakening fog around him. There comes a time when human nature seems unable to carry on any more. Every last vestige of strength has gone. How easy just to give up. Somewhere in the depths of his mind the idea was debated briefly, and then discarded. There was his daughter to consider. Her life and future were his responsibility, and he would survive in order that she might have the opportunity she deserved. The deaths of his wife and son must not have been in vain.

As he had predicted, the heavens opened and the rain fell heavily. There was sufficient shelter from the deluge to keep them reasonably dry, but the warmth of a small fire was denied them. They huddled together as the thunder became louder and lightning flashed its way across the dark sky. For one brief moment the immediate area was illuminated, betraying the silent presence of three warriors who had picked up their trail the previous evening. One man and a woman alone with eight ponies was a very tempting opportunity for any young brave wanting to build up a reputation amongst his people. The intruders stood stock still, seeking to identify where their intended victims were hidden. Two were armed with a knife and axe in each hand, while the third held a bow with an arrow in place ready to fire. It was this last Indian that James chose as the one most dangerous to Fiona and himself, therefore he would be the first to die. The heavy rain made the use of his rifle risky, for the powder may have become damp. His pistol however had been kept primed and dry, a habit that James always followed wherever he went.

He whispered his intentions in his daughter's ear. He would fire the pistol when the next flash of lightning appeared, then follow up his attack using his knives. Fiona, already poised with a knife in each hand, was to set upon the intruder on the right of the trio. The seconds passed before the flash from the lightning caught the three warriors in its brightness. James fired and the Indian recoiled as the ball struck him in the middle of the chest. The two groups came together quickly and for the next few moments the dangerous game continued against a backcloth of torrential rain, thunder and lightning. The whirling combatants performed a frantic dance to the death, where there would be no encore for the losers. The brave facing James lost his footing in the mud and the Scot stepped inside his attacker's guard and ripped his belly open with an upward sweeping thrust.

He struck again with his other knife and the Indian dropped, lifeless, to the ground. Fiona was still sparring with her opponent when James came behind the warrior, grabbed his hair and cut the exposed throat to the bone. The fight was ended.

Both father and daughter stood in the torrential rain, drained by their exertions, each checking that the other was unharmed. It had been a close run thing, for if the lightning had not flashed when it had, the intruders might not have been spotted. What was needed now was warmth and hot food. James started a small fire tucked in at the base of a tree and left Fiona to prepare some hot soup. He removed the bodies that he identified as Blackfoot, and after a short search found the ponies the Indians had tethered nearby. The creatures would be safe enough where they were until morning, when he could assess whether they were worth keeping or releasing. That done, he returned to find a hot soup waiting for him. The rain had eased off, and come morning they would dry out clothing and equipment and make any repairs needed before moving on.

The following morning James awoke to find that his daughter had let him sleep longer than he had intended. Although he gently chastised her he was grateful for the rest. There was a fresh feel to the land after the storm from the day before. As he ate his breakfast he looked at the surrounding area. The mountains hung in the misty far spaces, shadowy, elusive and forever changing. Were the mountains real, he pondered, or simply mirages playing tricks on the eyes. He stretched and yawned. It was time to sort things out before they moved on.

A closer inspection of the Blackfoot ponies confirmed his first suspicion that they were in poor condition. It was little wonder that their owners had tried to steal replacements! He turned the beasts loose and left them to their own devices. They would probably find a herd of wild ponies and join up with them.

The warmth of the sun was most welcome and the wet clothing dried out quickly. By early afternoon they had packed and were ready to continue their journey. There was a need to do less aimless travelling and to concentrate more on making better progress to reach Georgetown. Yesterday's attack had provided a reminder that the longer they took to reach their destination increased the risk of being set upon by hostiles.

From that day onwards they travelled at a sensible pace that ate into the many miles that lay ahead. They took no unnecessary risks however, and on at least three occasions opted to lie low for a few days, having spotted fresh signs of riders who would almost certainly have proved to be hostile. It was on enforced stops like these that James talked quietly about all aspects of the way of life of the whites. Fiona asked many questions of her father, and there were times when even he had to admit that he did not have an answer. On reflection it was time well spent and each of them gained a little more confidence with every day that passed. They were in this great challenge together and were determined to succeed in building a shared future.

James explained that he intended setting up a vantage-point on the road leading to Georgetown, in the hope that passing traffic might provide some indication as to the location of his friend Douglas. If the freight company that he and Douglas had set up all these years ago had grown, there might be wagons bearing the McDonald brand. It was also his intention, before reaching Georgetown, to exchange one or two of the ponies for clothing for himself. This would enable him to discard his Indian clothes and make him less conspicuous. It would also allow him to visit the town for a quick look around, although it might be a risky thing to do. James suddenly felt concerned. It had not occurred to him before now that Douglas might have moved away, or that the freighting business had failed, or even that his friend might be dead. In that event there were others he could hopefully ask for help, in particular, to provide a safe home for Fiona. He kept these anxieties to himself, for his planning was flawed, and he cursed his stupidity in not having realized the extent of the difficulties that lay ahead. Perhaps at least one of his other friends, William Porter or Hugh Mercer, still lived in the town. These thoughts helped to quell his fears a little, for at least he had identified other possible options to pursue if contact, for whatever reason, couldn't be made with Douglas.

It was many tiring miles and long weary months later before James pulled his mount to a halt, his eyes narrowed against the blinding glare of the noonday sun. Heat waves danced their hypnotic dance across the lower sky and his face was pummeled by the sweltering heat. Far away in the distance there shimmered a thin purple line, and his heart leapt within him. He turned to his daughter and forced a smile through his dry lips.

"Take a look Fiona," he pointed ahead, "those are The Appalachian Mountains. We are getting closer to Georgetown. If we push on we should make the foothills before nightfall."

He kicked his reluctant pony into motion as he spoke. During his years away he did not doubt that there would have been some settlement by homesteaders on the eastern side of the mountain range. Some hardy souls had already started out to do so during the time James had been in Georgetown. The opportunity to barter for some clothes for him to wear might well present itself soon. One thing at a time however, for once they had reached the coolness of the foothills they could rest the horses, and themselves, for the final leg of their journey.

CHAPTER NINETEEN

Newly promoted 1st Lieutenant Cameron McDonald sat in his room. He had just returned from a meeting with the Garrison Commander, Colonel Thomas Alexander, who had informed him of his elevation in rank. The promotion had come more quickly than expected, and at first Cameron was pleased. It was, after all, a lovely start to the day he was due to begin his stay with the McDonald family. However the young officer was not happy, indeed he was very angry, for there was a price to pay.

Colonel Alexander had stood looking through the window of his office, his hands clasped behind his back when Cameron entered the room. The Commander had been watching some of the latest reinforcements drilling and practicing their firearms skills. He had turned and smiled a welcome and motioned for Cameron to be seated.

After congratulating the young officer on his promotion, the Colonel had come straight to the heart of the matter. For the next two weeks Cameron would be residing with Douglas McDonald, a man of considerable standing and influence in the community, who enjoyed close friendships and regular visits from others of similar standing. During his stay Cameron was to keep his eyes and ears open at all times. On his return to the barracks he was to report back directly to the Colonel details of any discussions he might have overheard between Douglas and his visitors.

At this point Cameron had moved as though to speak, but was stopped by the senior officer's raised hand. The Garrison Commander was not unsympathetic to the disquiet his request had caused, but he reminded the young man where his duty lay. Any intelligence gathered may be of sufficient value to ensure the safety of his fellow officers and soldiers.

The Colonel had continued by explaining that there were times when demands were placed upon individuals that were distasteful. In this instance some may regard it as spying. He did not, but viewed it as an opportunity to gather intelligence that could prove of great value. Cameron must therefore accept that it was his duty to do so. There followed a lengthy silence during which both stared at each other. Finally Colonel Alexander invited the junior officer to speak.

"Sir, I will do as ordered, but I regard the task you have set me as a betrayal of my family's high regard for Douglas McDonald and his household." He rose to his feet. "May I have your permission to leave Sir?" The Colonel nodded his approval, acknowledged the smart salute given to him and watched the angry young man leave his office.

Colonel Alexander reached into the bottom drawer of his desk and pulled out a bottle of whisky and a glass. After a large dram had disappeared down his throat he felt no better. There were indeed times when soldiering did demand much of those who served.

"Damn it all," he scowled, "Damn it to hell." He poured another drink and emptied the glass but still felt no better. Indeed there was a bitter taste in his mouth that whisky could not remove.

Cameron finished his packing. The anger he felt had subsided somewhat. He had already decided that if he took care not to eavesdrop on any conversations during his stay at the McDonalds, he would have nothing to report. Before leaving his room he made one final check to ensure that he had packed everything he needed. His father, Ewan, had asked Cameron to deliver some gifts and correspondence to Douglas on his behalf. These were tucked away in the smaller of his two bags. He was due to meet David Wilson at the guardroom and the pair would then travel to the McDonald ranch on horseback. It took no time at all to make his way from his accommodation to where a patient Wilson awaited him. Within a few minutes they had set off, and Cameron began to relax with each passing mile. He was determined to enjoy his stay at the ranch, for there was news from home to be exchanged and he was very much looking forward to spending time with the lovely Anne. He smiled in anticipation, and by the time they had completed a further five miles the gloom he had felt earlier had lifted.

CHAPTER TWENTY

After two relaxing days rest at the foothills they were ready to begin the crossing of the Appalachian Mountains. James had shot a deer on the first morning of their stopover and they had eaten well during the remainder of their short stay. The ponies had gorged themselves on the lush green grass and were reluctant to leave their equine paradise. Eventually, after much persuasion and considerable curses from James, the party set off.

As they rode along, James was able to identify some of the more prominent features remembered from when he and Seth had ridden this way all those years ago. One who returns to a place sees it with new eyes. The mountains would not have changed but he had. He was certainly older, and he smiled wryly to himself because there was not much evidence to support any claim that he might be any wiser. There were many questions that would soon be answered if luck was on their side. How easily would they find Douglas? How could he avoid being recognized? He stopped himself from asking any more questions, for he had done so every day for what seemed an eternity. Time would provide the answers and he and Fiona must concentrate meantime on doing what must be done.

They travelled on. The higher they climbed the cooler it became, and the snow lying on the highest peaks shone blindingly in the morning sun. The clear air enabled them to see for many miles in all directions. Their breaths and those of the horses were steam in the coolness, and movement became more tiring in the rarefied air. There was no sense in pushing themselves too hard. It would take a week or so, at a sensible pace, to cross the mountains in safety. It would be foolish to needlessly tire themselves and the horses for the sake of a quicker crossing.

They had taken a cold mid-day meal then set off again. James kept a watchful eye for any likely spot that would be suitable for an overnight camp. By late afternoon they had found one and settled the horses before building a little, well hidden, fire at the rear of a small cave. The welcome heat reflected from the stone and the flickering flames threw dancing shadows around them. They huddled closer to the fire for there was an evening chill in the air. James announced that he would stand first watch and Fiona wasted no time in wrapping her blankets around herself before drifting off into a deep sleep. Her father stepped away from the comfort of the fire, for it would be easier to keep alert if he had to move every so often to stay warm. He would periodically check on the wellbeing of their mounts and ensure that the fire was kept alight during the night. The sky above was full of stars and the gentle shuffling of the nearby ponies was comforting, for they would raise the alarm if they caught the scent of any creature, man or beast, that they considered to be dangerous.

It was on the morning of the sixth day that they became aware of the faint thud of axes, a lovely and welcoming sound that echoed through the mountains. They were camped near the downward slopes on the eastern side where James had hoped to find some small settlements. He was pleased, for the activity below was an indication that settlers were nearby, for no Indian used axes the way the white man did. He smiled at Fiona who nodded in return, for she too understood what the sound meant.

After a hearty breakfast they packed up and set off, following the contours of the slopes that were becoming less steep the further they travelled. After two hours or so they topped a small ridge and the view before them was outstanding. The quiet morning and the beauty of the long green valley that spread before them somehow felt like a welcome from the land. Father and daughter drank in the scenery, enjoying the peace and tranquility of the moment.

The morning sun had driven away the chill of the dawn and as they continued their descent into the valley below, a cluster of three cabins came into view. Lingering smoke rose from the chimneys, beckoning fingers with a promise of security and shelter. A woman appeared in the doorway of the nearest cabin, her hand to her eyes against the sun's glare as she watched them approach. She called to someone inside the shack who came out to join her, a rifle in his hands. James motioned for Fiona to stop with the packhorses while he rode on slowly, taking care to keep both hands in view. When he was within fifty yards of the cabin he stopped his horse and shouted a greeting to the couple who were warily observing him.

"Good morning," he called, hoping that his greeting in English would soothe any concerns they might have over his appearance. "Do you mind if my daughter and I come in and rest a while?" His words had the desired effect and the couple visibly relaxed. The man beckoned for James to come forward, and spoke as he halted his horse before them.

"My name is Trevor Bird and this here is my wife Pamela," he nodded in his companion's direction as he spoke. "Don't see many strangers around here and can't be too careful," he added as he lowered his rifle. "Call your girl in and we'll have a bite to eat before you ride on." Even as he spoke his wife had scurried away to prepare something for the table.

James waved for Fiona to join them, and helped her secure the horses before Bird invited them inside. The cabin was clean and neat with some chairs and a small table taking pride of place in the middle of the room. James introduced Fiona and smiled to himself as she hid her curiosity well, for this was the first cabin she had seen from the inside. Hot cups of coffee and a large apple pie were placed on the table and they ate in near silence. This was a luxury James had not enjoyed in a long time, and Fiona never before. Pamela flushed with pleasure when James complimented her on her cooking skills and added that the pie was the best he had tasted in ages.

The Birds were curious about their visitors, but good manners forbade direct questioning of strangers, especially guests. To satisfy their inquisitiveness James gave them an imaginary tale about how they had spent time with some friendly Indians while he was trapping beaver for their pelts. The story was flawed but seemed to satisfy them.

Before leaving their hosts James exchanged a blanket for powder for his gun and some other odds and ends, including a whole fresh baked apple pie! When questioned by James, Trevor Bird was able to give directions to a small trading post run by a man called Valentine, which was situated about eight miles further down the trail. The best news of all however, was when he also confirmed that there was a large freight company based near Georgetown that was owned by a Douglas McDonald! James and Fiona were barely able to contain their excitement.

With a final thanks to Pamela and Trevor Bird for their hospitality they set off to find the trading post. At last they were in touching distance of their objectives. Confidence was high and hope was in their hearts that the next few days and weeks would bring positive results.

CHAPTER TWENTY ONE

William Manson was an unhappy man. In his career to date he had never come across any target as elusive as Douglas McDonald was proving to be. Pressure from Henri Chirac was relentless and he was demanding a conclusion to this contract killing within the next few days. Manson's attempts earlier in the week to sneak into the McDonald ranch had proved unsuccessful, due to the high level of security in place. Indeed, last night had he not spotted the flare of a match from a guard smoking while on watch, his presence would have been discovered. He had always rigidly adhered to his own rules about the stalking and method of terminating the selected victim. The knife was his preferred method for killing but he was proficient in a variety of alternatives, including the rifle. It was with some reluctance that he had decided to plan for an ambush, for McDonald usually travelled to Georgetown and Boston once a week. He was normally accompanied by at least one other armed rider. Manson had set up a firing point amongst the bushes near to where the trail from the ranch joined up with the Georgetown trail. He had calculated the angle for his shot and had carefully worked out two alternative escape routes. He would now wait. Patience was one of his strengths, and McDonald would eventually be within target range of the killer's rifle.

The sun had risen then passed its zenith and there had been no sign of McDonald. The trail was much used and there was a steady stream of riders and wagons in both directions. At least the activity helped combat the tedious task of checking that his target was not amongst those travelling along the trail. Two riders appeared, and as they drew nearer turned onto the ranch approach track. One was a young army officer who was in uniform, and his companion was a rider Manson identified as one of the ranch hands. They had come from the Boston trail he mused, the soldier probably based at the garrison. No matter, for there was nothing to suggest that he needed to alter his plan. The presence of one young officer made no difference to his strategy.

Cameron and David Wilson had made good time, and when they slowed their horses to a walk to give them a breather they had chatted. Amongst other matters, the ranch hand had told the young officer of the attempt on Douglas' life and the increase in the ranch security. It was a concern, but nobody was going to stop the owner from carrying out his business, and the family was safe enough as long as they stayed on the ranch.

Wilson pointed out the various main features as they approached the ranch house. By the time they drew up at the front porch Douglas and Isabel were waiting to greet them. Cameron dismounted and saluted them, a smile on his face. Isabel spoke first.

"Welcome to our home Cameron, we are delighted to see you again."

"It is a great pleasure to be here. Thank you for asking me."

Isabel took him by the arm and led him inside where it was cooler. David Wilson deposited Cameron's two bags on the porch and handed over some papers he had collected from the freight line's Boston offices. Douglas nodded his thanks then went inside to join the others. He stopped in his tracks, for his daughter Anne was wearing a pretty dress instead of the jeans and shirt she usually wore. Douglas smiled. Perhaps Cameron had made a good impression, not just on Douglas, but also on the youngest member of the family. Cameron's stay could prove to be quite interesting!

"There's an hour to spare before we eat," said Isabel, "so why don't the four of you take a ride around the ranch while I help Nan with the meal?" This had been agreed in advance of Cameron's arrival, with the intention of giving him the opportunity to get to know Douglas and the two McDonald teenagers better. There was only a minor delay while Anne changed into a pair of jeans and a shirt before they set off on the tour. The layout of the ranch had been carefully planned, and Cameron was impressed with the way the various activities dovetailed into each other. They were soon exchanging opinions on the breeding of beef cattle and the type of soil best suited for growing the lush grasses that would provide the high quality feed vital to rearing healthy bloodstock.

Douglas spoke about the circumstances that had brought Isabel and him together. She and her mother, Moira, had travelled from Scotland to join Andrew Smith who was Moira's husband and father of Isabel. They were never to meet, for he was murdered before they could be reunited. The following year Douglas and Isabel were wed. Around the same time Moira married a Scottish surgeon called Hugh Mercer who had befriended them shortly after their arrival. They had three daughters. Although of similar ages with Anne and James, the girls were their aunts and Hugh their grandfather! Douglas laughed aloud at the confused expression on Cameron's face. He already had some understanding of their circumstances and would work it out eventually.

They had ridden a wide loop around the ranch perimeter, and were approaching where the main trails to Boston and Georgetown converged with the ranch track, when Anne pulled up her mount. The pony had developed a limp, and James dismounted to examine his sister's horse while Douglas and Cameron continued onwards at a slow pace. Something ahead caught Cameron's attention. It was the shine of sunlight on metal from the bushes ahead! Wasting no time the youngster spurred his horse into Douglas' mount, calling out a warning as he did so. A gunshot rang out and Cameron was flung to the ground as the ball caught him in the left shoulder.

Douglas wasted no time assessing the extent of the wound, as a quick glance showed that it was not fatal. He shouted for James to get a doctor, leaving Anne to tend to Cameron, then spurred his horse into a fast gallop and headed to where he had seen gun smoke rising from the bushes. There was no doubt in his mind that the shot had been aimed at him, and only Cameron's speedy response had saved his life. He swiftly drew closer to the spot where the gunman had lain in wait. He drew his pistol from his belt and pulled his horse to the right, just in time to catch a glimpse of a horse and rider disappearing into a dip in the ground. Douglas stayed calm. He wanted this man alive but would not hesitate to kill him if necessary. The drum of hooves on firm ground came from his left and he cautiously followed, slowing his mount sufficiently to enable him to establish the direction his attacker had taken. Douglas now had the bit between his teeth. There was no way this man was going to escape, for Douglas had saddled up his best horse, an Appaloosa stallion, for the ride around the ranch. The chase might be a lengthy one but it was one he would win.

Manson was angry and not a little scared as he turned in his saddle and saw McDonald in pursuit. The killer whipped his horse, demanding greater effort, but the distance between them continued to close. He forced himself to think of a way out, although he knew that his horse could not outrun McDonald's mount. He would have to turn and face his pursuer and take his chances. Manson's horse was a brave mare and she ran her heart out for another five miles before almost falling with exhaustion. Now was the moment to turn and face McDonald who was close behind. Manson was no coward but he had never before met anyone as quick and deadly as Douglas. The killer savagely pulled his mare to a halt and turned in the saddle to aim his pistol at his pursuer. He never got to fire his weapon, for Douglas saw the danger and went for a shot to kill. To have done otherwise would have been too risky. Manson was dead before he hit the ground.

A quick search of the corpse revealed no information as to who he was. Douglas tied the body to the mare, pulled himself into the stallion's saddle and set off back to the ranch. The mystery of the dead man's identity could wait. His priority now was to find out how Cameron fared, for he owed the youngster his life.

CHAPTER TWENTY TWO

Anne had reacted quickly to her father's hasty orders as he rode off in pursuit of the gunman. Her time spent helping at the surgery in Georgetown now stood her in good stead. Cameron smiled weakly as she knelt down beside him and started to loosen his tunic jacket in order that she might assess the extent of his wound. She muttered an apology when he flinched as she cut away his shirt from the area where the musket ball had entered. The injury was not life threatening but would nevertheless prove to be painful. Anne stroked Cameron's brow and assured him he would live. After all, if he died while she was tending him she would forfeit her reputation of that of a nurse held in high regard!

He forced a half smile through gritted teeth, his face pale as he fought the rising pain. Young James would have alerted someone at the ranch before riding to Georgetown, and a wagon would be with them soon. In the meantime Anne continued to comfort Cameron, relieved that his wound was not as serious as it might have been. She was taken aback by her feelings for him despite the short time they had known one another. He had made a big impression on her, and his smile caused her heart to beat faster than was normal. It was a sensation that both scared and excited her.

The arrival of a wagon with Isabel and two ranch hands on board interrupted her thoughts. Anne gave her mother a brief description of the wound, while Cameron was lifted onto the wagon by the two men.

Within a short time the wound had been cleaned and Cameron was tucked up in bed. The ball was still to be removed, but this would be undertaken by the doctor when he arrived with James. Isabel waited anxiously by the front door of the ranch for any sign of her husband. That a second attempt had been made to kill Douglas was extremely worrying, and much as she knew her husband to be very capable of looking after himself she would fret until his safe return.

It was David Wilson who met up with a grim faced Douglas as he rode home with the dead assassin in tow. No words were needed between the two men. The cadaver's presence explained everything. As they approached the ranch Douglas gave an assuring wave to Isabel who was waiting on the porch. He pulled up and handed the reins of the horse carrying the dead man to Wilson. The corpse would be kept in the stables until the arrival of Sheriff Ricky Milligan from Georgetown. As he dismounted Isabel embraced her husband tightly. He had come home safely and she silently gave thanks for his return.

"How is Cameron?" he asked. "That young man saved my life with his quick thinking. If he hadn't acted as he did I would be dead." Isabel shivered at his words. It had been a close thing. Much too close for her peace of mind, and as yet there was no clue to who wanted Douglas dead. Anne hugged her father as he entered the room and informed him that the young McDonald was awake, although still in some pain, and that the musket ball was yet to be removed.

It was a further hour before Hugh Mercer, Sheriff Milligan and James arrived from Georgetown. Hugh attended Cameron straight away, and after a brief examination made ready, with help from both Isabel and Anne, to remove the ball from the young man's shoulder. It was a fairly straight forward procedure and Cameron was left to rest after being given a sleeping draught. Hugh had quickly realized that Anne was attracted to the handsome young patient and solemnly declared that someone should be stationed nearby to regularly check on his wellbeing. It was no great surprise when Anne quickly volunteered for the task.

Downstairs, Douglas and Ricky Milligan discussed the events leading up to the death of the gunman. The sheriff had carried out a thorough search of the dead man's clothes and saddlebag but there was no form of identification to be found. It was a complete mystery to both of them. Douglas had a vague feeling that he had seen the man somewhere before, but could not remember where or when.

The two men were friends of long standing and shared a glass of wine before the sheriff headed back to Georgetown. The corpse would be brought into the town on one of the freight wagons later that day. Sheriff Milligan would inform the Georgetown judge, R J Greaves, who was also the mayor, of the events leading up to the demise of the assassin. Beyond that there was little that could be done.

Hugh had washed up after treating Cameron and accepted Isabel's invitation to dine with them before his return to the surgery in Georgetown. He had been impressed by his young patient during the limited talk that had passed between them. He smiled broadly as he spoke, giving a nod in Anne's direction. "What a lucky young fellow he is to have such an attractive nurse tending his every whim. I shouldn't be surprised if he feigns sickness for as long as possible." Anne blushed at his remarks and Isabel gently chided him for teasing his grand-daughter.

"He has saved my beloved husband's life and therefore all of us are exceedingly grateful to him. He may stay as long as he wishes and visit with us anytime." Turning to Douglas she went on to suggest that he contact Colonel Alexander and inform him of the injury to Lieutenant McDonald. The young officer would, of course, be most welcome to stay at the ranch until he was able to travel.

A happy Anne nodded her agreement to her mother's proposal.

Chapter Twenty Three

Peter Lloyd and Consuella sat side by side on the porch of their rented mansion, enjoying the spectacular heavenly show provided by the stars and the full moon in a clear sky. A gentle but cool breeze rustled the leaves and Consuella pulled her shawl a little tighter. They had just returned from a most enjoyable evening spent in the company of Alexander McDougall, who had proved to be a most generous and amusing host. Regrettably, and not for the first time of late, Maria had declined to attend the dinner at the last moment, claiming a headache. Their hostess for the evening had been Mistress Nancy McDougall, Alexander's wife who was his cousin, and also from Islay on the west coast of Scotland. The McDougalls had entertained Consuella with tales of monsters and witches, each story becoming more unbelievable as the evening came to a close. Before they left, Alexander informed his guests that he and his wife were shortly returning to Islay on family business and would be away for about six months. During his absence an employee of his, Mr Norman Banks, would handle his affairs.

The Lloyds sat contentedly enjoying the beauty of their surroundings when Manuel Jamon, their manservant, appeared on the porch with some coffee and liqueurs. Manuel had been with Peter for many years and was trusted completely by his master.

"Tell me Manuel, have Ania or Simone noticed any changes in Senora Maria? We have concerns that the lack of response to her search for Esteban has affected her health." There was a moments silence while the coffee was poured before an answer was forthcoming.

"Both the maids have expressed their concerns to me Senor. There is no doubt that something has had an adverse effect on the Senora." He waited for a moment, before Peter nodded for him to continue. "The Senora has always been a kind and thoughtful lady and much loved by those who are in her service. However she has changed over these past few months and has become ill tempered and rude in the way she addresses her maid." Peter thanked Manuel who retreated back into the mansion.

Peter had already made his wife aware of his concerns for Maria. She no longer showed any interest in the business nor had she any desire to socialize, although there had been quite a few invitations from male suitors. Consuella had spoken to Maria enquiring if she was ailing of some illness, and had been rudely rebuffed by her friend. There was no doubt in either Peter or Consuella's mind that the Esteban situation was the cause of the unattractive change in their friend.

To make matters worse, Peter had received a worrying communication from Pedro Palacio in Barcelona. The young Hernando was proving to be too much of a handful for his uncle to control. Vast sums of his inheritance had been squandered and the debts were continuing to accumulate at an alarming rate. There had been talk by angry creditors of seizing some of the assets of the Cortez estates, part of which belonged to Maria. Pedro had advised her urgent return in order that she could protect her wealth from confiscation. When Peter had told her of Pedro's concerns Maria had little to say, except that she still hoped for some response to her appeal for information regarding Esteban's whereabouts.

Peter was close to finalizing his business dealings in the Colonies and, after discussing it with his wife, decided that it was appropriate to return to Spain within the next three weeks. Maria would have little choice but to accept that her quest to find Esteban had failed, and to return with the Lloyds to Barcelona.

The Gods in the heavens play the game of fate as the mood takes them. Lives are lost or destroyed on a whim. On rare occasions their meddling can create the opportunity for humans to find some good arising from their interference. Such a scene was set not sixty miles away from where Maria sat brooding over her failure to find Esteban.

James McDonald and his daughter Fiona had arrived on the outskirts of Georgetown. They were hidden close to the main route out of the town, keeping watch for any freight wagons showing the McDonald brand to pass by. It should not be overlong before they could follow such a wagon that would lead them to the McDonald ranch. And so they waited.

CHAPTER TWENTY FOUR

Henrick Swartz was a mule skinner held in considerable regard by those who knew what the job entailed. Most people meeting him for the first time noted the heavily muscled arms and torso, and wrongly assumed that there was little in the way of brain power in his shaven head. They were wrong. Henrick was quite content for his appearance of physical strength to cloud the judgement of those he met along the freight trails that he and his fellow mule skinners travelled. He had rarely been bettered in trading deals and could barter equally as well whether sober or drunk.

It had been a long and tiring haul up from the Virginian plantations, and he and his mules deserved the long rest he planned for all concerned. He was due a six day stop over at the McDonald ranch, and he knew that his animals would enjoy the best feed and care available. He might even have a bath as it was two months since his last one and his underwear would need changing. It was only around three miles to the turn off to the ranch and he was eager to sample Nan's cooking again. The McDonald freighting outfit enjoyed a good reputation amongst the various crews they employed, for they looked after both men and stock, unlike some other outfits that provided only the most basic support. The sampling of Nan's cooking was high on the agenda of those stopping over and she received an average of six proposals of marriage every year.

His thoughts were rudely interrupted by the appearance of a tall man, on foot, who stood in the middle of the trail. His arms were extended, shoulder high, to either side of his body and his hands were open as if to show that he was unarmed. Henrick had been up and down the trail too often to believe everything his eyes told him, and his pistol was quickly pointed at the stranger, just in case there was a hidden weapon somewhere. The man spoke in a calm friendly voice, making no move while he did so. "Afternoon to you, it's a fine day. I take it from your rig that you are headed for the McDonald ranch."

Henrick made no reply so the tall man continued. "It would be much appreciated if you could pass a message to Mister Douglas McDonald for me. Tell him that Seth's friend has returned and will be here at this place, at noon, for the next two days. If he hasn't come by then I'll ride on."

The mule skinner looked hard at the tall man. This was no fool who stood before him but someone who obviously wished to avoid being seen and possibly identified, otherwise he would have ridden into the ranch without hesitation. Henrick was curious but asked no questions. He nodded in affirmation to the request.

"I'll do as you ask, but for my peace of mind just you move away from me and keep walking while I turn off here. One thing stranger, I've got a good memory for faces and if what you are asking me to do causes them McDonalds any grief I'll be on your trail. Do I make myself clear?"

James nodded, turned with arms still extended and slowly walked towards the nearby bushes where Fiona lay hidden, watching, with musket at her shoulder. She waited until the wagon was out of sight before she rose. James looked at his daughter and smiled.

"We are almost there Fiona. It seems that Douglas is well respected if the mule skinner's words are to be believed. Come, we will move some way off and watch from there. I have no wish to be arrested before we meet my old friend." They set up a dry camp just over a mile from the turn off to the ranch and took turns at watching for signs of activity. There were still some lingering doubts in his mind but James hoped that his friend would help and most important of all would protect Fiona. Meanwhile they must wait.

CHAPTER TWENTY FIVE

Henrick approached the ranch house, slightly nervous, for he had wasted no time in handing over his beloved mules at the stables before making his way to speak to Douglas McDonald. His clothes were covered in dust from the trail and he had neither washed nor shaved in a coon's age. Plucking up his courage he rapped on the door and waited. Footsteps drew nearer and the door was opened by Douglas who ushered the mule skinner inside.

"I need a wash for sure Mister McDonald," he began, "but I got a message for you that could be important, or again it might not be." Douglas did his best to put the man at his ease.

"Come through Henrick and sit down. I'll get us a hot drink then you can tell me all about it." A few moments later both were seated, coffees in hand, and Douglas waited for Swartz to begin. After a few nervous coughs the mule skinner told of finding the tall stranger standing in the middle of the trail just before the turn off to the ranch. Even as he spoke, his words sounded hollow and he began to suspect that he had been the victim of some trick and was going to look foolish. He faltered and Douglas had to urge him to continue

"What did he say? What did he want from you? He clearly didn't try to rob you so what was he after?"

"He asked me to give you a message. He was quite clear about that. It was a message for Douglas McDonald. He said that he was Seth's friend and if you wanted to meet him he would be at the same spot at noon tomorrow and the day after. If you didn't want to meet him and didn't show up he would ride on." Henrick stopped speaking, watching for some kind of response from his employer. He was not disappointed.

Douglas leapt up from his chair and grabbed the mule skinner by the shoulders.

"Tell me what he said again," he demanded. "Come on man. Speak to me. What were his exact words?" A startled Henrick did as asked and sat bewildered as Douglas ran from the room shouting for his wife to come quickly. A flustered Isabel appeared by his side and both re-joined Henrick, who was totally flummoxed by the excitement his news had caused.

"Tell my wife what you have just told me, for this is wonderful news indeed if it is from whom I believe it to be."

Henrick repeated his story and noted the rising excitement on Mistress McDonald's face as he quoted chapter and verse of the earlier meeting with the stranger. She half collapsed into a chair her face flushed and she spoke to her husband in a voice shrill with emotion.

"Can it really be him Douglas, after all these years? Where has he been? Is Seth still with him? Oh if it is true then it is a miracle!"

Douglas thanked Henrick as he left the ranch house and promised that a fine bottle of whisky would await him when he attended the evening meal in the cookhouse.

The couple talked excitedly about the news. At one point Isabel wondered if it was a trick by those who wanted her husband dead, but this was dismissed, for few knew of Seth's involvement when James had fled Georgetown all those years ago. It was Douglas who made an educated guess that James was unaware that he was no longer a fugitive from the law for the killing of Marana. That would be why he had chosen not to ride up to the ranch in case this caused a problem for the McDonalds. There were clearly other factors involved but hopefully these could be addressed tomorrow when Douglas rode to the meeting place.

It was a highly excited household that dined together that evening. The McDonald family of four, plus Cameron, discussed the news about the appearance of James McDonald after all this time. Indeed as Cameron stated, he had found his father's friend and now had an uncle who had long been thought dead. It was a time to rejoice, for tomorrow held the promise of friendship and family reunion in a way that had previously not been thought possible.

CHAPTER TWENTY SIX

James awoke in the chill of pre dawn darkness and lay unmoving, enjoying the warmth of his bedroll. It had been a restless night and he was aware that Fiona had also slept fitfully. The events of this day would shape the lives of his daughter and himself forever. He had dared dream that this moment would arrive, that he would meet his old friend and a safe future for his daughter could be secured. He stopped to chide himself for thinking too far ahead. Douglas might not come today or tomorrow. He might not come at all for reasons that James was not aware of. The thought scared him, but he must accept that it was a possibility and consider what they would do if this was the outcome. His heart sank, for he was feeling mentally and physically drained. He constantly questioned his motives for bringing his family eastwards, and the loss of his wife and son sat heavily on his shoulders. Unless Douglas helped then Fiona's future would be a bleak one. As if reading her father's thoughts she spoke.

"You must believe father. It was a choice we made as a family and we owe it to my mother and brother to succeed in whatever the future demands of us." The rays of the rising sun started to filter through the leafy boughs above where they lay. "Look it is a fine start to the day and we must believe that we can achieve all that we planned to do, for their sakes as well as our own."

"You shame me daughter, but your words do not surprise me for you are strong like your mother." He rose as he spoke. Noon was some way away and in the meantime there was food to be prepared and horses to tend to. First things first, and then whatever was meant to be would be.

The time moved on as slowly as a snail crawling up a steep incline. They had eaten and tended to the horses. There was nothing for them to do but sit, watch and wait. They had a perfect view of the crossroads from where they now sat in silence. Every rider and every wagon were scrutinized as they passed by. The tension was mounting, although neither would admit to it. A lone rider was drawing nearer on an Appaloosa that stood all of sixteen hands. They held their breaths, for he had reined in and was now waiting at the appointed spot. Fiona looked to her father for some recognition of the horseman below. The seconds dragged by before he rose and started to walk down the slope, leaving Fiona hidden. He had earlier told her that she should stay out of sight until he was satisfied that there was no danger to her.

Douglas had spotted the movement on the hillside and watched as the figure drew nearer. God in heaven! There was no doubt at all! His friend was alive and well. He dismounted and was smiling broadly as he grasped James' hand.

"Welcome back. It has been too long." His friend merely nodded in response but the tears in his eyes betrayed the emotion he was feeling. The men took some moments to study each other. Time had been good to both of them.

Each had much to tell the other, and James suggested that they sit a while and talk before deciding what they would do next. He began by calling to Fiona to join them. As she moved towards them he spoke with pride in his voice.

"My daughter Fiona," he indicated with a sweep of his arm. "She is the main reason we are here as I need your help as never before, for I have great concerns for her future if anything should happen to me." Douglas stepped closer to Fiona and took her hand in his then held it to his chest. He began to speak in the old tongue of his native Scotland and James translated his friend's words in a soft voice.

"I, Douglas McDonald swear on my life that I will protect this woman to the best of my ability, and in the tradition upheld by my ancestors as Protectors of the chieftains and families of the McDonalds of Clanranald. My home is her home. My family is her family. This I swear."

No one moved for a highly charged emotional moment before Fiona smiled and bobbed a graceful courtesy towards Douglas.

"You honour me sir. I thank you from the bottom of my heart."

The trio seated themselves on the ground in the shade of the trees where James and Fiona had earlier set up their overnight camp. Douglas could contain himself no longer.

"I have something I must tell you before we talk further. You have been released from the charge of the murder of Marana. Solomon Jackson, a member of Marana's crew at the time of his death, gave a sworn statement to Judge Greaves that proved you innocent." Both James and Fiona were elated at the news and it was some minutes before they had calmed down enough to continue an exchange of the events since James and Seth had ridden away all those years ago.

Douglas was saddened to learn of Seth's death, and James did not go into any great detail of the killing of his wife and son. It was still too recent and painful a memory for both him and Fiona at this time. On the positive side, Douglas was pleased to inform his friend that the freight business they had formed together had thrived over the years. The other two partners in the venture were Hugh Mercer and William Porter, who was Moira's brother. They could have talked for hours but Douglas hinted that a pleasant surprise awaited them at the ranch, and he was keen not to keep Isabel waiting any longer, for she too was greatly excited at the thought of meeting James again.

It took very little time for the trio to mount up and head for the ranch house. It had been a day of great news that had far exceeded everything that James could possibly have wished for. He glanced sideways at Fiona, who returned his look with a little smile. The sacrifices made to get them this far had been hugely in excess of anything they could have imagined. There was, however, a shared iron determination that any opportunities that lay ahead would not be wasted by either of them.

As they rode closer to the ranch house it was obvious that word of their pending arrival had already gone before them. Isabel stood on the porch in one of her best dresses, for this was a very special day and she could hardly resist the temptation to rush out and greet them. She wondered who the young woman was who rode with them but put her curiosity to one side, for James had dismounted and she rushed into his arms and gave him a big kiss and a loving hug. He stepped back and held her at arm's length, both feeling slightly embarrassed at their show of affection.

"Hello Isabel, it is wonderful to see you again. May I introduce my daughter to you?" He beckoned to Fiona as he spoke and she stepped forward to join them. Isabel took Fiona's hands in hers then kissed her lightly on her cheek.

"You are most welcome here Fiona. Your father is a great friend of this family and our hearts are open to you. We hope that you will accept our hospitality for as long as you may wish." Isabel turned as she finished speaking for she felt the tears sting her eyes and she had promised herself that she would remain calm. She indicated to the porch where the others waited impatiently.

"We have a little welcome back surprise for you both. These two are our son and daughter, James and Anne, and this young man is Cameron, son of your brother Ewan and a cousin to you Fiona." Without pausing Isabel entered into the cooling shade of the house calling on those remaining outside to follow her.

Cameron smiled gently at his new found cousin and she replied in kind. They moved from the porch and entered the building. The size of the ranch house and the variety of furnishings it contained filled her with curiosity, for this was the first dwelling place like this that she had entered. She had noted the fine dresses that Anne and her mother wore, and she was aware that her own buckskin attire paled in comparison. Isabel informed all present that they would eat in about half an hour and perhaps James and Fiona would like to freshen up beforehand.

Anne asked Fiona to follow her and then led the way to her room, where a wash bowl and towel were to hand. She noted the hesitation in her visitor's face, so went through the motions of washing her hands then invited Fiona to follow suit. Anne sat back on her bed and studied her more closely as she dried her hands on the towel.

"I hope that we can be friends Fiona, for there are few girls of our age nearby." She paused, uncertain how to proceed without causing offence.

"Anne, I will need your help in so many ways, for much of this is strange to me and I have no wish to cause embarrassment or hurt to anyone. My mother was a woman of the Sioux and she and my father did their best to prepare me for this day when I would return to my father's people. I have been taught to read and write English but I have had little information on how white women should behave and dress."

Anne jumped up from the bed and clapped her hands in delight.

"Then I shall help you and you must tell me all about the Indian way of life. After we have eaten we will come back here and I can show you some dresses and under garments for you to try on." With agreement reached they returned to the main room downstairs to re-join the others.

The meal was a tasty trip back in time for James, and he encouraged Fiona to sample the various dishes on offer. Isabel had thoughtfully placed father and daughter together at the table so Fiona could follow James' lead on what cutlery to use for the different courses. Rarely had Nan's cooking been so highly praised, and the few crumbs left at the end of the meal were evidence that those sat at the table had enjoyed a meal that would be remembered for some time to come.

The hours that followed were taken up sharing news. Cameron spoke first and told of his father and mother and how they had eventually adjusted to life after the crushing defeat at Culloden. Both grandparents had died within a few weeks of one another and Ewan, as the new Chieftan, had struggled to ensure that the harsh regime imposed on the Highlanders did not destroy the McDonalds way of life. As he spoke those present listened in silence, for Cameron's words painted a picture of savage retribution by the victors upon those who had dared oppose the Government forces. Many innocents were put to the sword by a rampaging and blood thirsty army that left a trail of death and destruction behind them.

Cameron broke the silence with a smile and gestured at his uniform.

"As you can see I was 'volunteered' to show our allegiance to the Crown, and will serve for five years before I can return home. I am not sure that my uncle James will have the same choice, for a warrant for his arrest is still in force."

James made no attempt to answer the unspoken question regarding his future intentions, but began to tell of the events following his flight with Seth from Georgetown all those years ago. He was a born story-teller and soon had everyone laughing at the stinking consequences of his failure to avoid a skunk and other greatly exaggerated tall stories. He stopped short of telling of his life with the Sioux. That would keep for another day.

It was Douglas who suggested that they ride into Georgetown in the morning to meet with Judge Greaves. There would have to be a formal hearing in order that the arrest warrant against James could be overturned, and the sooner this was arranged the better for all concerned. There would also be an opportunity for the ladies to shop for clothes for Fiona, although any excuse would be reason enough, Douglas observed dryly.

Later that evening the two friends sat outside on the porch. So far everything had worked out much better than James could have hoped for. There were difficulties yet to be faced and his concerns for Fiona were not imagined, for although she had been made most welcome, there would be some harsh lessons yet to be learned. She was of mixed blood and this would mean that she would never be treated as an equal by some. James too had to re-educate himself, for the world he had returned to had changed greatly during his absence. Douglas had already touched upon their business partnership and that James would be entitled to his full share as agreed when it had first been formed. The offer was most generous, but James could not accept this for he had contributed nothing to the success of the enterprise.

The two men agreed to differ. James and Fiona would stay at the ranch house until suitable accommodation could be found for them nearby. James would begin work as an employee after the arrest warrant had been withdrawn. Once he had learned about the freighting business then, and only then, would he accept a reduced partnership. This agreement satisfied both of them in the short term and they retired for the evening.

James had opted to sleep outside near the stables, despite Isabel's insistence that he could at least use the bunk house where the hired hands slept. Fiona would sleep in a small spare room next to Anne's bedroom. The darkening sky above was resplendent with countless twinkling stars, and James was content to lie in his bedroll and enjoy the evening sounds from the horses and other creatures of the night. A movement nearby alerted him to the presence of another. A voice spoke, and he smiled for it was Fiona.

"I cannot sleep in the bed and I feel trapped inside such a large building. I will get used to it in time but tonight I think it is better out here otherwise I will not sleep. I have brought my bedroll." Within a few moments both father and daughter were asleep. A shooting star raced across the night sky. An owl hooted his challenge to the moon as the day finally gave way to the darkness of the night.

CHAPTER TWENTY SEVEN

It was some time after the cockerel had crowed his morning greeting to the world when they set off to Georgetown. Cameron rode with them for part of the way for he had been ordered back to Boston by Colonel Alexander, as he was now fit enough to carry out some of his duties. He and Anne had become close friends in the few short weeks they had come to know one another, and their parting was accompanied by a stolen kiss during a moment when they had found themselves alone. They would meet whenever circumstances allowed, and letters could easily be exchanged meantime using the freight messengers who regularly travelled to and from Boston on Company business.

Fiona wore an ankle length gingham dress given to her by Anne, but had insisted on retaining her moccasins. Shoes, she confessed, would take some time for her to master. The ladies rode in a small carriage driven by young James. Isabel, Anne and Fiona had excitedly been discussing what shops they would visit and had drawn up a list of the clothes Fiona should buy. Anne would of course advise her new friend on her purchases, for she had considerable experience in such matters. A bulging bedroom wardrobe would testify that this was indeed the case!

Douglas and James rode on horseback. Their first port of call would be at Sheriff Ricky Milligan's offices in order that he might be fully informed of what was happening. Douglas had suggested that the law officer would appreciate this courtesy, and it would do no harm to be able to fully brief him on the purpose of the meeting with Judge Greaves. Ricky had proved to be a most capable law officer and he had the respect of the law abiding citizens of Georgetown.

By the time they arrived James had readily acknowledged that Georgetown had grown much more than he had thought possible. There was considerable activity everywhere and the noise, consistent with a thriving community, was almost overwhelming. The main street offered a variety of premises that included shops, a barbershop and a lawyer's office. Fiona sat wide eyed at this great collection of buildings and the hustle and bustle of the townsfolk going about their business. Never in all her life had she seen anything like this. The carriage drew up outside Norman Taylor's store and the three ladies made their entrance, leaving the men folk to cross to the other side of the street where Sheriff Milligan had his office.

The coolness of the store made a welcome change from the mid morning sun, and after a cheerful exchange of greetings with the Irish owner the threesome began their shopping in earnest. Time flew by and the bundle of purchases grew steadily as a variety of different items of clothing were selected after much discussion and not a little laughter. They had been in the store for well over an hour when Fiona became aware that she was being openly studied by two other female shoppers. There was disapproval bordering on hostility on both faces as they loudly voiced their objections to the presence of a half breed Indian woman being allowed in the store. Isabel, her face tight with anger, was about to confront them but before she could speak Norman Taylor had already acted. He stood before the venomous twosome, hands on his hips, with increasing annoyance in his voice as he spoke.

"My family has been here for over fifteen years. During this time we have been welcomed by mostly everyone we have met. The exceptions have been small minded bigots like yourselves who have regarded the Irish as some lower form of life." His voice rose and his brogue thickened as his fury increased. "This is my store and any person who wishes to shop here is welcome to do so. This includes you two pillars of society, provided you behave." He glowered as he finished speaking and watched with satisfaction as the flustered duo made an indignant exit from the store.

"My apologies Miss," he said to Fiona, "I cannot control what people think, but while they are in my store I can control what they say, particularly if it causes offence." He wiped his hands on his apron and with a nod, turned to serve a waiting customer.

There was an embarrassed silence for a moment before Fiona spoke in a quiet steady voice.

"My father warned me of such people. They fear what they do not understand and this in turn can become hatred." She forced a laugh. "Come Anne, you have yet to explain to me the mystery of these undergarments that you tell me are so essential to my wellbeing." The tension eased at her words and the trio once more set about the selection of suitable clothing for Fiona with renewed vigour.

LESLIE H. ALLAN

At the offices across the street the discussion with Sheriff Milligan had come to an end. As Douglas had surmised earlier, it had been a good move to have informed the law officer of James' return to Georgetown and of the forthcoming meeting with Judge Greaves. After a handshake from the Sheriff they left and headed for the Judge's office which was only a hundred yards further along the street. The day had gone well so far and James was beginning to enjoy himself. The friends entered the legal offices that bore the sign of Judge R J Greaves and his associate Stuart Forbes. It was the latter who greeted them with a broad smile. He was a young Scotsman who had qualified in Edinburgh and had decided that he would like to practice in the Colonies. He had been in Georgetown for some eight months now.

"Come in gentlemen, please be seated and I'll let the Judge know you are here." As he spoke he knocked on a nearby door then entered. A few minutes later the four men were comfortably seated in the Judge's office, and after the usual pleasantries had been exchanged the Judge began to explain the procedure to formally nullify the arrest warrant against James. The process did not take long as Mister Forbes had meticulously drafted the legal documents needed, and they now only required signing by James and Judge Greaves. Once this had been accomplished the Judge produced four glasses and a bottle from the bottom drawer of his desk.

"I wouldn't normally drink this early in the day, but these rituals have to be observed," he declared, poker faced. "You are now no longer a fugitive from the law James McDonald. We wish you a long and happy life." He emptied his glass in one swallow then stood up, for he had some minor cases of misdemeanors to deal with at the courthouse and time was pressing. Douglas and James thanked the Judge and Stuart Forbes, then left.

The McDonald Freight Line kept a small office in Georgetown and young James had made his way there earlier after he had dropped off Isabel, Anne and Fiona at Taylor's store. Douglas suggested to his friend that they stop at the office to pick up any papers that needed his attention, and to let his son know that they would shortly be heading back to the ranch. The office employed three full time staff and was managed by Malcolm Slater, a highly efficient and competent accountant and lawyer who controlled the paperwork needed to service the Georgetown business needs. He had recently been appointed a junior partner in recognition of his value to the Company. He was seated at his desk and rose when the two men entered. Young James had already left to seek his mother and the girls at the shops.

After the introductions were concluded, Slater gave a short briefing to James on how the office was run and linked with the other premises the freight line had throughout the Colonies. There was a large map nailed to the wall and this was marked with pins showing the location of livestock holding areas, pick up and drop off sites.

To one side of the map there was a notice board and James found one of the notices of particular interest. It was concerning information sought regarding the whereabouts of a young man named Esteban Santara. James pulled the paper from the notice board and carefully read the wording again. This had to be the same young man whose diary he had in his possession. The pain of the loss of his wife and son returned with a hammer blow and the taste of bile rose chokingly in his throat.

He staggered to the door beyond a shocked Douglas and into the harsh sunlight. His lungs gasped for air, and he fought down the light headiness and weakness in his legs. He was aware that Douglas had grasped him by the shoulders.

"What in God's name is the matter James? Are you ill?" James shook his head but made no reply. He allowed himself to be led back into the office, where a concerned Malcolm Slater poured him a black coffee. After he had drunk it he excused his actions as having had too much sun. This failed to convince either Douglas or Slater but neither commented.

The ride back to the ranch was a muted affair. Fiona was very concerned for her father, but a whispered word in her ear in Sioux, told her he would explain later. When they reached the ranch house James apologized to Douglas for his earlier behaviour and promised that he would explain himself later. In the meantime he and Fiona had much to discuss.

Shortly after their arrival back at the McDonald ranch, father and daughter left the group and found the privacy they sought under the shade of a gnarled apple tree that was situated a short distance from the main ranch house. James showed Fiona the handbill he had removed from the notice board at Slater's office. The implications were not lost on her, and for a long moment she too again felt the deep pain at the recent loss of her mother and brother. Esteban's diary and the map leading to the gold had been the catalyst for the misfortune that had so brutally impacted on their family. James had already been close to discarding the diary on a number of occasions, but had not done so for reasons he was not entirely sure about.

Who was this woman seeking to find Esteban? Would the contents of the diary not bring her much sadness at the hopelessness of a young man on the verge of madness, as he sought to evade the pursuit of those who wanted him dead? The gold nuggets in James' possession would confirm the existence of a place where the precious metal came from. Would this not lead to some foolhardy attempt to seek out the source of the gold? The events that had recently taken place leading to the deaths of his wife and son, and the braves killed in the attack, would be talked about around the Indian campfires for some time to come. The location would be regarded by them as a place of bad medicine and few would venture there. James had found comfort in this and had hoped that the spirits of his wife and son would forever be left in peace, undisturbed by any intrusion.

The two discussed the matter at length, but were unable to agree what course of action to take. Was it right to stay silent when they had in their possession a diary that would give an explanation to Maria of what had befallen Esteban? James remembered his friend Seth's translation of the diary, and of the young man's love of this woman who had travelled from Spain, after all this time, on her quest to find him. Finally it was agreed that the advice of Douglas and Isabel would be sought. In such unusual circumstances four heads were better than one.

CHAPTER TWENTY EIGHT

It was three days after the decision had been taken to contact Peter Lloyd, and to seek a meeting with Senora Maria Cortez. James and Fiona, accompanied by Douglas, waited nervously in the reception room at the Lloyd's mansion on the outskirts of Boston. Douglas had swiftly arranged the visit once agreement had been reached that some preliminary discussion should take place before any disclosure of the existence of the diary.

They had not been waiting long before Peter and Maria entered the room. James thought that Maria looked pale and drawn, while she in turn faced a deeply tanned man with dark brown eyes that looked at her with no hint of whether or not he approved of what he saw. Douglas introduced everyone and normal pleasantries were exchanged as a maid poured some coffee then withdrew. After a few moments James spoke. He had carefully rehearsed what he wanted to say, and he started by explaining that he had fled Georgetown some years ago to evade his wrongful arrest for a crime he had not committed. His friend Seth had joined him and the two had ridden many thousands of miles westwards, before the onset of winter had forced them to build a cabin to enable them to survive the harsh and freezing conditions they would encounter. James looked directly at Maria as he spoke, and he could tell that he had her full attention.

"My friend had been married to a Spanish lady for many years and could read and write the language as well as being a fluent speaker. Tell me Senora please, what was your surname before you married?"

The silence in the room was absolute, and there was a lengthy pause before her barely audible reply.

"Valdez. My name was Maria Valdez."

"Where did you live when you first knew this young man Esteban?"

"We both lived in Bilbao in Northern Spain. His name was Esteban Santara." She straightened her shoulders and her head lifted proudly as she continued. "He was my lover and the father of my son whom he never saw, nor was he aware that I was carrying his child."

The expression on James' face did not alter before he spoke again, but only after a silent nod of approval from Fiona.

"Senora Cortez, I bring you news of Esteban that you may not wish to know, for I regret that he is dead. He had been badly mauled by a bear, and although my friend and I tried everything we could to save him it was not enough." He waited for a response, but there was none. Maria's eyes were filling with tears, but she eventually asked him to continue.

"I have in my possession a diary written by Esteban. May I suggest that you read this before we proceed further? Once you have done so I will answer any questions that you may have, including further details of his death. With your agreement Mister Lloyd," he said turning in his direction, "may we indulge upon your hospitality a while longer until Senora Maria has had time to read the diary?" As he spoke James gently placed the journal into her hands. She held it to her lips and kissed it before rising and leaving the room.

It was three hours before Maria made her reappearance in the company of Consuella. The others had meanwhile been offered a light lunch and had discussed a variety of subjects, whilst avoiding the contents of Esteban's diary. These would remain private unless Maria chose to divulge them herself.

It was clear from the puffiness around her eyes that Maria had wept a great deal during her time reading the words of her dead lover. She had been horrified at his ramblings towards the end of his writings, but took great comfort from his repeated declarations of his love for her. Before she allowed Peter to assist her to a chair, she offered the diary back to James, who insisted that it was rightfully hers to keep. Maria requested that everyone present remain in the room while she asked James to tell of the circumstances of Esteban's death. This he did as gently as possible, but without avoiding the failed attempts that Seth and he had made to save the young Spaniard's life. She was pleased to learn that he had received a decent burial, with Christian words being spoken as they laid him to rest.

"I am a woman who has lived a sheltered life, but I have learned to treat with some disbelief tales of gold that can be gathered from a stream as easily as grapes from a vine." She smiled wistfully as she spoke for she was convinced that Esteban was close to madness at the time he wrote of his great find.

"Not so Senora. He was quite correct in what he said. Fiona and I have seen this place with our own eyes." As he spoke James produced the small pouch containing the gold nuggets found amongst Esteban's belongings after his death. "These too are rightfully yours." James had no wish to inform those present about the killing of his wife and son while searching for the source of the gold. Fiona and he had previously agreed that nobody, not even Douglas, need know about this.

James rose as he spoke. He had given the diary to Maria and his task was ended. He could be contacted at the ranch if there were any more questions. Just as they were taking their leave, Maria came to James and gently kissed him on both cheeks.

"Thank you Senor James. You have answered the questions I needed to know. I can now begin to live the rest of my life" She then turned and left the room.

CHAPTER TWENTY NINE

"This is madness Maria, what on earth are you thinking about? Have you taken leave of your senses?" demanded a bemused Peter Lloyd. "You cannot possibly stay here any longer, for your finances in Spain are under great threat. Have you no regard for the warning from Pedro Palacio? In any case our ship sails in three days time and your passage has been arranged."

Maria, Peter and Consuella were in the dining room of their rented mansion on the outskirts of Boston. The morning had gone well and the three friends had enjoyed a stroll in the gardens before returning for coffee. Preparations for the return voyage were progressing to his satisfaction and Peter expressed his delight at the success of the trading agreements that had been signed with the various agencies in the Colonies. It was at this point that Maria had told the Lloyds that she had decided to remain in Boston for the time being.

"It is my intention to find where Esteban is buried and to provide him with a more suitable resting place. I am also of a mind to find the source of the gold he discovered, for it is rightfully mine and if my finances in Spain are as vulnerable as Pedro states, then I would be wise to take the opportunity to improve my situation." Peter exploded with anger at her words.

"In God's name, do you not understand the danger you would be in to undertake such a risky and foolish venture? Apart from the threat of hostile Indians, every thief and scoundrel within a thousand miles would be seeking to rob or murder you for such information. If you cannot see the risk to yourself you must surely recognize the danger that James and Fiona McDonald would be in, for both of them have been to where the gold is located."

As he spoke the guilty look on Maria's face confirmed his worse fears, for he was now certain, without asking, that Maria had made known to some of her acquaintances the existence of the gold. He held his head in his hands in despair. He must warn the McDonalds of Maria's foolishness, for there were many people who would kill without hesitation to gain either the map that would lead them to the gold, or to force someone who already knew its location to take them to it.

Even as Peter scrawled a hasty letter of warning for his servant Manuel Jamon to deliver to James, word of the existence of the gold mine was spreading like wildfire. With each telling the story became more exaggerated and greedy minds began to plan how they could possess the precious metal that would make them rich beyond their wildest dreams.

CHAPTER THIRTY

In the weeks that followed his return to Boston, Lieutenant Cameron McDonald had settled into his military routine quickly and had applied himself fully to learning as much as he could about the capabilities of the soldiers under his command. He had a small troop of fifty infantry soldiers, many of whom had arrived straight from training at the Military training centres in England. The troop senior non commissioned officer was an experienced professional soldier of many years service called Colour Sergeant Martin Smith. Cameron had quickly learned to seek advice from him, although the final decisions were always his alone to make. The pair had soon gained respect for each other and shared the same views that those under their command should be treated fairly, but firmly, as the need arose.

An increasing number of patrols were ordered to be undertaken by the Boston Garrison and the young officer led his troop on a number of these excursions. In the latest patrol they had formed part of a force of British soldiers that had been tasked with carrying out a search for illegal weapons in the small village of Lexicon which lay south west of Boston. A force of local armed militiamen defiantly faced the column of redcoats on the village green. Cameron was initially bemused by the ineffective and almost aimless tactics employed by the patrol commander Major John Pitcairn. This soon turned to dismay when Pitcairn ordered his men to form up in battle formation, an action that was both aggressive and challenging to the seventy or so militiamen facing them. In the cold morning light the two groups silently waited for the other to make the first move. Major Pitcairn took the initiative and rode his horse to within a hundred feet or so of the militiamen then called for them to lay down their arms and disperse. His demands were met only in part, for the militiamen did begin to depart the village green, but carrying their weapons with them. Pitcairn repeated his demand that the militiamen leave their weapons behind them, but this was ignored.

What happened next was unclear, but what was undisputed was that a shot rang out. A platoon of British troops then fired a volley into the ranks of the militiamen, which was quickly followed by a second volley. The redcoats then charged, leaving eight dead and ten wounded militiamen lying on the village green.

From the small window of a house that overlooked the scene before him, Henri Chirac glowed with satisfaction at the confusion that his musket shot had produced. Both sides would undoubtedly blame the other for the loss of life that had taken place. He smiled a contented smile. This, his most recent attempt to increase the distrust and animosity between the Colonists and the British had exceeded his wildest dreams. After today this episode would soon be regarded as a massacre, and would further kindle the fire of rebellion against the British.

Chirac and his agents had worked ceaselessly to ferment distrust between the Colonists and the British and had achieved considerable success. Even as he basked in the triumph of the events of the evening, two of his agents had organized attacks on the retreating British troops on the sixteen mile trek back to Boston. The militiamen exercised their superior skills and experience in guerilla fighting, and the redcoats suffered horrific casualties of seventy dead and over two hundred wounded before reaching the sanctuary of Boston.

Cameron McDonald had witnessed yet another, and too often to be repeated, example of the lack of good leadership and tactics by the officers leading the British troops. On arrival at his barracks he sought out information regarding the well-being of the small company of troops that had been under his direct command. Over half had been killed or wounded. He felt thoroughly miserable at the consequences of the bungled search for illegal weapons, and he vowed that he would learn from the events that had taken place. In the aftermath of the conflict the Colonists would seize the opportunity to release exaggerated versions of the alleged 'Lexicon Massacre' of innocent Colonists and their families by the murdering British barbarians, and the heroic bloody revenge taken.

Colonel Thomas Alexander was grim faced as he listened to his officers' reports on the debacle that had resulted in the high casualties amongst his troops and, he acknowledged to himself, the immense and damaging publicity that would follow. The loss of life on both sides was needless, and with decent leadership by the senior officers in command of the British troops could have, and should have, been avoided. The only crumb of comfort he took from the day's events was from Lieutenant McDonald's report that stated he was positive that the first shot fired had come from behind the troops and had definitely not come from the British ranks. Colonel Alexander had for some time been aware of attempts being made by an unnamed group to undermine the uneasy peace between the Colonists and the British. This latest incident would, he feared, bring the possibility of conflict ever nearer. Those who wished for peace were becoming a minority voice against the ever increasing numbers of those who saw a full scale war as inevitable. The situation called for calm thinking on both sides, and not the heated rhetoric from some of those political individuals based in the Colonies and the Parliament in London.

It was with a heavy heart that he wrote his report to be submitted to his superior officers. Doubtless his stated belief that outside agencies had inflamed the events at Lexicon would be ignored. He privately conceded that war would become inevitable unless drastic action was taken by the British Government. A minority of fair minded voices in the Westminster Parliament had called for the Colonies to be given due recognition and political representation. The Colonists demand for "No taxation without representation" was becoming ever louder and should no longer be ignored, but properly debated as a matter of great urgency. To delay would prove fatal.

A subdued Cameron had earlier spoken with Colour Sergeant Smith who was in agreement that the training of the soldiers in their troop needed urgent review. The militiamen had dealt a harsh lesson to the British. Tactics that had been so successful in previous conflicts were outdated against opponents who would not stand in the open, but who fought skirmishes then retreated before the massed British troops could respond. The young officer was both tired and depressed. The loss of life of men in his troop was, he believed, his fault and he re-lived the events of the day over and over in his mind. He was puzzled by the shot that had been fired and caused the tense situation to explode into a melee of random shooting and bloodshed. He was adamant that the gunshot had not come from within the British lines. His head ached, and he washed his face in a bowl of cold water before preparing for bed. He doubted if he would sleep much that night but he should try.

This latest conflict would increase the difficulty in his friendship with Anne. Her family was sympathetic to the Colonists who wanted a negotiated and peaceful agreement with London on their demands for a voice in government. They would however defend themselves if called upon to do so. Cameron was unsure if Anne felt as he did, for he was in love with her and he missed her terribly. He had written to her almost every day since his return to duty, although he had only hinted at his true feelings for her. It was early days and he had not wanted to risk scaring her away if she did not share his ardour. Perhaps she could meet him at the Boston offices of her father's freight line. He would suggest this in his next letter to her.

The sentry in the watch tower drew his cloak closer to him against the chill and damp of the night air. As with all things we take for granted, he told himself, the sun would eventually rise bringing with it the warmth he was currently lacking. Wouldn't life be easier if we could have what we wanted when we needed it? He stamped his feet to combat the rising cold. Another hour or so, he calculated, before he would be relieved, and in the meantime he would keep moving in an effort to retain his body heat and remain alert.

CHAPTER THIRTY ONE

The merchant ship 'El Torro' left Boston harbour on the morning tide for her return voyage to Barcelona. Despite the best efforts of Peter and Consuella, Maria had refused to change her mind about remaining behind. There was a tearful farewell before the Lloyds boarded the ship, leaving Maria alone on the dockside. The moorings were undone and the craft slowly eased her way into the channel leading to the open seas. The Captain ordered additional sail to be raised and 'El Torro' picked up more speed as the canvas began to bulge as the wind caught her.

Peter stood on the deck with his arm around his wife.

"There was no more we could do to persuade her to return with us. She is determined to stay, regardless of the danger she and the McDonalds may find themselves in as a result of her recklessness." Peter kissed his wife on the cheek and raised his arm in a last farewell to the swiftly diminishing figure of Maria on the quayside. Consuella nodded her agreement, and both remained where they stood until the land was no longer in sight, somewhat reluctant to retire below to their small but comfortable cabin.

On the previous evening they had hosted a farewell dinner at their mansion, and most of those invited had attended. Despite their best efforts, it was apparent to the Lloyds that there was a muted feel to the evening.

This was due to the main topic of conversation being the escalating number of clashes between the thirteen Colonies and the British. Even the more moderate minded were in despair at the aggressive stance being taken by the Parliament in London.

Maria had insisted that James and Fiona McDonald be included in the invitations sent out. Peter was pleasantly surprised when both accepted. James was clothed in a dark velvet jacket with matching trousers that set off his dark looks to great effect, and drew a number of admiring glances from many of the ladies present. His entrance however was overshadowed when Fiona followed her father into the room. She was stunningly beautiful in a dark green gown, tight at the waist with bare shoulders that exposed her lightly tanned skin to devastating effect. A small necklace sat tantalizingly at the base of her throat and her long hair had been arranged in ringlets. James took delight in seeing the effect Fiona had created, and was not in the least surprised when she was soon surrounded by a cluster of young male admirers.

George Washington was amongst those present and he spoke to James at length and asked, in particular, about the rumours of a huge source of gold that James and Fiona had found.

"Come sir," James smiled in reply, "do you believe that I would be relying on the charity of my old friend Douglas McDonald if I had access to a source of so much gold?" He sipped his wine before continuing. "It is certainly true that I have travelled many miles these last years, and I am proud that I have a daughter as thoughtful and caring as she is beautiful. I give you my word that I have no gold in my possession to speak of, nor do I seek great wealth for myself. With the help of Douglas it is my intention to apply myself to earning a living that will adequately provide for my daughter and me."

"Well then Mister McDonald I wish you well in your venture. This land has many opportunities for those who would give of their sweat and toil for the chance of a new life. I see Mistress Washington awaits me so I must go." He extended his hand and gave a brief shake before moving across the room to join his wife.

As the evening progressed James became aware that Fiona was having some difficulty from one particular admirer who had clearly had too much wine. His hands were constantly touching Fiona at thigh level and Peter, who had noticed the situation, moved towards the offender. Without warning the young man in question gave a startled cry and leapt away from Fiona, then fell backwards to the floor. In the stunned silence that followed the youth rose to his feet, and mumbling apologies hurried from the room.

When the chance presented itself James asked what had happened. Fiona explained that she had kept a straight face as she told the young man who had been pestering her, that his hands were dangerously close to the hunting knife that she kept strapped to her thigh. If he touched it, then Indian custom demanded that she cut his throat with it then take his scalp. Her words had had the desired effect and the young man had ceased to annoy her!

Several of the guests had departed before Maria approached James and asked if she could speak with him in private. He agreed with some reluctance, for he was reasonably certain that she wanted to speak further about the source of the gold. Maria led him to a nearby lounge and sat herself down on one of two chairs that were close enough to the fireplace to enjoy the warmth from the flames that burned invitingly within. She gestured for James to sit himself in the other chair before she began to speak.

"Senor James, it will be no surprise to you that I ask for your help in taking me to where Esteban is buried, and also to where the gold can be found. There are few that I can trust to help me, and although I have Esteban's map to the source of the gold, there is only you who can take me to where he is buried." The look on James' face clearly mirrored his rejection to her request, and she continued before he could reply. "I have been told that it would be dangerous, but you are the one person I know that I can trust to help me. I am determined to succeed in this matter and will hire capable men to take me if you do not," she added almost petulantly.

He studied her in silence and held her gaze before she looked away, irritated with herself that she had done so. The silence continued for almost a full minute before he spoke in a low but firm voice.

"Senora, you cannot begin to appreciate the dangers involved in such a journey. There are wild animals, poisonous snakes, hostile Indians, floods, drought, and both searing heat and freezing blizzards to contend with. The wilderness is a place of great danger where the slightest mistake or careless action can be fatal. When you journey there you are never alone, for the risk of death from thirst or starvation is a constant companion." He rose from his seat and moved towards the door. Maria was angry that her plan to have his assistance in her venture had failed. Nevertheless she would not give up and there were others who would take her to the gold using Esteban's map.

The location of his grave could wait meantime. She sat alone with her thoughts for some time before returning to join the few guests who still remained. James and Fiona had already left, having thanked their hosts and wished them a safe journey on their return to Spain.

In the carriage on the way back to the ranch, father and daughter exchanged their thoughts about Maria's intentions to seek out the gold and Esteban's grave. James was angry at himself for having given her the diary in the first place, for without it the current situation could not have arisen. They both were aware that they must take great care, for even Washington had heard of the rumours of the gold, and greed and temptation is a powerful mixture. Only James and Fiona had been to the source of the gold and they would be regarded by many as the key to the door that would lead to great wealth.

Chapter Thirty Two

Douglas was a worried man. The news of the Lexicon incident was on everyone's lips and the tension had risen to a dangerous level. It was a time for cool heads and leadership but neither was forthcoming. The recent events had him caught in the middle of a two horned dilemma, for he was not unaware of the strong bond that had developed between his daughter and Cameron. Douglas sighed in frustration. He could never forget that the young man, nephew of his dearest friend, had saved his life when Manson had lain in wait for him. He must nevertheless put this to one side, for his first concern was for the safety and wellbeing of Anne. Despite his earlier pleas in public debate with other politically minded Colonists, any attempt to seek an open debate on the grievances of the Colonists at Westminster was no longer an option. The escalating ill feeling between the opposing factions had made this impossible. Opinion on both sides had hardened and war was a real possibility.

It was with a heavy heart that he informed Anne that there was to be no more contact between her and Cameron. He tried to explain the reasons for this decision to a tearful daughter, whose ears were closed to her father's words from the moment he had begun to tell her of his decision. She had made a quick exit from the room, knocking a chair over in her haste to leave. Dinner that evening was taken with one empty place where Anne would normally have been seated. Isabel eyed her husband sympathetically, for she had been in agreement with his decision. She was still young enough to remember the euphoria that love can bring, and how it can blind lovers' eyes to the harshness of reality.

"It will take time Douglas, but she will come to realize the wisdom of this decision, although I suspect that it will not diminish her feelings for Cameron. I confess that I would have welcomed him to our family if circumstances had been different." She pushed her plate to one side. There was still the difficult task to tell James of what had been decided, for his response might be one of anger.

Douglas had already decided to wait for James and Fiona's return from the dinner given by the Lloyds prior to their departure to Spain. He liked Peter and felt that the contracts agreed between them were full of promise for a fruitful partnership. The rapidly deteriorating situation with the British was a major threat to peace and stability within the thirteen Colonies. If war did break out there would be many losers in the conflict, for it would set brother against brother and split families apart forever.

It was late in the evening, or to be more accurate, early in the morning, before James and Fiona returned from Boston. Douglas had fallen into an uneasy sleep in his chair in the study and was awakened by an amused James.

"Sleeping on watch again Douglas," he chided, "an offence punishable by death I believe." The lack of humour in Douglas' demeanour warned James that all was not well. Within a few minutes Douglas had explained his decision regarding Anne and Cameron.

It had not been an easy one, but given the worsening political situation, one that had been taken with the best of intentions. Perhaps surprisingly it was Fiona who supported the measures decided upon. She argued that there were times for love and times for war, an old Indian saying, she reminded her father. He nodded and made no comment. His thoughts would remain his own. There was no more discussion and they retired to bed.

The quiet of the night was pierced by the sound of crickets chirping their calls into the darkness. The six men were huddled around a small and inadequate fire as they planned their next move. Their leader, Alex Campbell, was a tough and unscrupulous man who had deserted from the British Army almost four years ago. There was no compassion in his heart, and he would use to his advantage any opportunity that presented itself. The main topic of discussion was the gold that the Spanish woman had openly discussed with her acquaintances. She was reported to be planning to ask James McDonald to lead a party back to the location where the nuggets had been found. If he refused she would hire men with knowledge of the western lands to seek out the source of the gold, using the map she had of the location. Campbell had thought about he and his men volunteering for such a venture, but discarded this option. There would be great public interest if the Spanish woman was to lead such a group into the hostile lands, and too many potential witnesses if she was to die somewhere along the way. No, the best option would be to force the squaw man McDonald to lead them to the gold. The key to this would be his daughter. Capture and keep her as a hostage until her father took Campbell and his gang to the source of the precious metal. Once this had been achieved both could be killed. He nodded to himself in satisfaction, for this was the plan they would follow. He began to outline his thoughts to his men on how they needed to prepare for the way ahead. By the time the fire had gone cold, each man present had been fully briefed on the part he had to play.

CHAPTER THIRTY THREE

In the weeks that followed, Maria, aided by McDougall's trusted assistant Norman Banks, set about recruiting experienced tough men to form a well armed group that would seek out the location of the gold. The excitement of those involved overshadowed the poor planning for the venture. Maria was the only person with access to the map, therefore nobody thought to question if she knew how to get to the area identified in the diary. In her rush to get the search started, coupled with her lack of any experience in such matters, she had overlooked this vital fact. She had also failed to inform the men who were recruited that she would be going with them. After all, she had reasoned, she was the owner of the map and she was not going to trust strangers to find the source of the gold and return to her with sacks of the precious metal. She was naïve in many ways but she was not stupid.

To his credit, Banks did his best to warn her of the dangers involved, but Maria disregarded his words. She had the bit between her teeth and was determined that the venture would succeed. Any suggestions made to her that might cause delay to the group's departure were treated with suspicion. The provisions for both horses and men were sparse and leadership sadly lacking. Already cliques had formed within the group and distrust simmered below the surface. Banks pleaded with Maria to delay starting out until a strong leader was appointed to lead the group, and to review the direction it would take. His words fell on deaf ears.

It was only three days before the party was due to leave that Bank's prayers were answered. A well known and trusted mountain man returned from one of his many trading ventures. He was laden with fine pelts and, as was his usual practice, visited his friend Banks to discuss the sale of his furs. His father was an Irish trapper who had taken the daughter of a Pawnee Indian chief as his wife. His childhood had been spent living amongst the Indians. Since the death of his parents in a raid by hostiles the young man had made a living trading with both the Indians and the white settlers. He was known as 'Pawnee' Rob Ahern, a man to be treated with respect by all who knew him. He had the proven reputation of someone who was a good friend to have in times of trouble, or a very bad enemy to those foolish enough to lock horns with him.

Banks welcomed the young visitor warmly, and reached in his desk drawer for two glasses and a bottle of Scotch whisky that had been made in the Highlands with all the fine skills of a master distiller. Ahern noted this generous gesture by his friend and raised an eyebrow in a questioning manner.

"Norman, I cannot remember when I last had a dram from you without there being a sting in the tail, so make sure you pour a large one before your speak." His tanned face broke into a smile as he spoke, and he waited in silence as the glasses were filled, the contents sipped and the levels of the amber liquid much reduced. Banks refilled both glasses before he spoke. Choosing his words with care, he detailed the situation regarding the expedition to seek out the location of Esteban's gold. As Banks continued to explain the state of affairs, the young trapper soon recognized that the venture was fraught with danger, and shook his head in dismay. It needed no genius to realize that what little planning had been attempted was totally inadequate and lives would be lost. An expedition into Indian country by white strangers, hungry with gold fever, had the potential to start a war. The older man finished speaking and waited impatiently for Rob Ahern to speak. Ahern emptied his glass before responding.

"I was only half joking Norman, when I said that there would be a price to be paid for a dram or two from your bottle. It was an understatement," he grimaced before continuing, "I should have been offered the whole bottle!" He drummed his fingers on the arm of his chair as he digested what his friend had told him. It was a mess, and a very dangerous one at that. The old clock on the office wall had registered the passing of a further five minutes before Rob rose to his feet and nodded his agreement towards a much relieved Banks.

"I need to meet with Senora Cortez immediately if I am to have any influence over what is being planned. I may not be able to stop this madness but I will try." The men left the office hurriedly and barely twenty minutes later arrived at Maria's residence. To Bank's dismay there were at least a dozen others seeking an audience with her. After a futile attempt to persuade a flustered young secretary of the urgency to speak with the Senora at once, Rob, dragging Banks with him, entered Maria's room unannounced. Two men were present in the apartment, along with an astonished Maria who looked on as Rob persuaded the men that their business was finished. The stern look on the trapper's face left them in no doubt that there was no debate invited regarding their presence, and the duo wisely departed quietly.

Norman Banks swiftly explained the interruption to Maria, who inspected the tall, tanned young man who stood before her. She noted that his clothing was a mixture of Indian buckskin and normal store bought pants and boots. Broad shoulders tapered down to a narrow waist where an ornate belt held a large knife and an axe. He had dark hair and his brown eyes surveyed her with open curiosity. Maria gestured for the men to be seated while she poured two glasses of wine, using the opportunity to take some control of the proceedings. She handed over the wine and seated herself with care before she spoke.

"I am aware that Mister Banks has severe misgivings about my expedition, but I am satisfied that every consideration has been taken to ensure that we are properly equipped, and the individual men trustworthy. What, may I ask, makes you think that you are in a position to criticize our planning?" The two held each other's gaze for fully thirty seconds before Rob responded, choosing his words carefully.

"Senora, of the people waiting outside in your hall, two are known horse thieves, another two are killers and the rest are as trustworthy as a rattlesnake in your bed. I have known Norman here", he gestured with his thumb as he spoke, "for a number of years and I rely on his judgement in many things. If he tells me that the stock set aside for your expedition is inadequate and the provisions badly selected, then I have no reason to believe otherwise." Irritation showed on Maria's face at his words.

"Am I therefore to abandon my plans on your advice? Who are you, that I should trust what you say above others who will be with me when we seek out the gold that is rightfully mine? Rob sat still, digesting her words before he shook his head and rose to leave. Banks blocked the doorway and pleaded with his friend not to go. His smaller frame was dwarfed by his friend as he addressed his words to Maria.

"Senora, you have questioned the honesty and integrity of my friend who came here at my request. If you were a man you would be held accountable for your words. Indeed, I would challenge you myself for the insult to be withdrawn." He turned to Ahern. "Please Rob, your help is vital here if needless loss of lives is to be prevented." Banks was an astute man and he knew that his words had found some acceptance with both Maria and Ahern. He grasped the opportunity with both hands and began to outline proposals that would be acceptable to both parties, and therefore ensure that the group would be better prepared for the journey ahead.

It was almost two hours later before all the details of the agreement were finalized. Maria would be consulted in all matters, but Rob Ahern would be responsible for the hiring and firing of all members of the group, the choosing of stock, and the proper selection of supplies. A start date of fourteen days was agreed before the trio finally parted. There was much to be done in the days that lay ahead, but Maria at least had no doubts that her agreement with Ahern was very much to her benefit. That night she slept more soundly than she had for some time.

CHAPTER THIRTY FOUR

Peter and Consuella sat together in silence. They had taken an early lunch in their dining room but neither had any appetite and the food prepared for them was left almost untouched. Their elation at arriving safely back in Spain only two weeks ago had quickly been dashed on learning that their dear friend Pedro Palacio was close to death. To make matters worse, Peter's initial enquiries into the state of Maria's finances showed them to be at an alarmingly low level. His attempts to gain access to either Maria's son Hernando or his guardian Don Juan Cortez had proved to be exceedingly difficult. In desperation he had waited unannounced in Hernando's favourite restaurant, and had followed him outside at a moment when the youth would not be in the company of his friends.

Hernando was taken by surprise when Peter confronted him and sought some explanation about the loss of much of Maria's inheritance left to her on the death of her husband. It did not take long however for the youth to gain his composure, and he taunted the older man with his reply.

"My mother was a common whore who was with child when she married my fool of a father, who was not my father. I have evidence to this effect, and have persuaded the courts to deny the legality of any claim she has to part of my father's estates. Her share has rightfully been returned to me. She is young enough to return to her old profession as a whore if she is in need of the resources to house and feed herself." Hernando was enjoying the moment and savoured the disbelief on Peter's face at his words. "In fact it would not surprise me if some have already enjoyed her favours. Have you been beneath her skirts Senor Lloyd?" he sneered.

In response an iron hand grasped him by the throat, threatening to squeeze the life out of him. Peter's low voice spoke in Hernando's ear in an angry growl, and the terrified youth realized he had gone too far with his insults.

"It is only the respect I have for your mother that stops me from choking the life from your worthless body. Doubtless your wealth has bought you friendships in high places, but I warn you that your life is forfeit if I hear of you insulting your mother, or indeed me and my family." He pushed the young man to his knees, disgusted at the words Hernando had spoken, and angry at himself for losing his temper and coming so close to taking the retching youth's life.

Peter had relayed the details of his meeting with Hernando to Consuella on his return to their home. He regretted his actions, and his wife had cautioned that he should be careful in all his future dealings. Spain was in a high state of excitement, for events were taking place in the American colonies that could well lead to a war for their independence from Britain. The French and the Spanish governments had publicly declared their support for the Colonists and had pledged to declared war on Britain if such hostilities broke out. Both countries had suffered greatly at the hands of their old enemy and were keen to take revenge. Peter and other British citizens living in Spain were now regarded by some with a degree of suspicion. He was thankful that he had earlier supplied the requested detailed information to the Spanish authorities about his views on the situation in the Colonies. Surely his actions had proved his loyalty to Spain, the land where he lived with his beloved Spanish wife? Time would tell, but in the meantime there was little that could be done to salvage any monies for Maria.

The following week Pedro Palacio died without having regained consciousness. Both Peter and Consuella were distressed at the passing of such a dear friend. Maria would have to be informed of his death, for Pedro had loved Maria as though she was his own daughter. Peter grimly prepared a letter telling of Pedro's death, and the loss of her estates to Hernando. It took several attempts before he found the words to convey the terrible news to Maria, whilst trying to assure her that there was still hope that the courts could eventually agree to an appeal being considered. Even in the best of circumstances such an appeal would take years to be heard, if at all. Peter now had a most difficult decision to make, although he knew that he had no choice in the matter. If he continued to try to intercede on Maria's behalf he ran the risk of incurring the wrath of those influential people who benefited from Hernando's generosity. The effect on his business, and therefore the wellbeing of Consuella, would be at risk. There was only one way to proceed, for he loved his wife above all else and he would do nothing to place her open to harm. He would cease to argue on Maria's behalf, but would maintain a low profile while keeping the business operating as a profitable concern. He must do nothing that could leave him exposed to charges that he was not loyal to his adopted country.

Consuella read her husband's letter to Maria with tears in her eyes. Peter had made the correct decision, as she knew he would, for she had his undying love and he cared for her above all else. Nevertheless he would feel a terrible guilt that his actions would leave Maria in a situation where only she could influence her own future, without any help from the Lloyds. Consuella gently kissed her husband on the lips before quietly leaving the room and making her way to her private little chapel. She would pray for her husband, and Pedro, and for the welfare of her friend Maria. She could do no more.

CHAPTER THIRTY FIVE

'Pawnee' Rob Ahern was made of stern stuff. He had promised to lead the expedition to the best of his ability and intended doing just that. His purpose was to do all in his power to minimize any Indian uprising that could follow if a huge gold source was found to exist. If this happened a large influx of gold hungry hordes into Indian country would prove to be a disaster. He was hoping that there was no big source of the precious metal at the place shown on the map, but that what gold there was would prove to be limited in both quality and quantity. He had known of numerous 'big strikes' that were over very quickly and interest in these locations had soon died.

Time was of the essence and he called together all those involved in the proceedings to date. There was no faltering in his resolve, and he quickly dispensed with the services of a number of known trouble makers within the group. Only one, a scarred faced bully called George Smith, protested and advanced towards Ahern making threats as he did so. Rob remembered the words of his father who was an Irish fist fighting man of repute. He had stated that street fighting was an art and that it was always best to deliver the first punch. His son acted on this advice and Rob's fist landed on Smith's chin, giving off the sound like a great tree being struck by an axe. That was the first and last protest from any of those whose services had been dispensed with.

The quality of the stock available was examined with care, and replacements brought in for the animals being rejected. Weapons were tested to confirm their proficiency and condition. Saddles and personal equipment were assessed and unsuitable items discarded. Each man was to carry his own musket balls and powder. Alcohol was forbidden, as was any form of gambling or fighting between themselves. Discipline was to be maintained at all times, and anyone guilty of any misdemeanour would be severely dealt with. Rob was at pains to explain that the safety of the group depended on everyone understanding what was required of them. Mistakes could be fatal for one or more persons within the party. They would be setting off with the intention of avoiding trouble at all times. The expedition would encounter heat and dust and thirst that many of them would never have experienced before. Every person must stay alert to danger at all times. They must ensure that great care and attention was taken to attend to the wellbeing of the horses and mules. The health of the stock was of paramount importance to all concerned.

There was a week left before the agreed date of departure. Rob was a troubled man, for there was a problem that needed dealing with, but he was at a loss how to resolve it. He confided in Norman who listened carefully and agreed that something had to be done. The difficulty they faced was regarding Maria and how she would cope with being in daily close contact, over many months, with the rough and ready ways of the men in the group. Her privacy would be minimal and her personal needs would have to be attended to by herself within the close confines of wherever the party stopped. It would be too dangerous to wander away out of sight of the others. After a great deal of head scratching Norman eventually came up with a possible solution. There was a couple who ran an eating place nearby, who had recently retired from running a small ranch. They had made a living roping and breaking in horses which they then sold on to a variety of customers.

"Marlene McGregor is the lady who just might help us out here, because I know that she and her husband Roy used to drive herds of horses to buyers on the remote cattle ranches and farms. They hired extra hands for these drives and Marlene is a capable lady who can advise Maria how she managed being a lone woman when on the trail." Ahern readily agreed to his friend's suggestion and the following morning Mistress McGregor met up with Maria and the two men. Norman had already briefed both ladies of the purpose of the meeting, taking particular care to talk in generalities when discussing the matter with the Senora.

"You men can go now and leave us ladies to talk in private. I've brought my horse and buggy here with me and Senora Cortez and I will take a short drive into the countryside once we've become better acquainted." She smiled as she spoke, and was pleased to note that Maria visibly relaxed on hearing her friendly words. Marlene McGregor was a fine looking woman who could ride a bronco to a standstill or be equally at ease when mixing socially with the great and the good people of Boston. From the moment she had entered the room, Marlene had acknowledged that the Spanish lady was indeed quite beautiful. A lengthy journey with tough men of the calibre going on the expedition, mixed with the presence of this attractive woman, was inviting trouble. At the start of the excursion Maria would be regarded by all as a lady. After some weeks on the trail, and in the constant sight of the men she travelled with, she would cease to be a lady to some, but would become a woman whose every movement would be watched with naked desire. Marlene warned that she must neither flirt nor tease nor play women's silly games. Maria must avoid smiling, but remain polite and slightly aloof. Above all she must act like a lady at all times. To fail to do so would invite disaster.

The afternoon came and passed all too quickly. Many of the practical issues were discussed, cautiously at first, but much more openly as the day wore on and Maria began to appreciate the value of the advice being offered. The two ladies enjoyed each other's company, and even laughed together at some of the situations that Marlene confessed to have found herself in while on the trail. By the late afternoon they were on first name terms. Maria was invited to have lunch with Marlene at her restaurant on the following day. Once they had eaten the pair would go shopping for 'sensible' clothes to wear on the journey.

"Nothing tight," Marlene cautioned, "only loose and baggy will do. We must do all we can to hide that lovely shape. Anyway, tight pants are not desirable when you are in the saddle for hours every day." She stopped her horse drawn buggy outside Maria's residence, and Maria gracefully stepped down, one hand holding her dress clear of the ground.

"Until tomorrow Marlene," she said, "thank you for a most informative day. I am very grateful to you."

"Until tomorrow Maria," her new found friend replied, adding in a whisper, "God be with you for you are about to enter a Hell of your own making."

—⁂—

The remaining days before departure came and went quickly, until finally they were as ready as they could be. Maria and Rob sat together on the porch at her house. The sun would be gone soon for it was late in the afternoon. Rob took this final opportunity to attempt to erase any lasting romantic notions Maria might have about what lay ahead of them. As he began to detail his concerns to her, she merely smiled at him and nodded her head gently. His words were having no impact at all, indeed he might as well have been speaking in some Indian dialect for all the good it was doing. The danger they would face in the many long and hard months was beyond her comprehension. He was tempted to physically shake her out of her complacency until she grasped some understanding of his concern for the whole expedition. He realized that this would achieve nothing for she was as stubborn as a mule, a trait that could cost lives. Rob eyed her profile which was outlined by the light from a lamp positioned on a small table close to where they sat. When they had first met, Rob admitted that he found her attractive. The more he had come to know her however, the feeling lessened. He found her girlish pout annoying and she was still, on occasions, playing the helpless little girl, despite the warnings given by Mistress McGregor.

Those who knew 'Pawnee' Rob Ahern often said that his wanderings would be the death of him. He smiled to himself, for there had been a number of times when they had almost been proven to be correct. He had survived numerous brushes with hostiles over the years, and the occasional run in with thieves had also left his body carrying a number of scars. The love he had for the mountains, and the plains that lay beyond the far horizons, was as irresistible as the human body is to a man of medicine. His prime consideration remained unchanged. He would do everything in his power to avoid trouble with the hostiles. He still hoped that the quantity of gold, when and if found, would prove to be greatly exaggerated. If his worst fears were confirmed and the site of the gold was a bonanza, then he would do his best to deal with this, although be admitted he did not know what he could do. The possible repercussions sent a shiver up his spine and he pushed the nightmare scenario to one side.

The expedition, consisting of twelve men and one woman, would set out the following morning, come what may. Hopes were high in many hearts, although the chances were that not all of them would return alive. Those who seek adventure and riches must be prepared to take the ultimate gamble. There is no second chance available to the majority who fail. Fate plays to win, and with great relish takes those who fall by the wayside, no matter how close they may be to the winning line.

CHAPTER THIRTY SIX

Colonel Thomas Alexander was close to despair. He was led by fools at Military Headquarters and governed by bigger fools from the Parliament in London. Despite clear evidence that a soft approach was necessary by the Military, an escalation of confrontation had been ordered. Resistance by the Colonists against British rule was to be put down at any cost. Already, in protest against further tax increases, a cargo of tea had been seized by some hot headed Colonists, poorly disguised as Indians, and dumped into the waters of Boston harbour. In response a blockade had been imposed stopping all craft leaving or entering the harbour without the approval of the Royal Navy Admiral in command. Chaos had ensued and the mood had turned very ugly indeed. Recently appointed General George Washington was openly gathering an army together and the opportunity for any reconciliation between the two sides was quickly disappearing. The stressed Garrison Commander swallowed the last of the contents of the glass of port he had poured only minutes earlier. He threw the empty glass against the wall of his office and he momentary enjoyed the foolish gesture before his anger returned. The world was in a mess. How could sane and intelligent people allow this senseless situation to race out of control? Nobody wanted conflict, yet neither would extend the olive branch that would enable talks for reconciliation to begin.

His anger abated somewhat and he turned once more to the map that lay spread across his desk. His orders were clear, and despite his grave misgivings he must follow them to the best of his ability. He sighed heavily. He had grown to love this land in the few short years he had lived here. Regardless of the outcome of the impending conflict he knew he could never stay, for his memories and affection for the people would be sullied forever.

"Enough Thomas, you are beginning to sound like an old maiden aunt," he chided himself, "It is time to issue the orders to the Company Commanders." By the time he was halfway to the adjoining door leading to his Adjutant's office, his thoughts were focused on how best to deploy his soldiers. Despite his best efforts there were too many recent arrivals from the training depots in England, whose basic skills fell short of the high standards he demanded of the troops under his command. His concern also applied to some of his officers, who seemed much more skilled at backgammon than having the tactical awareness they would require in the field of battle. The training centres continued to place far too much emphasis on foot drill and too little on the proper use of the weapons the soldiers would carry into battle. A great deal of extra weapon training had taken place, despite the restriction on the provision of musket balls and powder placed upon the Garrison by Headquarters.

The Colonel returned to his office, having instructed his Adjutant to arrange meetings with various groups within his command. The bellow of a Sergeant Major at some unfortunate soldier filtered into the office, but was unheard by the officer who was once again studying his map. Alexander was no fool. He had experienced at first hand in the war against the French, how efficient and deadly a fighting force the volunteers had proved themselves to be. In the opinion of some of the British Military hierarchy they were viewed with derision because of the casual approach they had to discipline. They also had a tendency, on occasions, to only follow orders if they felt so inclined. None of this affected Alexander's opinion in the slightest. If there was a weakness with the volunteers at all, it lay with some of the senior officers who, although not lacking in courage in any way, had little experience of command and battle tactics. If the two opposing foes were to meet on the open field of battle the superior tactics of the British would, nine times out of ten, win the day. If, on the other hand, the British were forced to chase an army who fought at a time and place of their own choosing, then they would struggle to win the conflict.

The Colonel was not a pessimist. He preferred to be regarded as a realist and had rarely failed to give an honest reply to an honest question. The dice, he reasoned with himself, were loaded against the British winning any war that broke out against the Colonies. If General George Washington applied hit and run tactics against the British and avoided any major face to face conflict, and the French entered the war and provided troops, then Britain could not win.

His thoughts were interrupted by a sharp rap on his office door and his Adjutant entered, saluted smartly, and informed the Colonel that the first of the series of meetings he had ordered was ready to begin.

Thomas Alexander was a soldier to the core of his soul. He donned his cap, quickly checked his uniform was in good order then strode from his office. The game of war, with all the savage and bloody battles gloriously depicted in books and newspapers, was fated to begin within a matter of weeks if not days. Of this he had no doubt. History repeatedly showed time and again that the heroics and the sacrifices made by many would quickly be forgotten in the mists of time. Grand monuments erected in memory of the dead heroes provided perches for the birds, rather than a reminder that war was a filthy business that scarred people's lives forever and should be avoided at all costs. There had been too many wars, too many widows, and too many children left without fathers. Dead heroes could not feed hungry families. How many years after this war ended he wondered, before the inept politicians of this world would again lead their nations into another preventable needless conflict?

A passing company of his soldiers presented a salute which he returned smartly. The war might well be lost to us but, he promised himself, he would do all in his power to increase the chances of survival of every blessed soldier under his command.

CHAPTER THIRTY SEVEN

Alex Campbell was furious. In this kind of mood he was liable to lash out at any unfortunate within striking distance. Sandy Young, the bringer of the bad news, had prior knowledge of Campbell's temper and made sure that he was well out of range when he delivered it. Young tried to ingratiate himself with his leader, while having regrets about passing the information he had learned onto Campbell.

"I only just got to hear that McDonald had left Georgetown in the company of Malcolm Slater, the manager of the McDonald freight offices there. It seems that they had arranged to visit all the freight stations belonging to the business as far down south as time allowed. They planned to be away for up to six weeks or thereabouts." He watched carefully for any reaction from his boss before he continued.

"Maybe this isn't such a bad thing. We were going to grab the squaw and force McDonald to lead us to the gold if he wanted his daughter back, but why can't we just force her to lead us to it?" There was a silence while Campbell digested this suggestion. His unshaven face broke into a wide grin, exposing dirty black tobacco stained teeth. He released a deep hoarse chortle and slapped his thigh.

"Sandy, you're the only one in this outfit with any brains, apart from me of course. I was waiting to see how long it was afore somebody realized that the girl knows where the gold is and she can lead us there. All we got to figure is a way to make her take us to the place. Have you got any ideas?" He looked at his underling with raised eyebrows. Young already had a proposal in mind but waited a few moments while pretending that he was addressing the question before replying.

"Why not take Douglas McDonald's daughter Anne as a hostage? She and the Indian woman are friends, and we'll tell the squaw that if she won't take us to the gold then we'll kill the girl. If we cover our faces when we snatch them we can blindfold them. One of the boys can stay behind with the McDonald girl for a couple of days, and then release her before catching up with us. She won't be able to identify us and she can be told if she opens her mouth about us and we are followed, then we'll kill her friend. Meantime we can head out avoiding the main trails until we are away from this area and with less chance of being seen. The squaw won't know we are no longer holding her friend and will take us to the gold." He sat back, content that he had come up with a plan that clearly appealed to his boss. Campbell's eyes narrowed as he thought through the suggestion. The tricky part would be to get the two girls alone together, but the idea was a good one. He decided it could work and turned to his companion who was waiting impatiently for an answer.

"Get to it Sandy. Find out when they go to town, or ride out, or whenever we can catch them on their own. Take two of the men to help you. The sooner we can get our hands on the squaw the sooner we can start out after the gold." Young nodded his head in acknowledgement and left quickly. Campbell would not admit it to himself, but the lust for the gold was getting into his head like a deadly silent disease that clouded his normal cautious approach. He wanted to see it, touch it and hold the yellow metal in his hands. To do this he would steal and cheat and, he admitted to himself, he would kill for gold. Anyone who got in his way would be eliminated. In his mind he was already planning how the money might be spent. He could begin a new life in a big house with servants to tend his needs, wear only the finest clothes, and enjoy expensive wines with food prepared by his own chef. His stables would house only the best horses money could buy. Most of all, he would have women at his beck and call. He warmed at the thought for he was not a man who appealed to the ladies, but with his new found wealth they would find him irresistible!

A day passed and then another before Young reported back concerning the movements of the young women, who proved to be creatures of habit. It made the planning for the kidnapping much easier than they had hoped. Almost every afternoon after lunch the duo took a horse ride around the ranch boundary. Sometimes they would journey in a clockwise direction and, for a change, sometimes in the other direction. Either way they would have to pass anyone lying in wait for them, Campbell smilingly informed his gang as he explained his plan for the kidnapping. Providing everyone carried out his instructions there should be no trouble. He restated the details once more and made each of his men repeat what task they had to carry out. Satisfied that his orders had been understood, he stubbed out his cheroot and moved towards his horse.

"We meet here first thing tomorrow. In the meantime stay away from the whisky and the saloons. I want no loose talk from any of you. Check you have everything you need for the journey to hunt for the gold. We've already agreed what every man should take. This is our big chance boys, let's take it." There was a muted murmur of agreement from the men. There was no turning back now.

CHAPTER THIRTY EIGHT

James McDonald and Malcolm Slater had travelled hard over the last three weeks and had stopped overnight at one of the freight company's stations just south of Williamsburg in Virginia. It was early in the morning and a watery sun appeared rather reluctantly in the sky. James was enjoying a piping hot cup of black coffee as he stood outside the bunkhouse door. He stretched himself in a tired but contented way. The various stations visited had proved to be efficiently run and were situated in key locations along the trading routes used by the Company. Douglas had done a very professional job of setting up and expanding the business during the years James had been away. Those employed at the stations were hard working and tough men, who made sure that everything was done to enable the movement of goods to take place quickly and safely. The McDonald brand was highly respected and those employed by the Company enjoyed good working conditions. Such consideration was a policy put in force from the very start and had resulted in a loyal and dedicated workforce.

Whilst the health of the business was good, the events taking place throughout the Colonies were extremely worrying. The increasing incidents of violence were clear evidence that unrest amongst the Colonists was heading for open rebellion unless some calming action was taken by both sides involved. Like a stampeding herd of cattle, the situation was out of control and heading for the inevitable conflict that would result. James shook his head. The effect that the outbreak of a war would have on the business would be catastrophic. Some of the employees at the stations had declared themselves to be on one side or the other, and such divided loyalties could only lead to trouble. He consoled himself that wise heads, such as William Porter and his friend Douglas, were openly calling for calm from both sides and for urgent meetings with the British. Surely common sense would prevail in the end. War was a mad disease that was to be avoided at all costs, and he had no wish to be forced to choose sides. He had great hopes for Fiona, and that she could enjoy a normal happy life. What would happen to Cameron, his newly found nephew and an officer of the Crown?

His thoughts were interrupted by Slater who had risen, shaved and dressed and was now ready for breakfast.

"Time for food James, then, if you're happy with what we've seen here, we can start back for home."

James nodded his agreement and emptied the coffee dregs from his cup before turning and following his companion inside.

They were about a thousand miles south of Boston, but had the advantage of stopping at any of the stations on route for overnight accommodation and a change of horses. Weather permitting they could travel at a reasonable pace on the return journey. After thanking the men at the station for their hospitality, the duo set off northwards towards Georgetown and home.

CHAPTER THIRTY NINE

Everything was in place. Campbell and his men were hidden in some shrubbery close to the boundary fencing that marked the perimeter of the ranch property. The band of men had moved into their positions early that morning, taking great care to avoid being seen. The mid-day sun was hot and the shade provided was sparse. One of his men was heard to grumble about the heat as he wiped the sweat from his brow. Campbell glared in his direction and motioned to those close by to remain silent and alert for the expected appearance of the two young women.

Time passed slowly, and only the drone of insects broke the monotony of waiting. In the blue sky above a few puffballs of flimsy white clouds were gently scattered by a warm breeze. Nerves were beginning to show in one or two of Campbell's men and he nodded in their direction, more as a warning to be still than of encouragement. If they made a mess of this, or if the women didn't show, it would be over before it began. They waited.

Anne and Fiona were in somber mood as they rode along their normal circuit. Despite her parents' decision that Cameron and Anne should end their friendship, the two had continued to secretly write to each other. This was a situation that the young couple did not feel at ease with. Anne was overwhelmed with guilt at her betrayal of her mother and father, and Cameron was adamant that he must be allowed to approach her parents to declare his love for Anne. He was ashamed of himself, for his actions were not that of a gentleman. His latest letter to her had insisted that she permit him to make a formal approach to Douglas in order that he might openly declare his affection towards Anne. It was this latest letter that she was discussing with Fiona.

"I know that we are young and that Cameron wears the uniform of an officer of the British Army, but I must be true to my feelings for him, and yet I cannot continue to lie to my parents." She dabbed her eyes with a handkerchief and drew her pony to a halt before continuing. "Papa has always told me to be honest, no matter how difficult this may prove to be. I cannot sleep or eat properly and it has not gone unnoticed by my Mama, who has already asked me if I am unwell. Oh Fiona, what should I do?" The two friends coaxed their mounts into a walk and there was a brief silence before Fiona spoke.

"It must be said that I have little knowledge of your customs in matters of the heart, therefore I am reluctant to offer much in the way of advice. I am only certain of one thing, and it is that you must not allow the situation to continue as it is. If your parents find out that you have been deceiving them they will be deeply hurt. If your friendship with Cameron continues for any length of time before your secret becomes known, then the fact you have kept it from them for such a long time will cause them more distress. To delay further would also show Cameron up in a bad light, for he wants to inform your parents of his love for you, and moreover wishes to do this openly as a gentleman should. All parents who care about their children have to act as they think best. It is the same everywhere I believe." Fiona glanced sideways at her friend, hoping that she had not overstepped the mark. Although she had spoken from the heart she had yet to experience the kind of love that Anne had for Cameron, and felt at a disadvantage as a result.

Without warning a voice rang out.

"Hold up ladies," ordered Campbell as he and his gang stepped from cover. All of them were masked and armed with pistols at the ready. Two seized hold of the halters of the horses being ridden by the young women. The ambush had been a complete success, catching them totally off guard.

"Sit still and be quiet and no one will get hurt." The order was then given to the two friends to dismount and blindfolds were applied. Their hands were bound together and Anne and her horse were led away, leaving Campbell with two of his men and Fiona, who was silently chastising herself for having failed to have stayed alert and allowing Anne and herself to be captured so easily. She remained silent, listening for any clue that might help identify the men at a later date. Faint cries of protest by Anne were quickly silenced. There then followed the sound of horses being mounted and ridden away. Even blindfolded, Fiona was able to calculate that there had been three in the departing group, including her friend. She waited in silence for only a moment before she was roughly led into the cover of the bushes and away from view of any passersby. She uttered no protest as she was pushed to her knees, before one of her captors began to speak.

"Listen very carefully to what I say, for your friend's life depends on you doing everything I ask. Any failure on your part and she will end up dead. Do you understand?" Fiona nodded in agreement.

"Good. You will be allowed to leave here unharmed once I have finished giving you the instructions that you must follow in every detail. You will have your hands untied before we leave you here, but the blindfold will remain in place. You will wait until you can no longer hear our horses before it can be removed. You will ride to the ranch and tell the McDonalds that we have their daughter. We are not to be followed, and any attempt to do so, or to find where she is being held, will result in her death.

You will pack everything you need for the long trek we will be going on. You will no doubt have guessed by now that you will lead us to the location of the gold that you and your father discovered. If you fail to do as I ask, your young friend will die." Fiona was in no doubt that these men were desperate to find the gold, for their actions so far would be treated as a hanging offence. The kidnapping of women was a crime that was not tolerated in these parts. Adding murder to their wrongdoing would make no difference to any punishment meted out to men who were certain to die by the noose if caught.

"You would be foolish to leave any message for your father on his return from his business in the south. Be sure that any attempt by him or the McDonalds to find us, or your friend, will result in her death, and of course yours," he added. "Once you have packed I want you to head west on the trail, heading for the trading post run by a man called Valentine. It lies about forty miles from here. Be there before nightfall or else. One of my men will then contact you and you will go with him. Again I repeat that any attempt to follow us will lead to the deaths of your friend and yourself." At this point her hands were untied and the sounds of the men mounting up told her they were about to leave her.

"Your horse is back in the brush and should be easy for you to find, you being an Indian and all," the speaker sneered. His words were followed by the hoof beats of the retreating horses until they were no longer audible, even to Fiona's keen hearing. She removed the blindfold and studied the sign on the ground left by the horses. It did not take her long to confirm that there had been five in the party plus the mounts of Anne and herself. It was little enough information, but a small start to the task that lay ahead. She was sure that both the McDonalds and her own father would attempt to hunt these men down. In the meantime she must follow the instructions given to her and inform the McDonalds what had taken place. Fiona mounted up and set her horse into a steady gallop towards the ranch house. The game was just about to start, and there was a long way to go before any conclusion was reached.

CHAPTER FORTY

Fiona's news was received in a shocked silence as she carefully related the details of Anne's kidnapping to Douglas and Isabel. Neither parent spoke as they listened intently to every last word. Isabel's eyes filled with tears and her husband's features were white and tight, with a mixture of fear and anger, as Fiona told of Anne's capture. She calculated from the tracks at the scene of the kidnap, that there were five men involved. When she finished speaking a flood of questions burst forth from the McDonalds. Did she recognize the voices? Was Anne unharmed? Fiona shook her head, for she could add no more facts to those she had given. Time was passing, and the young woman ended by stating that she would now pack her things together before riding out to meet up with the kidnappers near Valentine's trading post. The McDonalds were aghast at her decision to do so, and protested that she would be placing herself in great danger.

"If I do not return they will kill Anne. These men are blinded by the thought of the gold. It is a long journey over dangerous lands before we will reach the place they seek. This will give you time to find out where Anne is being held and to free her. My father will follow these men, as I will take them on the same route we travelled getting here. I will also leave some small sign for him to pick up along the way."

She smiled at the protests made by the McDonalds, but was adamant that it was best for all concerned.

"If by some chance my father has not contacted me in some way after a month I will escape from them whenever I can. He will find me or die trying, of this I am certain. In some ways I feel sorry for these men who have taken Anne, for my father is a warrior and there will be no mercy in his heart." She reached as far as the door before she turned, and after some hesitation told them of the earlier conversation that had taken place with Anne regarding Cameron.

"It was her intention to tell you both of their shared affection, and for Cameron to meet with you and seek your approval. You may wish to make him aware of her kidnapping, even if you disapprove of his failure to approach you earlier." She left the McDonalds, went to her room and started packing. She changed into her Indian clothes which would be more comfortable than any of the latest additions to her wardrobe. She strapped her hunting knife to her inner thigh and wound a belted knife around her waist. She expected this to be taken from her but hoped that her hidden knife would be overlooked if she was searched. After one last look at her room she headed towards the stables to put together some items for the care of her pony. It would be a long journey and a heavy demand would be placed upon all of the horses over the many months of travel that lay ahead. She decided that she would also take one of her father's pack horses to help spread the load, and even to ride occasionally to give some respite to her pony.

After a brief farewell with Douglas and Isabel, Fiona mounted up and set off westwards for the arranged meeting with the outlaws near Valentine's trading post.

The search for the gold would then take them across the far distant Appalachian Mountains and the great endless prairies that lay beyond. Her father was due to return soon from his trip down south, and Douglas had dispatched a rider to head down that way to meet him and hasten his return to the ranch. The messenger carried a scribbled note from Douglas to be delivered to James, giving him a brief outline of what had taken place. Meantime Douglas gave serious thought to what needed to be done next. Any knee jerk reaction was to be avoided, as any sign of pursuit or increased activity in the surrounding area might panic the kidnappers into killing Anne. He would wait. While the abductors felt that all was going to plan they would grow in confidence, perhaps become over confident. This could result in them making some small mistake that might lead to Anne's whereabouts. It was a dangerous game to play, but his daughter's safety was of paramount importance. His thoughts touched briefly on Cameron. He was a fine lad and his friendship with Anne might develop into something serious or not. Douglas would contact him as soon as possible.

CHAPTER FORTY ONE

Maria was trembling with excitement. Her heart was beating with the speed of an antelope in flight and her eyes shone in anticipation. Today the journey would begin, the search for Esteban's gold was at last underway, and the future was full of promise! The cavalcade of twelve heavily armed riders, excluding Rob and Maria and two Susquehanna scouts, set off from the outskirts of Boston. Their departure was accompanied by the cheers of those who had come to see the party set off. It was an open secret that others would follow the procession in the hope that they would be led to the gold. The harsh conditions and dangers that lay in wait would soon discourage most of these dreamers.

The next three weeks brought the travellers within sight of the white capped peaks of the Appalachian mountain range. Rob had used this time to assess the men within the group and to identify and correct security lapses. A careless rider had neglected to properly care for his horse. This had resulted in sores on the animal's back caused by the blanket not being placed with care, and rubbing with the movement of the saddle. It was an opportunity for Rob to show that he meant business and he sacked the man on the spot. The message given was a clear one, obey the rules or ship out. He again spoke to them about the need for discipline in all matters. Any careless action within the group placed them all in jeopardy.

He also had a quiet word with Maria, who had earlier asked one of the riders to take her on a jaunt to see some of the surrounding countryside. The man, an experienced former soldier named Laidlaw, had the good sense to refuse and reported it to Ahern.

"Senora you must understand that these are men who would never cause harm to any decent woman, for it is their code. Lower your standards however, and in their eyes you will be quickly regarded as a woman of no morals and therefore available to all." He continued to plead with her.

"You must remain aloof and be seen to behave as a lady at all times, and who is above them in station. Please remember what Mistress McGregor has told you, for failure to do so would be disastrous for your safety." Her response was not what he wanted to hear. She was a lady, she said, as anyone could see, and she had no fears that even the roughest amongst the hired help would fail to regard her as such. Rob was in despair, for Maria had no concept of the rough and ready morals held by many of the men in the group. They were on this expedition to seek and find, whatever the cost, the Holy Grail of gold.

To make matters worse, some of the men within the group became more demanding for information on where they were headed. How long would it be before they reached the landmarks that would lead to the source of the gold? The bolder men within the group approached Maria directly when Rob was out of hearing. She had fended them off with a smile and a promise that all would be revealed in due course. It was only then that she began to realize that she had no idea where the party should be heading once they had crossed the Appalachians. She had no knowledge of the general area that the map referred to, and in a panic drew Rob aside and blurted out a jumbled confession of the situation. Although horrified at her revelation, he reasoned that all was not lost, for James McDonald and his daughter were known to have been in Sioux country when they found the gold. That covered a huge territory, but it was a pointer to the area into which they should travel on their search. Rob tried to be positive about the situation, but realized that the consequences of the others within the group learning the truth would lead to an explosion of anger that would be impossible to contain. He cursed his stupidity in failing to insist on seeing the map before agreeing to lead the expedition. However, he had made his bed and now he must lie in it. They would travel onwards until they entered Sioux country, then review how they would proceed from there.

The change in Maria's manner did not go unnoticed amongst her hirelings, and two of the group approached her that evening. They stood before the small fire where she sat and demanded to know where they were next headed. Tom Black, a huge man, spoke first.

"The scouts need to know in order that they can seek out the best trail. They also need to know to be able to find water for us and the horses. We don't want to be held back from finding the gold any longer than need be, so that we can avoid them hostiles and get back safely." He leered at Maria as he spoke.

"We all know what them Indians does to white women when they gets them alone. Think about it Spanish lady. We are getting impatient." Black and his companion left her and returned to the main group that was sat nearby.

Maria's face was pale in the firelight from her own small fire. The cold hand of fear clutched at her heart. She now began to appreciate the warnings about her own behaviour that Ahern and Mistress McGregor had tried to give her, and she had so foolishly disregarded. However, her biggest mistake by far was to insist that no other person should see Esteban's map before the group set off. Had she confided in Rob earlier about the limitations of the map, more detailed planning may have been possible to deal with this major shortcoming. Suddenly she was once more the young woman of yesteryear who felt alone and vulnerable, her mind frozen of any thoughts of how to escape her predicament.

The small campfires had dimmed and there was little light apart from that provided by the myriad of stars that shone through the dark sky. The limited warmth of the late evening sun had departed and the hint of a mild frost was in the air. The occasional sounds from the creatures of the night could be heard as they went about their task of finding food. The picketed horses nearby huddled a little closer, ever alert to any scent picked up that might warn of danger. Apart from the two guards on duty, sleep descended on those lying there. Some would sleep well, and some, including Ahern and Maria, would not.

CHAPTER FORTY TWO

James McDonald had received the note from Douglas and was riding back to the ranch as fast as he could without killing his horse in the process. He had left Slater to make his own way back to Georgetown, and took an extra mount from the company freight station so he could switch horses along the way. He was deeply concerned for Fiona's safety, but consoled himself with the knowledge that no harm would come to her until her kidnappers had reached the source of Esteban's gold. He knew his daughter well and was sure that she would make no foolish attempt to escape. She would go through the motions of leading the outlaws westwards, while waiting for some sign from her father who would be on their trail. James McDonald had never been known to push a horse to the limits, but the safety of his daughter and her friend was now at stake. He silently apologized to his mount as he kicked it into more effort, for this was a matter of life or death.

Four days had passed since Anne's capture by Campbell and his gang. Aware that the ranch might be watched for any sign of pursuit, Douglas had made no move that could place his daughter's life in jeopardy. To any watching eyes, life at the ranch continued as though nothing untoward had happened. A cool head was needed at this time and Douglas concentrated his thoughts on where Anne may have been taken. He disregarded the possibility that she was dead, as much to reassure himself as for the sanity of his wife. Isabel was close to breaking point, and the deep shadows under her eyes were confirmation of the sleepless days and nights endured since the kidnapping. The strain on both of them was a burden beyond belief. Isabel veered from accusing Douglas of not caring enough to do something to bring Anne home, to lying sobbing in his arms for lengthy periods of time.

Young James volunteered to ride to Boston to inform Cameron of what had taken place. However, on his arrival he found that most of the garrison troops had been deployed elsewhere as the move towards open rebellion loomed ever closer. He left no message, but before returning to the ranch he had a brief meeting with his uncle, William Porter, to advise him of Anne's kidnapping. It was at this time that Porter informed him that his grandfather, Hugh Mercer, had joined Washington's volunteers in anticipation of the conflict with the British that was now viewed by many as inevitable.

"It is a bad time for everyone concerned. It also means that there will be few resources available at this time to search for a missing young woman. I too am due to leave shortly, for there is much to be done if we are to unite the thirteen Colonies together against the British. Your father will also be pulled into the conflict, for his freighting company will be regarded of great value to either side. He will have to choose, for neutrality is not an option." Porter shook his head sadly. Despite his best efforts, and of those others who shared his views, there would be war. He shook his nephew's hand.

"Give my love to your parents. My thoughts are with you all at this difficult time. I will pray for Anne's safe return." The young man nodded in acknowledgement of his uncle's words and left, in low spirits, to ride back home.

—⚡—

Douglas was alerted to the sound of a hard ridden horse approaching the ranch house. It was his friend James astride a mustang that was on the verge of collapse. David Wilson appeared from the shadows and took the reins from the exhausted rider who slid tiredly from the saddle.

"Look after him well David, for he has given me his all this day," he instructed the ranch foreman. He made a half hearted attempt to brush the dust from his clothes before being ushered inside by Douglas. As he entered the room he gratefully accepted a piping hot mug of coffee from Isabel. Before he had time to be seated Nan appeared carrying a plate of food which she placed beside him. James had forgotten how hungry he was and he ate as Douglas briefed him on what had taken place, including Fiona's words before she had set off to meet up with the kidnappers.

There was a lengthy silence after Douglas had finished speaking. James' eyes were hooded and he chose his words with care before responding.

"It appears to me at this stage that we should be looking for Anne. It can be no easy thing to hide a young woman for any length of time without someone some-where noticing. I would suggest you go public on the kidnapping without any mention of Fiona's involvement. Stir things up, offer a reward, and get everyone you can to ask around." James acknowledged the unspoken question in the eyes of his friend.

"There is a danger that by taking this action, she may be harmed in some way," he hesitated to say 'dead' but Douglas was all too aware of this possibility. "On the other hand, she may have been left in some remote place and even now is waiting to be found. Remember, these outlaws have Fiona, and Anne is only of value to them if she remains alive." He did not add that Fiona would not know if any harm had come to her friend, but she must assume that Anne would be unharmed at least sufficiently long enough for the gang to have a head start from any possible followers.

It was clear that urgent pursuit of those holding Fiona must be launched without delay. At the same time a massive search should begin to seek out and find anyone who might know where Anne may be held. A large reward for any information could perhaps help to loosen some tongues. James wasted no precious minutes debating with Douglas about who should do what. It was logical, he argued, that Douglas take control of the search for Anne as he knew the area and the various contacts locally that would speed up the process. James, on the other hand would make his way alone back into Indian country. By travelling unaccompanied he would only have himself to worry about. There was no argument from Douglas, and James left to pack and grab two hours shuteye before he left to hunt down the outlaws.

In the meantime Douglas had all the available ranch hands brought together and told of Anne's kidnapping. He split his men into various small groups and detailed tasks to each. Some would search among local, but remote, areas identified as possible places for hideouts.

Others would pass word of the reward on offer for Anne's safe return. Douglas would ride to meet with Sheriff Milligan and Judge Greaves and seek their help. At last, Douglas told himself, he was doing something that could, no would, lead to the safe recovery of his daughter. He gave a reassuring hug to Isabel then set off for Georgetown.

Two hours later found James riding towards the Appalachian Mountains. He was astride his own horse and had a spare mount and a packhorse in tow. The sun was in the process of retreating out of sight, but its dying light flickered for a few moments more before fading from view. The final darkness of night descended, but James rode on. He would not travel much further before he made camp, but it felt of some consolation to be in control of what he must now do. His heart was once again that of a warrior and there was no mercy in his soul.

Chapter Forty Three

Fiona had been awake for some time. She viewed the poorly assembled group around her with contempt. Campbell stirred nearby and she closed her eyes and pretended to be asleep. Her legs were bound together at the ankles and one of her arms was tied to a nearby sapling. She could have escaped during the night if she had chosen to do so, but she knew that she must wait for her father to make contact. Anne's safety was what concerned her most. If she was safe, or indeed dead, then she and her father could act. He would contact her at some point, of that she was certain. He would not fail her unless he was wounded or dead. Looking at the men around her, she doubted if any of them, or indeed all of them together, had the capability to keep her father away.

The night coolness had gone and the air was barely moving enough to shake a response from the surrounding trees. The morning sun strode gently onto the earth below, a welcome guest as the warmth of its fingers spread into corners of the darkest places. Fiona pretended to be awakened by Campbell's words of command. She was to make food for the group, and nodded her agreement to the order while pointing to her bound feet and arm. He smirked his pleasure at her submissive action and untied her, while his hands explored her body in the process. She made no effort to respond to his touch. He snarled an angry curse. He would teach her respect and she would do well to be good to him, for her life was in his hands. Fiona made no reply. If she had wanted she could have slit his throat while his hands had fondled her breasts. Her time would come and he would pay.

After breakfast the outlaws mounted up, with Fiona tied to her saddle, her horse tethered to another, and set off along the trail towards the search for Esteban's golden bonanza. Fiona could not believe how ill prepared this band of thieves was to even begin to think that they could safely travel for many months though Indian country. Her concern was real, for although she had not seen sign of hostile presence it was only a matter of time before they were attacked. She was grateful for the fact that she had changed to Indian dress and that she was clearly a captive. If taken by a band of victorious Indians however, she could well end up worse off than she was at present.

Even now, after only a few weeks travel with the outlaws, she saw the consequences of poor provision for food, water and care of the horses, start to emerge. One horse became lame and soon afterwards another fell foul to the same condition. Campbell became angrier by the minute. When one of the pack horses had to be used as a replacement for a lame mount he exploded in rage.

"The next one who loses his horse goes on foot. Anybody don't agree and I'll kill them. Understood?" He looked around for any argument but there was none. Despite the problems with the horses, the group still travelled too fast, tiring out their willing but weakening mounts with each passing hour. In the end it was Fiona who spoke up, much to Campbell's surprise.

She deliberately acted as though she had little knowledge of English and signed as she talked.

"Too much for horse, too much without rest. They die soon," as she spoke she pointed to the exhausted band of horses that stood with bowed heads. "Rest or we never find place you seek. With no horses we die here." She stood impassive, waiting for a response. Campbell looked at her with a scowl.

"The squaw is right. We need to rest the horses and slow down. After all, the gold ain't going anywhere meantime. Just don't forget what I said, anyone who loses their horse walks." He glared at his men, daring any one of them to challenge him. None did.

The suggestion to rest the horses had not fallen on stony ground. Campbell saw the wisdom of the group taking a day off from their trek. The horses would benefit if given some respite from the harsh and exhausting use they had been subjected to. The men took it in turns to enjoy the chance of some uninterrupted sleep, while Fiona cooked some stews and soups. The speed at which they had travelled since leaving Georgetown had prevented her cooking anything other than the most basic food. Under the watchful eyes of one of the men who accompanied her, she had been allowed to wander nearby to dig for some wild edible roots and gather a small collection of herbs. Her efforts were well received and the mood of the group improved as a result. Fiona knew that this would be short lived, and she was ever aware that some of the outlaws rarely took their eyes from her. She was not regarded with respect by any of them, for she was just an Indian woman and not entitled to the consideration that any decent white woman might expect. She must take care at all times.

The presence of her knife, cool against her inner thigh, gave her some comfort. She would not succumb easily.

The evening drew to a close and the night was very still. Fiona gathered her blanket closer to her body. Above her the stars hung low in the dark sky. Her thoughts were of her father and she silently implored him to come to her rescue soon, for she was afraid of these men. It was only a matter of time before they were seen by some hostiles and attacked. When this happened they would be killed or taken by the Indians to face terrible torture, before death would ultimately claim them. She forced herself to remain strong of resolve, and eventually sleep came, giving her troubled mind some temporary peace.

CHAPTER FORTY FOUR

The search for Anne had begun slowly but was gaining momentum by the hour. It was now four days since James had ridden off in pursuit of Fiona. In the meantime an ongoing hunt was being carried out in areas where someone could be kept captive and away from prying eyes. Enquiries elsewhere, and a payment to an informer, had pointed to Campbell and his gang as the possible kidnappers. They were known to have occupied an old disused shack that lay some ten miles south of Georgetown. Douglas and four of his men had located the run down building and lay watching, hidden in a nearby hollow some three hundred yards away. They had been there since early morning and had seen no sign of movement. It was decision time. They could wait longer or move in. Douglas chose the latter course of action. He and David Wilson would approach from either side of the building, leaving the others to keep watch on the front.

The two men carefully skirted either side of the shack, using whatever cover was available. Douglas had a great deal of experience of fighting and had built up a well deserved reputation for being a cool head in stressful and dangerous situations. This time, however, it was his own daughter who could be lying in the shack, either alive, hurt, or God forbid, dead. Throwing caution to the wind he cocked his pistol and forced open the flimsy door with his shoulder. Hearing the noise from the entry by Douglas, Wilson forced his way into the shack from the other side. Douglas quickly entered the second of the two rooms within the half ruined structure and gave out a great cry of relief and joy. A wide eyed and gagged Anne lay on the floor, trussed up like a turkey. Her father quickly released her and held her tightly in his arms.

"I knew you would come for me Papa" she sobbed. "I have been here for three days since my captors left me. They have not been back since". On hearing her words David had signalled for the horses to be brought to the shack by the other three searchers. He took a canteen of water from his mount and re-entered the building, after giving orders for the men to spread the news that Anne had been found alive and well.

Douglas was a mighty relieved man. He acknowledged to himself that as the days had passed he had hoped for the best but expected the worst. He took the canteen from his foreman and gently encouraged Anne to take a few sips. He pulled it away as she fought to drink more than she should.

"Gently, gently" he coaxed, "too much too quickly will only make you ill". She heard his words and relaxed sufficiently for him to put the canteen to her lips one more.

"That's better" he encouraged, time for me to take you home now so you can rest up and tell us what happened". Anne made a small protest that died quickly as the effect of the lack of food and water hit her and she fell into a deep troubled sleep. She had wanted to ask about Fiona, but her exhausted body fought to stay awake in vain, and she gave way to its demands. Her father gently covered her in a blanket and carried her outside.

He mounted his horse and David Wilson helped place the sleeping Anne into her father's arms. Douglas smiled gently at his daughter. She was so very tired, and he believed that a stampeding herd of cattle could have passed close by and she would not have stirred. He kicked his horse into a steady trot and headed for the ranch. Isabel would have received the news that Anne was safe and well and would be anxiously awaiting the arrival of her daughter. As they rode along Douglas held tightly onto Anne and promised himself that he would be more understanding of her affection for Cameron. His child was no longer dependent upon her parents for guidance on her journey into adulthood. She was a young woman with her own views on life, who would make her own decisions and her own mistakes as she made her way in the world. He sighed, partly with a deep sense of relief that she was safe, but also with a little sadness that the innocence of childhood was now behind her. She had changed, and so must he, for nothing remains the same forever.

It was a tearful, deliriously happy Isabel who stood on the ranch house porch awaiting the safe return of her daughter. She fussed constantly with her apron as she anxiously sought for a sign of their arrival.

At last her vigil was rewarded as they rode into view, Anne still sleeping despite the bumpy ride. Douglas drew alongside the porch and smiled broadly as he handed her down into the welcoming arms of Isabel and Nan. Together they carried Anne gently into the coolness of the house and to her bedroom, where a hot tub and a change of clothes had been prepared in readiness for her return. After being bathed and given a light meal she would be left to sleep again. The many questions about her ordeal could wait until she was ready to talk.

Later Douglas quietly entered the parlour and placed his arm around Isabel. She looked up at him and then laid her head against his shoulder. The strain and worry over the days since Anne was taken finally broke the last vestige of her resolve and she began to sob deeply. He held her tightly until her shaking subsided. Their daughter was home and they had much to be thankful for.

Outside the ranch house the sun was starting to fade and the distant peaks began to point lengthening dark shadows over the surrounding lands. It had been an eventful day that had ended well. Tomorrow would bring whatever fate decreed, good or bad, but tonight was a time to be thankful, a time to rejoice in the safe return of their daughter.

CHAPTER FORTY FIVE

'Pawnee' Rob Ahern rode at the head of the cavalcade, his mind full of questions but with few answers. A single flimsy white cloud hung unmoving in the blue sky above. The atmosphere was stifling and their progress was a hot, sticky and uncomfortable journey. Heat waves rose into the heavens creating shimmering mirages that faded as the travellers drew nearer to them. Nothing stirred and no animals were to be seen, for even they had acknowledged that this was a time to seek shade from the inferno around them. Ahern nodded to himself in silent agreement at his decision to stop at the first opportunity where water and shade were available.

He had earlier tasked his two Susquehanna scouts with finding such a place and he was hopeful that they would soon return with news that they had found a suitable location. Meantime the group rode on. His thoughts returned to how he should deal with the shattering realization that the map held by Maria was virtually useless. It would remain so unless one or more of the key landmarks could be found once they had entered Sioux country. Over and over Rob debated his options, limited as they were. What would be gained by telling the men the reality of the situation? Would it not be better to let them keep the dream of gold, and deny them the truth of the inadequacy of the map?

There would be hell to pay and some might react in a violent way. The choice that appealed most was to simply do nothing and hope that something would turn up. When he repeated these thoughts to himself he felt sick to the stomach, for it was a feeble excuse. To travel onwards was really just an escape, that would enable him to delay the decision that he knew would have to be taken at some point. He would hope for the best but prepare for the worst.

Rob had faced death on too many occasions for his own liking. His body carried numerous scars in confirmation of the dangers he had encountered in his life so far. Those who knew him often said that it was only a matter of time before a stray musket ball, or a warrior's knife, would put an end to his existence. He sighed deeply, partly in frustration and partly in the thought that his demise would bring an end to the opportunity to explore this land, for there were many places he had yet to see. He had a deep love of the mountains, the vast prairies and the deserts that lay to the south.

His attention was drawn towards two iridescent riders that were emerging through the heat waves. He signalled for those behind him to stop, while he sought to confirm that it was his scouts returning from their search for a suitable place to rest. He relaxed as the two Susquehanna Indians drew to a halt beside him. The older scout called Senga was agitated, and with words and sign informed Rob that they had come across fresh tracks of up to twenty Piankasha warriors. All in the band were mounted and there were no signs of any camp followers. It was clear that this was a war party on a raid, and there was a risk that the tracks left by the gold hunters would be spotted. The scouts had however identified a location nearby with water, good grass and shade. It would also be a place that would offer some protection from attack. Ahern quickly informed those closest to him of the situation and told them to pass the news down the line. He signalled to Senga to lead the way, but not too quickly, or they would raise dust that could be seen some distance away.

The ride to the small but deep pool was under three miles away, and it did not take them long to reach it. The water was provided by a sheltered spring that gently fed the pool throughout the day and night. The surrounding trees of pecans, willow and dogwood provided welcome shade. Defensive positions were taken up without the need for any such orders to be given by their leader. The canteens were collected by two of the group and filled, before being returned to the respective owners. Only when this had been done were the horses allowed to drink, two at a time to avoid the edges of the pool being churned up by their hooves. The canteens were again filled up to ensure that water was available to all in the event of having to leave at short notice. Only an idiot or a tenderfoot would leave his canteen less than full when water was available. Rob noted with approval that everyone within the group took time out to care for their mounts. Even Maria had stripped the saddle from her horse and was giving her mare a rub down. Cold food was distributed and a small fire was permitted, barely sufficient to boil enough water for coffee. There was a risk in this, but the little smoke from the fire was quickly dissipated among the branches of the trees and the hot drink boosted the morale of the group.

They waited in readiness. Had they been seen? Had the Piankasha discovered their tracks? Were they, even now, being watched by the warriors? Ahern quietly went around the members of the band, giving a word of encouragement here and there. They were in a good position to defend themselves, he told them. They had water, shade and good cover and each of them was a capable shot. Meantime everyone must stay alert for any movement that might indicate the presence of the hostiles.

An hour came and went followed by another, and still the time dragged on. Half the men were detailed to watch while the others dozed if they could. The sun above had moved onwards and the heat of the day left behind the coolness of approaching night. Rob did a check of those on guard before returning to lie within a few yards of Maria who watched him wide-eyed, her face pale in the fading light. He smiled his reassurance before closing his eyes in the hope that he could doze for a while. The safety of the group now relied on the alertness of those on guard. A failure to spot any warning signs of an attack by the Piankasha could be very costly indeed.

The last shadows of the day reluctantly faded away to conceal themselves in the concluding darkness of the night. A passing owl flew silently overhead. The stars shone brightly in the pitch black heavens, like millions of tiny diamonds that twinkled endlessly. Rob was aware of movement near to where he lay. It was the faint echo of whispered words exchanged between the guards, trying to avoid being heard by those who were at rest. It was time for a change over after a two hour watch, which was long enough for most, for the senses lost their edge around this time.

Spotted Pony, a feared warrior of the Piankasha, watched from his hiding place amongst the bushes. He had chosen this place of concealment well, for he could see without being seen and had carefully noted the position of the guards. The war party had come across the tracks made by the white men shortly after they had set up camp in the place below. Spotted Pony had been selected to trail the group, obviously white men, as the horses they rode were shod. The warrior was feeling in a good mood and he gave a silent prayer to the great Manitou for His deliverance of the travellers into the land of the Piankasha. There were many scalps, ponies and weapons for the taking, and his sharp eyes had noted the presence of a woman. His medicine was good and he turned, silent as a ghost, and made his way back to his pony that was tethered a mile away. His brothers would be pleased with what he had to tell them and an attack would be planned without delay.

CHAPTER FORTY SIX

James opened his eyes at the first hint of daylight. He had wakened to the morning song of a blue jay that had perched in a nearby tree. He lay still, his ears alert for any sound that might mean danger. The bird's presence indicated that there was little chance that other humans were in the vicinity, for they were cautious creatures. Nevertheless James rose stealthily, his eyes searching for any sign that might indicate that unwelcome company was nearby. He coaxed the dying embers of his small fire into life and pushed his coffee pot, containing the remnants from the previous evening, closer to the flames. He surveyed the surrounding landscape with appreciation, before checking his horses that were picketed on a small nearby area of lush grass. There was a splendour in the surrounding peaks and the clear panoramic views of the far distant horizons provided a magnificent backdrop. He never tired of such vistas, and he gave way to nostalgia as he remembered the many happy times spent in the mountains with his family. There was only Fiona and himself left now and he gave himself a mental shake. The focus was now on the rescue of his daughter. He must not fail her.

James finished what was left in his coffee pot. The thick liquid was as hot as Hades and black as night, just the way he liked it. After a tidy up of the area, he saddled his horses and then set off westwards. The trail he followed was the reverse of the one Fiona and he had taken when riding towards Georgetown many months before. He kept his eyes open for any signs that travellers had recently stopped overnight and made camp. Any such site would not necessarily be one used by the thugs. However, if he did find one of their camps he was sure that Fiona would have left some sign for her father to find. During the next eight days he found indications of two recent overnight sites. Both had been used by small groups of Indians including women and children. On the ninth day he struck lucky. He found a place with signs of recent use that had clearly been occupied by whitemen. The tracks of the shod hooves and boot prints led him to believe that there were six men in the party. His heart leapt at the clear footprint of a moccasin! He searched around and discovered the sign he was so desperate to find. Three bunches of long grass had been knotted into an arrowhead indicating the direction the group was taking. Further searching of the area provided the remnants of a discarded meal and horse droppings. These enabled him to calculate that he was four or five days behind them and he gave serious thought on how best to proceed.

James was in no doubt from the various clues left behind by the gang, that they were ill disciplined and would be poorly prepared to defend themselves if attacked by hostiles. He must not delay, for Fiona's life was increasingly at risk with each passing day. He decided that he would push on as quickly as possible in a direction that would enable him to get ahead of the group. He knew that Fiona would stay on the same trail as at present, for she would realize that her father would anticipate her doing so.

The next four days and nights were hard ridden by James. He covered as much ground as was safely possible, taking no unnecessary risks. His capture by hostiles, or indeed his death, would spell the end for Fiona and he disciplined himself to stay calm and careful in respect of every move he made. At last he was satisfied that he was ahead of Fiona's captors. He had positioned himself on a high bluff that gave a commanding view of the trail he expected Fiona to lead the men along. He waited nervously as time passed without any sign of activity. Doubt began to creep into his thoughts. Had he miscalculated? Had Fiona been forced to take a different trail than the one below? He began to rethink his options. He would give it until morning, then would have to travel more openly in a bid to locate where the outlaws had gone. Another hour passed with no movement on the trail below. It started to rain, heavily at first, before warm sunshine enticed the remaining rain clouds to disperse, leaving behind a fine gentle wetness.

Suddenly, without warning they came into view, Fiona riding side by side with a large man at the front of the gang. James was relieved beyond words and he noted how well his daughter rode. She knew how to get the best from her horse, but then she had grown up spending more time on the back of a horse than walking. They would not ride much further before making camp for the night. He intended to follow and scout the area. If the chance presented itself he would make contact with her, or even help her to escape. He waited another hour before descending from the bluff, and tracked the outlaws for about a mile or so. He pulled to one side of the trail then led the three horses deeper into the woods, where he tethered them in a place with sufficient cover to keep them hidden and safe. He had decided that he would continue on foot, and he changed into a pair of moccasins which were much more suited to making a silent approach than his boots.

He set off, taking time to stop now and again to listen for warning sounds of movement. He also checked the fresh tracks left by the gang. James shook his head almost in disbelief, for no effort had been made to cover the signs of their passing. He continued onwards, careful as ever, and was not surprised to hear voices nearby. Someone was ordering Fiona to prepare a meal while one of the men prepared to light a fire. God in heaven, he told himself in bewilderment, what are the fools doing now other than making their presence known to every Indian in a twenty mile radius! He would wait until they had settled, then sneak closer and try to make contact with Fiona. The next five seconds brought about an abrupt change to his plan! Off to his left a young Indian was creeping closer to the camp, before stopping and watching from the cover of the shrubbery. James slowly moved his head from side to side trying to identify the presence of other hostiles. To his relief he could see none, although there could be others nearby. The warrior watched for over an hour before silently retreating from the area. James followed, unsure of what might happen next, but determined to prevent any attack on the camp that would endanger Fiona.

The Indian had gone just over a mile before he shouted a welcome to three others braves who sat cross legged, finishing off a meal of buffalo steaks that had been cooked over a small fire. The young warrior excitedly told his companions what he had found and they began to prepare for an attack on the camp. James identified the party as Tamaroa, a tribe who were reknown for their hunting skills rather than as followers of warfare. Taking a deep breath, James stood up some fifty feet or so from the four braves who sat before him.

"My brothers, I come in peace and would speak to my Tamaroa friends." His words and presence caused the astonished warriors to respond with shocked cries before they advanced slowly, weapons raised. He continued to speak.

"I seek your help for I am Shouts Plenty of the Sioux, and my daughter has been taken prisoner by the white eyes in the camp that your brother has told you about." He waited for a moment before moving closer to them, aware of the wary looks from the four Indians. Eventually a brave who seemed to be the senior in the party spoke.

"I have heard stories around the campfires of my people of a Waschitu called Shouts Plenty. He became at one with the Sioux and performed many brave deeds. This is you?" he asked while the others listened with interest to his words. James nodded his assent.

"I am he. I will help you kill all the white eyes, and their horses, scalps and weapons will be yours to take back to your village. I want nothing except the safe return of my daughter." The Tamaroa could not believe their luck. To be led on a raid by someone like Shouts Plenty would be an honour, and the story would be told over many a campfire. The braves' agreement was immediate.

The plan was simple. James would contact Fiona while the camp was asleep. He would disable the guard, quietly if possible, and the braves would then attack the sleeping outlaws with knives. The onslaught would take the camp by complete surprise. The victory would be a great one.

It was less than an hour later and the four Tamaroa warriors led by James were close to the camp. He signalled for the Indians to wait while he crept closer. Fiona was lying within ten feet of where her father lay hidden. He picked up a small stone, and with care tossed it so it landed on her face. Her eyes opened immediately, and she moved carefully and signed that her feet were bound and one arm was tied by a length of rope to a nearby tree. James rose silently towards the lone guard who, although awake, had made the unforgivable mistake of gazing into the fire, and in doing so had destroyed his night vision. It was the last mistake he would ever make. He never knew whose hand held his mouth closed or whose knife it was that slit his throat from ear to ear. He was dead within a few seconds. James threw a spare knife to Fiona and indicated to the watching braves to begin their attack. The surprise was complete and it was Fiona who ended the carnage. Holding a dagger in her hand she told a terrified Campbell that never again would his filthy hands touch a woman. A thrust of her blade through his heart sent him to meet his maker.

"Are you well daughter?" asked James, holding her as though he would never let her go. Fiona smiled and hugged him in return.

"I thought you might have come sooner father, but better late than never. Now let us leave this place for I would welcome some decent food and your company, as well as the news from home. Please tell me that Anne is safe?"

They took their leave of the jubilant Tamaroa warriors, Fiona riding her pony while James ran beside her, and soon reached the glade where James had hidden his horses. A welcoming snicker told him that all was well with his mounts and the pack horse.

They set off again almost immediately, for they desperately needed to find somewhere safe to enable both themselves, and the horses, to rest up after the exertions of the last few weeks. It was almost first light before they eventually came across such a place, a small cave where they could spend some days in relative safety.

As they dismounted the sky was coloured by a strange light, nature's warning of a storm to come. There was only time to picket the horses in the shelter of an overhanging rocky ledge before the heavens opened and the rain fell in a solid wall.

CHAPTER FORTY SEVEN

George Washington, General-in-Chief of the army of the American Colonies, was in a foul temper. Not a man known, at the best of times, as the possessor of a mild disposition, today was one of his worst outbursts ever. Standing facing him, grim faced and waiting for an opportunity to speak, stood General Hugh Mercer, a trusted aide and a trained surgeon. He had been in the chilly cabin at Valley Forge for fully thirty minutes listening to his Commander, and friend, rage about the incompetent Continental Congress and its lack of the promised support for the army.

"They give me fine words and promises when we need food, uniforms, weapons and medical supplies." He paused for breath before he continued. "I have explained to them on numerous occasions that my strategy is to avoid meeting battle hardened, better trained and equipped troops in open conflict. Our army is superior when we employ hit and run tactics. To pretend otherwise would be foolish. What do I get in response to my urgent demands for supplies? I get orders to face the British and their German mercenaries in the field and win a glorious victory or two!"

"Calm yourself George, for heaven's sake. Your voice will reach everyone within a hundred miles of here." Mercer poured a black coffee from the pot balanced at the edge of a small stove in the corner of the cabin that doubled as Washington's office and sleeping quarters.

"Here, take this and let me speak if you will. Our nation is in the grip of a smallpox epidemic, but despite our earlier efforts to inoculate our soldiers, we are losing more and more of our men to this dreadful disease. What I am proposing is that we arrange to provide the smallpox inoculations here, and only here, at Valley Forge. This will ensure that a proper programme of prevention and treatment is provided under our own strict quarantine. We will need to recruit as many nurses as possible, and augment that number with volunteers who have some experience looking after the sick. I will not minimize the risks involved to either those affected by the disease, or those caring for them. You do not need me to tell you that we are losing the fight to keep our army operational. Drastic action is called for."

Washington pondered over his friend's advice in gloomy silence. The bitter winter winds rattled the doors in the cabin, and the freezing chill penetrated every tiny chink in the cabin walls. He was already aware that the enemy troops were largely immune to smallpox as they came from countries where the disease was endemic. Morale amongst his soldiers was low. Philadelphia had been taken by the British in the autumn, and Washington had retreated to Pennsylvania and set up winter quarters around Valley Forge. The main meals provided consisted of 'fire cake', a mixture of flour and water that had been baked on a stick or in hot coals. It was not only food that was in short supply, for there was also a severe lack of medicines, clothing and munitions. The General had only that morning dispatched a strongly worded letter, by courier, to the president of the Congress. In it he had warned that if immediate aid was not sent then the army would be faced with three options. To starve, dissolve or disperse.

The suggestion made regarding the inoculation of the soldiers was agreed. General Washington issued urgent orders that the nursing staff needed to tend to his men were to be assembled as quickly as possible, to enable the process to start.

By springtime the procedure was in full swing and the much promised supplies and armaments were arriving on a regular basis. It had been a close run thing, but Washington's army was now becoming a much more efficient force and better prepared for the conflict that lay ahead.

One further boost to morale had arrived in the shape of a volunteer, Baron and General Friedrich von Steuben, late of the Prussian army. Hugh Mercer had it on good authority that the title was a fabrication and the gentleman had in fact held the rank of a captain prior to his discharge. Ignoring those minor discrepancies, his services were readily accepted and he quickly built up a rapport with the soldiers. He helped them to speed up their accuracy and rate of fire, how to use a bayonet effectively and to hold formation in both offensive and withdrawal situations. General Mercer in particular was impressed by von Steuben's insistence that proper sanitation procedures must be adhered to. Latrines were provided and sited on opposite sides of the camp to the kitchens. Prior to this troops had relieved themselves wherever they felt the need to do so.

Explaining his success with the troops, who showed a willingness to absorb his methods, von Steuben's reasoning was simple and to the point. Had he tried to impose drill, tactics and discipline using the Prussian method of blind obedience he would have been unsuccessful. He had quickly learned to explain the reasons why various orders had been given, and having done so, most of his instructions were carried out.

Further gains by the British forces included the taking of New York, Savannah and Charleston, although they were keen to avoid an all-out conflict. There was recognition by both sides that the priority was less about territorial gains but rather the winning of 'hearts and minds.' The British were doing their utmost to persuade the Colonists to end the rebellion, while at the same time seeking to destroy their morale by bringing about the annihilation of Congress's army.

Chapter Forty Eight

The weeks and months since her safe return had done little to dampen Anne's need to be doing something worthwhile. She was searching for a challenge, but she knew not what it was. A restlessness had grown within her since the departure of her beloved Cameron, the kidnapping and her rescue. There had been two short letters from him, which she had received some weeks after they had been written. He had again declared his love for her, but cautioned that any hope of their being together in the near future was unlikely. There was no return address in either letter but he promised that he would do his utmost to maintain some form of contact with her whenever and however he could. Isabel had watched her daughter struggle to come to terms with her rapid change into adulthood, while also experiencing the delicious agony of young love. Her words of comfort fell on deaf ears, and everyone in the household very quickly learned to tip toe around an increasingly ill tempered Anne.

It was sight of a paper calling for nursing volunteers to help the army at Valley Forge that caught Anne's attention. This was what she was looking for. This was something she had been trained for, and there would be the added bonus of working with her grandfather General Hugh Mercer. Anne was adamant. She would volunteer to help with the care of the soldiers during the inoculation programme. It was her duty as a well trained medical nurse to do so. She was not surprised at her father's objections, but was taken aback by her mother's support. It was, Isabel informed Douglas, a good opportunity for their daughter to keep busy doing a worthwhile undertaking that would keep her occupied. Anne was no longer an immature tomboy. She was a young woman who was keen to sample life with all the peaks and troughs involved in the journey.

Douglas was no different from many fathers throughout the world who suddenly find that the years have passed by so very quickly, and his young daughter is no more. He was taken aback that this fledgling woman before him was once the little child who called to her mother or to him in times of trouble. It mattered not whether it was a scary presence in a darkened bedroom, or a broken toy, or why a rainbow suddenly appeared after a rain storm. He and her mother were the ones who knew everything and would make it right. It was, he realized, time to move on. He now acknowledged the wisdom of Isabel's words. They could still be there for her, but in the background, always ready to rejoice in her achievements or to offer a comforting hug in the bad times. A surprised Anne was delighted when Douglas gave his blessing to her decision to become a volunteer nurse with Washington's troops at Valley Forge.

There followed a somewhat frantic few weeks after the acceptance of Anne's application, before she was finally packed and ready to set off for Pennsylvania. Douglas had made arrangements for her to travel with two wagons that were taking some badly needed medicines to Hugh Mercer at Valley Forge. He doubled the armed escort for the journey, for there were British sympathizers amongst the freight company's own employees, and it was becoming increasingly difficult to keep his business neutral. He intended for normal trading to continue as much as possible, while seeking to secretly supply the forces of the Congress with much needed medicines and food. Douglas was a realist and did not expect that these activities would go unnoticed for any length of time. What would happen then was in the lap of the Gods.

It was a tearful farewell, and young James gave his sister a hug and a kiss as he whispered for her to take care of herself. Isabel managed to hold back her tears until the wagons had travelled some little way down the track in front of the ranch. She sobbed, and continued to wave her little lace handkerchief until the wagons were almost out of sight. Douglas would accompany them as far as Georgetown where he had business matters to attend to. Anne was both excited and saddened to be leaving, but was determined to betray no silly female tears, at least not while she was in the presence of others. There would be time enough for that when she was alone.

The parting between father and daughter took place at the crossroads on the outskirts of Georgetown. Douglas, still on horseback, leaned over to where Anne sat beside Henrick Shwartz, the muleskinner who was driving the rig.

"Take care Anne, and tell your Grandpoppa Hugh that we send our love." He stretched over and gave her a quick peck on the cheek before turning his horse towards Georgetown and setting off at a gallop. It wouldn't do to let anyone see the tears in his eyes. He was entitled to a few private moments, he reasoned, for it was very rare that a father said goodbye to his little girl twice in as many months as he had. His greatest wish now was for the safe return of this young woman who had entered his life almost unseen, replacing the little girl who was no more, except in the precious memories that would remain with him forever.

Chapter Forty Nine

Lord George Howe stared out of his barrack room window at the dark skies above. The storm clouds had been gathering strength these past few hours. He viewed them with distaste as he pondered over his latest decision to approve the forming of a company of carefully selected men for what could ultimately prove to be a suicide mission. The wind was building up in its intensity by the minute, and would soon unleash a force of power and noise that would drive men everywhere to seek cover. He grimaced, the irony of the moment was not lost upon him. He wanted his volunteers to cause the rebel Colonists to experience the same fear as those now facing the wrath of the coming storm. His windows shuddered under the power of the wind, and nearby a loose shutter banged fiercely against the side of the building. The wind was relentless and unforgiving as it charged, thundering across the hills, into the valleys and bending the trees into a rage of activity, taking no prisoners as it sought to destroy everything in its way.

When nature unleashed such fury it was time for man and the beasts of the wilderness to seek shelter and safety wherever it could be found. The screaming wind scattered death and destruction on its way, unselective of the victims caught up in the rage of its passing. The great heaving leaden skies above tossed and swirled in a mad frenzy, as though seeking escape from the torment created by the wind's destructive passage.

The storm continued unabated for hours, before the wind decided that it was time to rest until it might reappear again with similar intensity upon the earth below. The General had continued to examine his plans for the deployment of his volunteers. He had sought out an old comrade in arms from the war against the French, Brigadier Thomas Alexander, to seek his advice regarding suitable officers and men for his special company. He had emphasized that they had to be fit, able to perform with initiative and be capable of living off the land for months on end. If wounded they would be left behind, although they would always be in uniform, and, if taken prisoner would be treated with the respect due to a captured enemy. This last statement was stated with fingers crossed, for there were no guarantees of such treatment if captured by those who had witnessed the death of comrades during the conflict.

The General had introduced similar tactics during the earlier war against the French. Although successful, it had nevertheless not had the full support of some of his fellow officers who regarded such actions as not 'playing by the rules of war.' He snorted in disgust at the thought. War was a madness that all humans with any sense would avoid. If, however, conflict was unavoidable then it should be fought to win, whilst recognizing that most of those doing the fighting were also victims of the inability of inept and weak politicians to avoid hostilities.

The list before him contained his final selection from those who had volunteered. It consisted of three officers, twelve non commissioned officers and twenty five other ranks that included four backwoodsmen. The group had been narrowed down from eighty brave souls who had undergone a rigorous selection process. They were taught how to adapt to war in the wilderness. How to travel light, adopting camouflage and abandoning parade ground tactics. There would be no women camp followers, for the volunteers had to be self sufficient, doing their own cooking, washing their own clothes and making running repairs on their equipment. Their clothing would be of a nondescript dark green with no long coats that could hamper quick movement. All regimental insignia would be painted over in black and all indications of rank would be of cloth. Their role was to strike at the enemy quickly then withdraw with speed. No prisoners were to be taken, nor were they to engage in anything other than minor skirmishes. The object of their operations was to create uncertainty and fear of attack that would result in an increase in the number of military required for guard duties. To achieve this, more of the enemy soldiers would have to be released from the frontline. The plan had worked well during the war with France, although the survival rate amongst the volunteers was low. The General grimaced. Such was the price of war.

He had arranged to host a small supper in the Officers' Mess that evening for Brigadier Alexander and the three volunteer officers. The company would march out tomorrow in the early morning light, an hour before Reveille was called. The General and Brigadier Alexander were sat in a private room in the Mess awaiting the arrival of the three guests. The time for talking and planning was over. The two senior officers had drawn on their not inconsiderable experience to give the operation every chance of succeeding. There was a knock on the door and the three young men were ushered into the room by a mess steward, who poured drinks for the new arrivals before quietly taking his leave.

Major Jack Boyd, the senior officer and leader of the newly formed company saluted.

"Good evening General, Brigadier, it was kind of you to invite us here." Lord Howe nodded his acknowledgement of the salute.

"Relax gentlemen, please help yourself to a drink," he motioned to the full glasses that the steward had poured earlier. "This is an opportunity for you to ask any questions or raise any points before you leave tomorrow, after that it might be too late," he smiled.

Captain Cameron Greaves was seated between Major Boyd and Lieutenant Mark Ingram. He hesitated before speaking, choosing his words carefully.

"What I am unclear of Sir is when, or rather at what point, do we withdraw from our activities? Is it to be after a given period of time, or a number of raids, or when our strength has been depleted to a certain number? The General's reply was delayed by the entrance of two stewards who began to serve soup to the seated officers. After the stewards had left the room the senior officer responded to the question.

"There are no hard and fast rules. What is expected is that all of you will do your upmost to keep the enemy guessing. The targets are at the discretion of Major Boyd, but all three of you will have your say on what may or may not be regarded as a suitable target. The Major has made this stipulation himself and I agree. The success or failure of this mission will be in your own hands. Rest assured that you have my full backing, and that of the Brigadier," he nodded in Alexander's direction. "If you return after one attack or ten, only then can we assess the merits of such ventures. Any more questions gentlemen? Good, now let us enjoy our supper." He rang a small bell to summon the stewards, its chimes bringing the business to a close, and the meal began in earnest.

It was two in the morning and the Brigadier had not yet undressed for bed. Prior to meeting the others at Lord Howe's supper, he had walked through the company lines, stopping to talk to the men as he passed. There had been a nervous tension apparent to his experienced eyes. Some men dealt with their inner fears in different ways. Some became quiet, while others sought company rather than facing the lonely period between bedtime and the blessed refuge of sleep. The nightmare of cowardice hung unspoken in many minds. There are those who would avoid conflict, not from cowardice but from the fear of such weakness. The dread that when the moment of truth comes they find themselves lacking the courage to face and conquer it. He offered a silent prayer for the safe return of these men. God alone had the power to select those who would live and those who would die.

CHAPTER FIFTY

Rob Ahern woke suddenly. A quick look at the stars told him that he had been asleep for three hours or so. It was close to dawn, but the darkness of the night still held the upper hand over the first fingers of morning sunlight. He lay unmoving in his bedroll listening to the surrounding quiet. He sat up slowly, eyes searching the camp area. His every instinct told him that something was not as it should be. His attention was drawn to the horses, for they had their heads up and were looking in the direction of the nearby willows. Where was the guard? His post required him to remain within a few yards of the horses at all times. Rob gently shook awake the men nearest to him. A warning finger to his lips cautioned against any talk and he signalled for the others to be roused quickly and quietly.

Maria had been lying awake and was alerted by the whisper of movement around her. Something was very wrong, and her heart beat faster than if she had run a hundred miles! She felt the bile of panic rise in her throat, for it could only mean that the Indians were attacking the encampment. She reached for the pistol that Rob had patiently coached her how to use. Grasping it in both hands she held it, primed and ready to fire. She lay still in her bedroll as all hell let loose nearby. Shots were fired and these mingled with the screams from the attacking savages. All around her was an explosion of violence that she never thought possible. She lay trembling in fear for she had never believed that such unbridled hatred and brutality was possible.

Moments before, Rob had spotted crouching figures move swiftly towards the horses, while other hostiles rose with a chorus of screeching war cries and ran towards the encampment in a sinister and threatening line, bows and war clubs at the ready. Rob waited no longer. He cocked his musket and shot the Indian who was nearest to the horses. His years spent living with Indians told him that the main objective of the first attack would be to steal the horses. Once this had been achieved the hostiles could choose whether to wait for the defenders to be weakened by hunger, or to launch sporadic attacks on them until they ultimately succumbed. Rob rose and ran in the direction of the horses, shouting as he went.

"Protect the horses, for without them we are lost!" Even as he ran he could see three or four attackers cutting the lines of the tethered animals that were becoming increasingly panic stricken by the shots and screams surrounding them. Ahern pulled a warrior from the back of a frightened bay and struck him a brutal blow to the head with the butt of his musket. On his left a pistol shot by Laidlaw, who had responded to Rob's shouts, blasted another Indian to the ground. The next few minutes were a deadly melee of shots, stabbings, and hand-to-hand fighting as both groups fought with a savagery where no mercy was expected, nor given.

Maria watched wide eyed as defenders and attackers fought only yards away from where she lay. The screams of the Indians and the curses of her companions mingled in a verbal and visual nightmare. Without warning she found herself looking upwards into the hateful face of a warrior. For a split second he paused before raising his arm, holding a war club. Maria closed her eyes and pulled the trigger of her pistol. The ball caught the hostile under the throat and for a second or two he stood unaware that he was dying before he fell on top of her. Maria screamed, tried to push him away, failed to do so, and then fainted.

As quickly as it had begun, the attack ended. A head count revealed that one man was dead, another who had been on guard was missing, and three were wounded, one seriously. Two horses had been taken by the hostiles who had carried their dead and wounded with them when they retreated. Maria was found, white faced but unharmed. When asked by Ahern how she was, she simply shook her head and sat down upon her bedroll, her arms clasped around her knees, and wept.

Rob ordered that the horses be fed and watered and examined for any injuries they may have received during the attack. He also instructed that a fire be lit and a hot meal provide for everyone. There was no need for pretence anymore, for the Piankasha warriors knew where they were. In the meantime the wounded men were tended to by Laidlaw, who was proving to be a valued member of the expedition party. As a former soldier he had some experience of wounds and how to treat them. There was, however, little he could do for the badly wounded man who died less than an hour after the attack.

Senga approached Rob and motioned that he wished to speak with him. The scout was in no doubt that the Piankasha would be calling for others to reinforce their numbers. The lure of many horses and scalps would be impossible for the Indians to ignore. The group must either retreat back eastwards or continue to head west. It would be suicide to remain where they were. Regardless of what option they chose, the hostiles would not let them go without pursuit.

The scout's words confirmed Ahern's own assessment of their predicament. He nodded his thanks to Senga and went to check on his horse. How easily, he thought, for men and women to seek to achieve wealth or greatness, when so often these things are too far out of their reach. They too readily embrace schemes that are impractical in the cold light of day. Already two men were dead, with a third unfortunate captured and as good as dead. For what purpose did they die? What was so desirable, so all consuming that enticed them to risk that most valuable of all things, their lives?

The dead man was buried in a hastily dug grave and a few words spoken over him. It would be his lonely and final resting place here in the wilderness. It was an unspoken thought amongst those present that it would not be the last death to be witnessed. However the lust for gold still burned deep within the very soul of most of those remaining. To turn back was not an option, and Rob realized that it would be pointless to suggest otherwise. They would ride on as soon as they had prepared themselves. Water bottles were to be re-filled, and the dead and missing man's weapons and clothing distributed amongst the members of the group. The Piankasha would have men watching the encampment, but that was only to be expected. They would ride out fully prepared to stop and fight a rearguard action against the pursuing hostiles. The two Susquehanna would lead off and the main party would follow behind, just keeping them in sight. This would enable early warning to be given of any possible ambush.

The cavalcade set off, grim faced and silent, with only the wind for company. Unseen eyes were watching their every movement and the hostiles would soon be giving chase.

The band of men and one woman rode westwards. Most of them were determined to continue their quest regardless of the increasing threat to their lives. The lure of gold silenced the voices inside that warned of danger and even death. Ahern was all too aware that the vision of great riches had taken hold of the minds of most of the fortune hunters. He pushed that thought to one side, for he was aware that Piankasha scouts were now clearly visible on the skyline on both the left and right flanks of the group. The message was clear. The cavalcade would be shadowed until the hostiles were ready to attack. There was nowhere to run, no place to escape the menace of the savages. He registered the sound as hooves made contact with stone. Saddles creaked as they rode onwards into the rising glimmer of morning. The band dismounted and paused for a short breather for the horses. There was no point in trying to outdistance the shadowing hostiles, better to save the strength of their mounts until needed. There was a quiet nervousness amongst them, for the realization had registered with some that their situation was as bad as it could possibly be. They dipped into a hollow and walked to the far side before mounting up and setting off again. A miracle was needed if they were to survive. They were being shepherded by the Indians until the time and place were to the liking of the attackers. To stop and make a stand would be a mistake. They must keep moving and hope for an opportunity to make a dash for safety.

Ahern was watchful of the deterioration of the weather that had taken place in the hours since they had set off. The skies above were becoming dull and angry, the clouds swirling in agitation at the intrusion into their midst. The winds were rising by the minute, and in the distance flashes of lightning drew nearer and the gusts increased in ferocity as the storm gathered momentum. Thunder crashed and a fearsome onslaught of wind enveloped them, accompanied by a wall of water as the rain pounded down upon them. This was their chance and Rob Ahern wasted no time in leading the band in a desperate dash for safety. He reached for the reins of Maria's horse, shouted to her to hang on, and spurred his horse into a frantic gallop. There could be unseen dangers ahead from hidden gullies but this was an opportunity that had to be taken, for to remain where they were was to die.

CHAPTER FIFTY ONE

Captain Cameron Allan McDonald was distraught, the sickness of despair deep within him. It had been a successful mission to begin with and the guerilla tactics employed by the special task force had created havoc amongst the Colonist army. The last six months had exceeded all expectation, with every surprise raid carried out causing considerable damage to the morale of the enemy. There was however, a sting in the tail. Each attack had cost men, either killed or wounded. Supplies of food and medicines were scarcer by the minute. It was becoming increasingly difficult to move from place to place without being seen, as word spread to be on the lookout for the British raiders. Major Jack Boyd had been wounded on the last raid but one, and had ordered Cameron to take command of the unit and to leave him behind.

The command strength was now down to a paltry sixteen. His right hand man, Colour Sergeant Martin Smith, had been caught in some cross fire on the last raid and had died instantly from the many musket balls that had torn through his body. He looked at the exhausted men around him. Very few did not have a wound of some sort, and the lack of food and water, and above all the need to rest, had taken its toll. They had escaped from the raid carried out that morning by the skin of their teeth.

An alert young farm boy had spotted the British scouts and informed his brother, who commanded a company of the local militia, of what he had seen. An ambush had been set up and the task force had walked into it. Only a brave rearguard action had prevented the annihilation of the British troops, but they had not escaped unscathed. More than half of their comrades had been killed or wounded. Even now the jubilant Colonist militia had their men searching for the remnants of Cameron's command. It was just a matter of time before they were discovered. The young officer had already decided that his men would continue to resist capture while the pitiful small supply of ammunition lasted. After that he would seek an honourable surrender, for his men had given of their best and deserved to survive.

"They're coming sir," whispered a soldier to Cameron's right. The sound of the approaching militia could be heard as they drew closer. Cameron waited, for he wanted every last ball to count. He arose, sword in hand and gave the order to fire. The resultant volley from his men was met by a greater response from the superior numbers of the Colonists. A searing pain caused the young officer to stagger backwards, and he dropped his sword and fell to his knees as a second musket ball tore into his side. Darkness descended, and his last thoughts were of Anne and the belief that he would never see her again.

The commander of the militia was a veteran of the war against the French and had ordered for the few remaining British soldiers to be spared. The losses by the Colonists were eight wounded but no deaths. Only four of the task force had survived, including the badly wounded captain who had led them. All the injured were loaded into three wagons and driven to a tented field aid station that had been set up only a few weeks beforehand. On arrival the wounded men were taken from the wagons into a hospital tent where a medical team awaited them. Amongst them was Nurse Anne McDonald.

As her beloved Cameron was placed on the surgeon's table Anne recognized him, and almost fainted with the shock of seeing him so pale and covered in blood. The surgeon noticed her reaction.

"Do you know this man Nurse McDonald?" he demanded. Anne made an effort to stay calm.

"I do indeed sir, for he is the man I wish to marry. You must save him, for if he dies then part of me will die with him."

"Then we must do our very best to save him, otherwise General Mercer will ensure that my promotion prospects will be very limited indeed," he responded grimly. The wounds were serious and it was apparent that it would be touch and go as to whether the young man on the table would survive or die. The surgeon would do his best. He began.

It is the threads of chance that weave the tapestry of our existence. The small tented field hospital had only recently come into being due to the foresight of Surgeon General Hugh Mercer. He had argued that medical care for the wounded should be made readily available, as close to the battlefield as was possible. General Washington's acceptance of this proposal had lead to six tented mobile hospitals being brought into use. It was in one of these facilities where efforts were being made to save Cameron McDonald's life.

Anne watched anxiously as the surgeon, Major P.S. Martin, used every ounce of his skill to remove two musket balls, and staunch the flow of blood from the body of the young man lying before him on the operating table. Sweat dripped from Martin's brow as he peered at his patient in the limited light provided by four lanterns held by nursing staff. The shadows cast onto the sides of the tent danced and moved in the surrounding dimness. The tension felt by everyone present was an oppressive malignant thing, an unwanted presence as the fight to save Cameron's life continued. Finally, over two hours later, the surgeon took a step backwards from the table, wiping his bloodied hands on his smock as he did so.

"He is in God's hands now, for I have done all I can for him." His face was grey with exhaustion and he staggered as he left the tent. "Call me if there is any change in his condition. I will be nearby."

Outside the darkness arrived and a gentle coolness descended. An owl hooted its challenge to the stars and a quarter moon shone its limited light onto the earth below. As the day finally drew to a close another stood ready to take its place.

CHAPTER FIFTY TWO

Fiona and her father had chosen their hideout well. Although constantly alert to any possible danger, they had nevertheless enjoyed long periods of rest and hot meals. The horses too had benefited from the plentiful lush buffalo grass that grew within a short distance from the cave where James and his daughter had based themselves. The cooking had taken place nearby, outside the cave, and against the exposed roots of a tree that had been pushed over in a previous storm. This helped hide the small fire from all but the closest inspection by any watching eyes, while the surrounding bushes spread the smoke before it became visible.

James sat crossed legged just inside the cave, his musket close to hand. Fiona lay sleeping on some blankets further inside. They had used the days together to discuss what each thought they should do next. He smiled as he remembered her words. Little laughter lines appeared at the corner of his eyes where they had lain unused for too long a time. When Fiona gave her opinion she gave it without reservation, but in such an honest way as not to cause offence. They had totally opposing views on one thing only, and that was regarding Maria and her party of gold seekers. James wanted to meet up with them before they came too close to the location where the gold was, a place that was near to the burial site of his wife and son. He castigated himself for having given Maria the map. Without it there would have been no hunt for the gold, and she would have returned to Spain and safety.

Fiona took the view that the group was unlikely to find the place they sought. The map, she reminded her father, was lacking in sufficient detail for those unfamiliar with the land to locate it. They themselves had only found it after a great deal of searching and, she thought silently, at an enormous cost to their family. Maria, she reasoned, was foolish and greedy and had disregarded the risk to herself and those in her group. Most of all she had dismissed the possible consequences that her search for gold could spawn. If, against all the odds, Maria and her companions did find the source of the gold, the invasion of large numbers of other fortune seekers into the Sioux lands would start an Indian war. With hindsight it would have been better that the existence of Esteban's map had never been disclosed. It was too late now, for what had taken place could not be forgotten.

James was going to try to intercept Maria's group. He would set up a static observation point where he was reasonably confident of avoiding discovery by the Sioux. The location would be within a few miles of the source of the gold. If Maria's group did not appear within one month he would assume that they had been killed, captured, or had turned back. He hoped that Fiona would not join him in his venture but would choose to make her own way to the McDonald ranch and to safety. She was highly skilled in travelling unseen, and he saw no need for her to put herself in more danger because of his decision to seek out Maria and her followers.

The horses needed to be cared for and he rose as quietly as possible and left the cave. Fiona opened her eyes as he did so, her senses alerting her to the slightest of noises made by his leaving. Those who lived in the wilderness must be at one with their surroundings. All senses are quickly honed, fine tuned to identify any change to the normal sounds, sights and smells around them. Survival is never guaranteed, but the risks involved can be reduced by constant vigilance by those who choose to exist in this way. From an early age she had been taught that a forest is a living thing that breathes. There is life and death there. The creatures, the plants, the trees and all living things depend upon each other to survive.

She rose and started to make preparations for a meal, her musket never far from her side. Her father could be a stubborn man at times and, despite her strong objections, had insisted that he would continue alone and seek out Maria's group. There was little in her view to commend such action. The Spanish woman and those who rode with her had made their choice and would be fortunate to escape with their lives. They were undeserving of any sympathy, and it angered her to know that her father was going to risk his life to help such people. Her mind was made up. She would go with him. They did after all make a good team. Four eyes were better than two, and the sooner they started the sooner they could return to their new home at the ranch. She looked out of the cave a little wistfully, as she took note of the beauty of the wild flowers lying at the edge of a stand of aspens. There were pink roses and bluebells carpeting the ground in vivid splashes of colour. Although she could not hear them, she could imagine the gathering of busy insects that would be attracted by such a multitude of scents. Her father's re-appearance interrupted her thoughts. It was time to eat, and then she would inform him of her decision to go with him on his quest to find the Spanish woman and her group.

CHAPTER FIFTY THREE

Rob Ahern hid his concern as he regarded the exhausted faces of his fellow travellers. It had been almost two months since the first attack by the Piankasha, and the Indians had hounded and harried them relentlessly ever since. He doubted if they had made more than five hundred miles during this time and the morale was at an all time low. Rob had broken up half a dozen fights amongst the men, and their limited supplies of food and water were now rationed. The care of the horses was of paramount importance, and he had to continually cajole some of the riders to attend to the needs of their mounts.

The greatest loss had been the disappearance of the two Susquehanna scouts three days ago. They had ridden ahead of the cavalcade as usual, but had not been seen nor heard of since. In the meantime the spasmodic attacks on the column continued unabated. By this time most of the group carried a wound of some sort, and Maria and Laidlaw were tasked with treating these as best they could under the circumstances. Due to their wounds, two of the men were incapable of carrying out anything other than the most basic of tasks. This increased the resentment amongst some of the more able bodied within the group.

Ahern sat on his horse at the head of the column, his eyes shaded by the brim of his hat. The glare of the fierce sun made it difficult to see clearly though the shimmering landscape. His horse stood with ears pricked, ever alert for any sound that might warn of danger. Rob gently coaxed him into movement, and horse and rider moved together in a slow plod towards the faint outline of distant hills. He avoided taking the party in a straight line, but changed direction now and then in the hope that this action would make it more difficult for the Piankasha to prepare an ambush. His eyes caught movement in the skies ahead, and within a few seconds he had identified it as circling vultures. They drew closer and the cries of the black feathered carrion eaters could be faintly heard as they performed their obscene dance in celebration of the dying or dead creature that lay below. Ahern kicked his horse into a trot and was soon close to where twenty or so of the screeching scavengers were feasting on what he realized were the badly mutilated bodies of the two Susquehenna scouts. The vultures voiced their displeasure at the interruption of their feasting and reluctantly made way as he came closer. The sight before him brought bile to his throat. Even he, who had lived for years among the Pawnee, had never seen such repulsive, nauseating acts of torture carried out as those on the unfortunate scouts. There was nothing he could do, and he turned and rode back to re-join the column. Anger burned within him, and he spoke loudly enough for all those present to hear his words.

"You have two choices. You can either stay with the group or you can go your own way. Anyone who leaves will take with them a share of what food and water we have left. Those who stay will do so on the understanding that I will no longer tolerate any fighting amongst ourselves. You will carry out my orders to the letter or leave. Any one of you who fails to come up to the mark will answer to me, and believe me after what I have just witnessed over yonder I am in no mood to be lenient." He looked at each of them in turn before he continued. "No more reminding you to look after the horses or to stay alert when on guard. I will kill the next man who crosses me or my orders. If you want out of this situation alive then I am the only one who can do it, and even then only if we are very lucky. We move out shortly. Any of you not coming with us can say so now and draw his share of supplies." He dismounted and began to check his horse's hooves, then his weapons in that order. When he mounted his horse the others followed his lead. No one wanted to leave the group. Ahern headed to the right of where the vultures were continuing their noisy feast, and headed for the hills. He reasoned that there would be more chance of finding some shade and water than on the flat where they were at present. It was going to be risky, but he intended that they should find a place that could be defended against the hostiles and give some respite to both the men and horses. This tactic might well prove to be a bad one, but they could not continue for much longer without rest for themselves and the animals.

It took a further two days for them to reach the foothills. During this time they had fought off three attacks, although they had managed to kill two of the attackers without suffering any further injuries to themselves. Rob was pleased, as the defenders had shown a fresh determination to give of their best following his earlier ultimatum. When they were a mile or so from the foothills Laidlaw volunteered to scout ahead for a place where they could rest up. Ahern decided that they should both ride ahead, with one watching for any sign of Indians while the other sought out a suitable location.

They rode out together, eyes searching for any sign of movement, ears alert for any sound that might mean danger. As the hills drew closer rocky outcrops were visible amongst the lower slopes. Fingers of green grass extended into the shadows cast by the stands of trees growing on the fringes of the rising ground. When they had reached further into the area they found that water was readily available and the lush grass needed for their horses was in plentiful supply. So far so good, but now they must find a place they could defend while they rested. Laidlaw kept watch while Rob followed a faint trail that dropped off into a deep black canyon. After a hundred yards or so the narrow passage opened into a fertile meadow that was surrounded on three sides by rising rocky cliffs. They had found the spot they were looking for and could defend if necessary.

Within the hour the group had settled into the bowels of the canyon. Guards were posted in positions that gave the maximum view of the surrounding areas, with particular emphasis on the security of the narrow passage that led to the meadow. The horses were hobbled and allowed to feed on the grass, and fresh water was available from two separate sources nearby. Traps were set and an antelope that strayed within musket range was shot and prepared for cooking. The mood of the group rose in response to the change of circumstances, although Ahern cautioned against complacency, for the Indians would not give up easily. He ordered that the opportunity should be taken to carry out necessary repairs to clothes and equipment. Those men not on guard duties were grateful for a chance to catch up on missed sleep, and did so without the need to be told. Ahern made a small screened off area near to the stream available to Maria in order that she might wash in privacy. He undertook the responsibility of ensuring that nobody ventured near until she had finished her ablutions.

The meal that evening was carried out in two shifts, to enable both those on and off guard the luxury of fresh meat augmented by wild onions picked from the meadow. Rob slept in snatches and every two hours or so throughout the night did a check on the guards. The Piankasha had shown that they were determined to pursue them to the end, for the lure of horses, scalps and weapons was a powerful one in the eyes of the Indians, where such things were highly prized.

'Pawnee' Rob Ahern lay awake in his bedroll. He had never given much thought of what he wished from life. His upbringing had been one of little restraint. He had gone where he wanted, when he wanted. There were moments when he thought that he would like to settle down with a like minded woman who would live away from the towns and cities he so disliked. Such a woman would be hard to find in a land where the males greatly outnumbered the females. Maybe no such person existed, but who could tell? Perhaps she was out there seeking someone like him.

He listened to the noises of the night, some caused by the winds and some by creatures of the darkness. Sound has a greater importance when the sun has gone to sleep and the clouds have screened the moon and the stars. Sight is denied on these occasions, and the ears of both the hunter and the hunted are tuned to identify the source of any sound heard. To err in judgment could result in the hunter becoming the quarry. So it was with those who chose to live in the wilderness. His years spent growing up with the Pawnee had developed his hearing to act as a filter that could recognize different sounds from the everyday noises that would safely be ignored. His ability was in hearing the uncommon sounds, or indeed the absence of any sounds, and to alert him to this. When the birds and the insects cease to sing it is because there is a reason for their silence. Something has caused them to believe that a possible threat is nearby.

He allowed himself to drift off into sleep, for morning would come all too quickly, bringing with it many questions to which he had only few of the answers.

CHAPTER FIFTY FOUR

Anne awoke with a start. Cameron was dead! He was no longer breathing! She had only closed her eyes for a few moments, having failed to fight off the tiredness that had finally overwhelmed her. She reached for his hand in a panic, her mind in utter turmoil, for she had not been there for him in his final moments. The tears welled up in her eyes and her shoulders heaved in her grief. She had sat by his bedside for three days now, eating little and sleeping even less. Her head leaned forward onto the bed in a gesture of utter despair. She had lost the man whom she loved beyond all measure, and he was gone forever. She moaned, misery a gigantic black monster that ate into her very soul. How could she have let this happen? His hand pressed hers gently and his eyes opened slowly.

"Anne, Anne, is that you?" he asked hoarsely. "I cannot see very well, but please tell me it is you, for it is your love that has kept me alive during these dark hours." He gasped at the effort his words had demanded of him, and his eyes closed. Beads of perspiration covered his brow and his pallid colour gave him the look of a corpse. His breathing came in painful gasps and the fever burned inside him like the coals of the furnace from hell. Anne applied a cooling cloth, crooning soothing words as she did so. She was unaware that her Grandpoppa General Hugh Mercer had entered the tent and stood behind her. His hand gently grasped her shoulder, and she looked up in surprise at his presence.

"He needs rest Anne, Major Martin has done a fine job and Cameron has every chance of surviving his injuries provided there is no infection. Stay with him as you will, but allow others to share the burden with you. The next day or so is crucial and he is not out of danger, but he is a fit young fellow who has much to live for. Sleep here in the tent if you wish, but let one of the other nurses attend him while you rest." He gestured towards Nurse Elizabeth Paton who stood beside him. "You must be strong for him Anne, if you are to help him recover. Come, lie here on this cot and get some sleep. Nurse Paton will let you know if there is any change in his condition." He held his hand up, palm towards her in gentle rebuke as she began to protest. He wrapped a blanket around her shoulders and led her to the cot. There was no further resistance left, and she lowered herself downwards onto the bed and was asleep within seconds

Mercer was a realist. The chances of Cameron surviving were finely balanced. This was a fine young man and someone who would make Anne a happy woman. He cursed this war and the unnecessary killing and maiming of those caught up in it. There was no glory, only pain and worry, and hate and the helplessness of those who could not escape the conflict. He kissed Anne on the cheek. She had much to live for and he prayed that Cameron would be there to share in her future. He left the tent and paused outside to light a cigar. There was coolness in the night air and the sun had almost vanished. A tiny hint of golden tentacles clung to the sky, their dying reflection mirrored in the remnants of a small number of flimsy pink clouds.

Mercer missed his family and the daily routine of a previous life that he had left behind, and once taken for granted. He remembered with fondness the moments of silence when he and his wife sat alone, enjoying each other's company without the need for words. He recalled the sound of laughter of his daughters and the simple pleasures of sitting in the sun, or enjoying a good debate over a glass of malt whisky with a friend or two. He finished his cigar, and with a final flourished threw it to the earth at his feet where he ground it into oblivion. He was tired. It was time he was in bed and he headed towards the loneliness of his tent.

It was a worrying three days before Cameron began to visibly rally from his wounds. He was utterly convinced that it was the loving care from Anne, and not the skill of surgeon Major Martin that had brought him back from the brink of death. His injuries were severe and it was obvious that he would not be capable of soldiering again for many long months, if at all. He was technically a prisoner, but the love he and Anne shared caught those around them in a bubble of hope. Love could survive even in the midst of conflict and death. There was something for everyone to cling to in these troubled times, a dream and a crutch to help them to get through times when there was little sunshine, only darkness.

The days grew into weeks and Cameron regained sufficient strength to walk short distances with the aid of a stick and the support of his beloved Anne's arm. Neither broached the question of how long he could remain there, for the conflict was now approaching its peak and the hospital would soon be on the move. Cameron was in no doubt what he wanted to do, and with little preamble he asked Anne to marry him.

"In the present circumstances I have little to offer you but my love, but it will not always be so for this foolish war must end sometime and life will begin again." He kissed her lightly on her lips and smiled into her beautiful brown eyes. "It is only a matter of time before I am taken under escort to some prison or other for those who have been captured. Rest assured that I will survive it, for I have you to keep me and my dreams alive. In the meantime, you must follow your heart and continue to provide aid to those who are wounded fighting for their beliefs. I would not have it any other way." For a second his despair showed through before he made light of the difficulties that lay ahead for them both. "There is neither time nor options regarding my proposal of marriage. I know not where your parents are at this moment or even if they would give their blessing, but I want you as my wife above all else. General Mercer could arrange for a priest today or tomorrow if you ask him." He waited in agonizing suspense for her reply. After what seemed like an eternity, although it was actually less than a minute, she smiled.

"What time tomorrow would suit you?" She threw herself into his arms, tears of joy flooding her eyes as she spoke.

Together they approached the General who was in the process of making arrangements for all of the field hospitals to move to new locations. When he heard the request from the young couple before him his face clouded over. A decision had already been made at headquarters on the previous day regarding the removal of the British prisoners to a place of internment. An exchange of the wounded prisoners between the two sides was in the early stages of agreement. Cameron and the other prisoners were to be taken there by a guard detail that would be arriving later that afternoon. Anne wasted no further time on discussion.

"Then we must marry now, without delay. Please Grandpoppa, do this for me," she pleaded.

The ceremony was a simple one, with few people in attendance. The priest offered a short blessing and General Mercer gave his grand-daughter away while Nurse Paton acted as a witness. Meanwhile the escort to take the British prisoners to a place for captives had arrived, and watched in mild disbelief at the proceedings.

There was barely time for a brief embrace before Cameron and his fellow prisoners were manacled together and loaded onto an open wagon. The newly-weds shared a last lingering look before the detail set off, leaving a tearful Anne in the dust of its departure.

Chapter Fifty Five

The morning drew on. James and Fiona rode towards the place where they planned to watch for sign of Maria's group. The pair stopped every so often, always alert to the threat from hostiles. James leaned on the pommel of his saddle and scanned the horizons, before turning his attention to his daughter.

"We have done well to come this far without any indication of being watched. I will be much happier when we have reached our destination and can stay put for a while. The longer we are on the move, the more chance there is that we will be seen." Fiona nodded in silent agreement.

Both of them continued to scan the surrounding areas for any sign of Indians, and also to seek out and memorize landmarks that would be invaluable if ever travelling through this territory again. It was the way of the wanderer to do this, as the landmarks provided guides to the location of water holes and places of safety. There were endless miles of grass as far as the eye could see, and it swayed to and fro in the wind like an ocean. Here and there were tracks of buffalo and deer, as well as other smaller creatures. They rode onwards after a short rest.

It was later, well into the afternoon, and hunger pangs reminded them both that they had eaten little since setting off earlier that morning. They stopped where there was a dip in the ground, picketed the horses and ate a cold meal. There was a brief shower of rain which was followed by a rainbow that showed all its colours in a magnificent arc that stretched from one side of the sky to the other. The horses were enjoying the grass, but they too were ever watchful of danger and would occasionally stop eating, ears pricked, until satisfied that no threat lurked nearby.

There was a cool breeze upon them as they mounted up later and rode onwards towards the faint ridges of the distant foothills. The grass underfoot was fresh from the earlier shower, and the sounds from the unseen small animals that lived there ceased until the travellers on horseback had passed by.

Fiona watched her father as he rode slightly in front of her and the packhorses. She had wished for so very much when the family had set out to go westwards to find and embrace the world of the white man. Her mother and brother were now gone, and she would mourn their passing until the day she died. There had been great hope in her heart when they had set off, that she could join this new world, be a part of how it would grow and, she acknowledged, find a place where she would raise a family. Her father had cautioned all of them before they had travelled westwards, that there were some who would not welcome those of mixed parentage, nor a man who had lived with the Indians and taken a squaw for his wife. These things she could live with, for people distrust that which they cannot always understand. She felt that there was much to like in this new world, but other things she would miss, such as the taste of ice cold fresh water from the hills, and the morning frost melting under the sun as it spread its warmth on the land below. To be able to walk amongst the wild flowers in a mountain meadow, and feel and hear the sounds of the living things that dwelt there. The snow flake upon the rising river, a moment of beauty, then gone forever.

But what of her father and his hopes and dreams? He too had suffered greatly, much more than he would admit to. She felt ashamed at her doubts and the pain of her loss, for they were no greater when compared to his. Knowing him as she did, she was in no doubt that his main concern now was for her safety and for her to have the opportunity to lead a full and happy life. Fiona concluded that it must be tempting when a person attained a certain age, to look backwards with regret at opportunities not taken, rather than facing the uncertainties of the future with the hopes and expectations of the young.

They rode onwards, and after a further three weeks of careful travel found the place they sought. They would now wait for any sign of Maria's party. The position they had chosen was one that gave a panoramic view of the surrounding countryside. A small cave provided shelter from the hot sun, the wind and the rains, while there was a good supply of grass for the horses. They must be patient and alert to any danger, and stay hidden from hostile eyes. Both father and daughter settled down into a routine whereby one was on watch while the other slept, cared for the horses or prepared a meal. And so they waited.

CHAPTER FIFTY SIX

Rob and Maria had agreed on two things. They must now give details of the map to everyone present, and the group must make a bid to escape from the safety of the canyon. It was tempting to stay in the relative safety of where they were, but in reality their haven could soon become a trap. The purpose of holing up had been to rest themselves and their horses, and it had proved to be a good decision. It was time to move on. Rob explained the decision to leave. He then asked Maria to produce the map and for every member of the group to study it. There was great excitement at first as Esteban's document was eagerly viewed, but some of the more experienced men quickly realised that there were limitations in the directions given. Rob let the men discuss their disappointment before speaking.

"Nobody said that finding this gold was going to be easy. You've already fought off Indians, and will have to again before we can leave this place. Do you want to give up now?" There was a muted murmur at his words. "Most of you are good at reading sign, and have travelled long distances many times. There are numerous landmarks detailed in that map that will help us find what we are looking for, if we want it enough." He inwardly cringed at his words for he did not want the gold to be found, but equally he needed to move the party out of the canyon. Survival was the priority at present.

"Everyone take a good look at the map so that we know what we are looking for. Have a good feed this evening, because I plan for us to ride out of here at midnight come what may. Some Indians don't like fighting in the dark and we might just get away with it" There were no dissenting voices raised in response to his words, so he turned and went to tend his horse. Inwardly he gave a big sigh of relief, for the past few minutes had been crucial. If the men had not accepted his reasoning, but had rejected his assessment of their situation, it could have proved to be very nasty indeed. He was joined sometime later by Maria who had Esteban's map in her hand. She had accepted Rob's words at face value and was a little bit more confident that they would succeed in finding the gold.

"What will you do with your share Senor Rob?" she asked. He gave no reply immediately, but continued to groom his mount. After a few moments of silence he stopped what he was doing and turned to face her.

"Well Senora Maria, I think that if we get back to Boston in one piece, then I'll be full of thanks for whoever it is up there above who is looking out for me. If I have a pocket full of gold then that would be a real bonus. I'm a man who doesn't need much to keep me happy. As long as I can still see a fish rising in a clear mountain lake and hear the call of the geese flying overhead in their hundreds, then I guess that I'll be as contented as a man can be." His horse stamped his feet and snorted as though in agreement at his master's words. Maria shook her head in a mixture of exasperation and disbelief.

"You do not want to enjoy the good things in life?" She took a step backwards. "You do not want good clothes and to eat the very best of food and drink the finest wine?" Silence descended as she awaited a reply that was not forthcoming. Finally, with a stamp of her foot and a small gesture of annoyance with her hand, she left him alone.

Rob confided to his horse his relief at her leaving. Senora Maria was a beautiful woman, that was plain for all to see, but she made him uneasy. There was something about her that didn't sit right. He pushed these thoughts to one side, for he wanted to check his weapons then confer with the others as to how they were preparing for the departure at midnight.

It had gone surprisingly well to begin with. At midnight they had moved as quietly as possible through the narrow neck of the canyon, the dark walls on either side towering above them. A hoof struck stone and the sound seemed to be as loud as a gunshot. Surely they must be heard. They continued onward, the tiniest noise amplified by the tension within them as they edged their way carefully with only the light of the stars to aid them. Leather creaked and there was the occasional whisper of sound as some horse or rider rubbed against unseen brushwood. They were almost through and the opening widened before them. Without warning there was a pistol shot followed by another, leading to a desperate mad dash as horses and riders fled from the scene. The enraged cries from the Piankasha went unheard by the escaping band of gold hunters as Rob led them into the welcoming darkness.

They had been very lucky indeed. Some negligent brave had paid dearly for his failure to stay alert, for

Laidlaw had spotted him and his first shot had caught the warrior in the chest. His second shot was into the falling body of a brave who was trying to get out of the way of the lunging horses. The stampede continued for a few more miles before they slowed down and a quick head count was taken. Everyone was accounted for, with only a few minor scratches amongst them.

The cavalcade of men, one woman and their horses, continued at a steady pace through the darkness. Ahead lay the emptiness of the open plains. There was no hint of light from the absent moon, who had failed to overcome the dark heavy clouds that lay between him and the earth below. The next few hours were spent riding at a steady tiring trot on horseback, broken by a spell of walking by the riders to give some respite to their horses. They continued onwards, wanting to put miles between the Piankasha and themselves, but also seeking a place of concealment and safety. There was no way that they could hide the tracks left by their horses, but the hope was that the Indians would be less keen to follow them, for the travellers were now close to what Rob calculated was Sioux territory.

At last, just as dawn was breaking they came across a stand of aspen, which they bypassed and rode on into a meadow where a small shallow stream gurgled its way contentedly into the distance. They would stop here and rest. Lookouts were positioned to observe all directions from where they now found themselves. They had escaped the Piankasha for the moment, and without loss of life. For this they were thankful.

CHAPTER FIFTY SEVEN

Lone Wolf, the Sioux renegade and an outcast, was in a foul mood. He had woken that morning to find that the young Crow woman he had taken prisoner weeks earlier was dead. She had been disobedient during her brief captivity and he had beaten her half to death on two or three occasions. Last evening he had thrashed her for far too long and she had apparently bled to death during the night. It was an inconvenience he could have done without, for there was now no woman available to cook for him amongst his meagre band of followers. Next time he must take care, he promised himself, but he knew this would not happen. He liked to beat his women into submission before abusing them in any way that would satisfy his lust.

He looked around the camp where ten of his followers, all outcasts like himself, were watching the approach of a brave, Man Who Smiles, on a hard ridden pony. His name came about as the result of an accident when he was a very young boy, when he was kicked in the face by a mustang. He was permanently disfigured and his mouth was fixed in what resembled an ugly smile. Like all Lone Wolf's followers he was a man with no morals, only a heart full of hate. He pulled his pony to a sliding halt that kicked up a cloud of dust and stones, much to the annoyance of the others. There was a look of excitement in his eyes and he ignored the complaints of those around him as he stopped in front of Lone Wolf.

"The Gods have been good to us today," he exclaimed, "for I have discovered a band of Wasitchu camped not far from here. There are many horses and there is a woman with them!" His news caused a commotion amongst his companions, for this was great news indeed. Few of them had seen a white man before, and the news of a white woman being with the travellers whetted the warriors' appetite for an attack. Lone Wolf calmed his men down before he questioned Man Who Smiles about the numbers of Wasitchu and horses he had seen in their camp. Everyone present listened, intent on missing no detail of the reply.

"I counted this many men, and this many horses," he responded, showing five fingers then three fingers. "There were four on watch, each facing in a different direction. The ponies were together near the stream, and another two Wasitchu watched over them. None of the ponies were hobbled, only held within a rope corral." The listening warriors nodded at the words of Man Who Smiles, for this was good news. Guards on watch were at their most vulnerable when placed in an isolated position. Similarly, horses not hobbled, but tethered to a square of ropes, were much more easily stampeded. The Indian spent his early years learning how to steal horses, for this was a way to prove his ability to provide for his family. A good horse thief was a warrior who was highly respected by his fellow warriors.

Lone Wolf was many things, but he was no fool to go charging in without as much knowledge of the intended target as was possible. His disgrace after the attack on

Shouts Plenty and his family many seasons ago was a hard lesson that he had never forgotten. He motioned to Man Who Smiles and two others.

"Come with me and we will have another look at the Wasitchu. Meanwhile the rest of you make ready, for we will attack before dark once we have seen how they have placed their defences. Man Who Smiles has brought us the chance to take many scalps and ponies. If we plan this attack well we will be able to return to our people with proof that we are worthy to be accepted amongst them again." Within a few minutes the four warriors were mounted, and set off led by Man Who Smiles.

It was some time later, and the returning Lone Wolf felt confident that the planned attack on the Wasitchu encampment would succeed. The first phase of the assault would involve the removal of the four sentries. It was essential that this was done quietly and he selected eight of his force, in groups of two, for this task. Meanwhile, Lone Wolf and Man Who Smiles would kill the two men guarding the ponies, cut the ropes and stampede them away from the encampment. Once this was achieved the Indians would be able to reduce the number of the Wasitchu further, or, if resistance proved stronger than expected, to retreat and recover the stampeded ponies. Either outcome would be a great victory for the Indians. It was agreed, and they painted up for war, sang their songs, and then rode off towards the Wasitchu camp. They were confident that victory would be theirs, for the Gods had led Man Who Smiles to the place where the Wasitchu were camped. Their medicine was good and they were experienced in this kind of warfare. There were many scalps and ponies to be taken tonight. Lone Wolf also had his mind on the white woman and what he would do to her. He looked forward to what lay ahead.

—◦◦◦—

'Pawnee' Rob Ahern was the kind of man that others respected. If he gave his word then he would do his utmost to keep it. Very few of those who knew him could call him a friend, but those few who did had someone who would die for them in times of need. His upbringing was split between his happy years living with the Pawnee, and the less happy times being forced to attend school for two years to learn his alphabet. He lay on his bedroll looking upwards into the fading sun. It would be dark in an hour or so. There was much on his mind. Had they shaken off the Piankasha? Were they now in Sioux territory as he suspected? How could he persuade those with him that the search for Esteban's gold was a dream that was impossible to achieve? He rose from his bedroll. There was time for a quick check of the sentries before he caught some shuteye. He held his musket in one hand and his pistol was tucked into his belt. His first port of call was the horses, and he was pleased to note that both those on duty, Laidlaw and another man called Carter, were alert and challenged him before he got within ten yards of them. After a few minutes exchanging small talk he went to the first of the four sentries on the unmarked boundaries of the encampment. The hair on his neck stood up. His every instinct told him that something was wrong. He could see no sentry. He called softly for the guard to identify his whereabouts, but there was no answer. As he opened his mouth to raise the alarm two dark figures rose close by and rushed at him. Rob lowered his musket and fired into the belly of the nearest Indian. He dropped his weapon and grasped the wrist of the other attacker's hand that was holding a tomahawk. They grappled together and the hostile wrestled with Rob forcing him backwards to the ground. Still holding the Indian's wrist that held the tomahawk he head butted his assailant, who grunted as his nose broke and splattered blood over both of them. Rob followed this up with a fearful right hook to his attacker's jaw that knocked him out cold. Rob drew his knife and slit the Indian's throat. He would not attack anyone again.

All around the encampment were scenes of brutal hand to hand fighting that was terrifying to behold. The evening sun was casting long fingers of fading light, and in the glow the devilish death dances of attackers and defenders were illuminated as if a dreadful nightmare had come alive. Without warning all was still. The Indians had retreated. Two wounded attackers had been left behind and they were quickly dispatched to join their ancestors by a grim faced Rob. The defenders had not gone unscathed, for a quick check showed that there were few of them left unharmed. Maria, Laidlaw, Carter and Rob were the only survivors. Two of their men were missing, presumably the sentries who had been taken alive or killed. Two more were mortally wounded and would not last long. Thankfully eight of the horses had been prevented from stampeding due to Carter's efforts.

Rob wasted no time and ordered for the horses to be saddled up. The remaining survivors of the attack would leave now. He checked the two wounded men. One had died and the other was in the last stages of death. He could not risk leaving him to be found and tortured. As quickly as he could he finished the man off with a merciful thrust of his knife.

The four rode away into the gathering darkness. They would doubtless be trailed by the attackers come dawn. In the meantime they must get away as quickly as possible from the bloody scene they were now leaving behind them.

CHAPTER FIFTY EIGHT

James stood on watch while Fiona slept nearby. They had eaten earlier but he felt restless. He never tired of looking at the mountains, for ancient as they might be they were always changing in some small way. He listened as he looked around him and could identify the call of the nuthatches and the blue jay, a particular favourite of his, as the birds sought out a meal from the variety of insects on offer. Further away he could see an ever vigilant deer venturing into the edge of a meadow, tempted by the green grass that swayed in tune with the gentle breeze. Every so often the animal would lift his head, standing stock still, and look around for any sign of danger. Even as James watched, the deer turned and swiftly disappeared into the timber line of trees. The birds had also ceased to sing. Someone or something had caused alarm amongst the animals.

"Fiona, wake up, I think we are about to have company," he searched the surrounding area as he spoke, "I can hear horses coming closer." He crawled forward, musket in hand, and stared in astonishment, his eyes wide in disbelief at the sight below him. There were four riders, three white men and a woman! He could scarcely believe his eyes. The woman he recognized as Maria Cortez! James wasted no time in debating whether or not the riders were being pursued. It was obvious that their horses had been hard ridden, and one of the quartet lagged slightly behind the others, checking their back trail as he rode. James stood up and stepped forward into the open. He put his fingers to his mouth and gave out a long high pitched whistle. The three men below responded immediately by pulling up and searching for the source of the call. Maria meantime had continued to ride on, having failed to hear the signal from James. Carter rode after her, caught up, and turned the horses back to rejoin Rob and Laidlaw, who had seen James waving for them to join him. The tracks left by the eight horses would leave a trail that a half blind five year old Indian could follow, and Rob made no effort to erase signs of their passing before the group rode upwards to join James.

It was Laidlaw who spoke first for he recognized the man waiting for them.

"Mister McDonald it's been a long time since we last met, when you and your friend saved Captain Campbell and me from some unfriendly hostiles. Don't suppose you could do the same again do you?" He smiled grimly as he spoke. Turning in his saddle he motioned to the others. "I believe you may already know Senora Maria Cortez, this is Josh Carter and this gent is Rob Ahern." James helped bring the horses into cover before replying.

"Good to see you are still alive Laidlaw, let's hope it stays that way." He looked at Maria in annoyance. "You couldn't let it be Senora, despite my warnings. Gold is of no use to the dead, and you are now in Sioux country which is not good for the health of strangers." Fiona appeared with some cold food and water for the foursome. Rob could not take his eyes off her, and she smiled at him in return, before moving to a spot where she could watch for any sign of pursuit.

"My daughter will let us know if you have been followed Mister Ahern. In the meantime tell me what has happened so far. I am surprised that you allowed yourself to be caught up in this mess, for I have heard talk of you, and you are well thought of by people whose opinions I hold in high regard." He cocked a questioning eyebrow. Before Rob replied he told the two men with him to change the saddles to the spare horses, for they might have to move on at short notice. He sat down on a boulder, finished the last of the food that Fiona had given him, and began to talk. There were no excuses, only an honest explanation of his wish that the gold would not be discovered, and that no lives would be lost. He had hoped interest in the gold would fade if the source was never found. Esteban's map was greatly lacking in detail, and the chances of anyone finding the gold, if it even existed, were very slim. So far, he conceded, he had failed on all counts, for there had been a high loss of life and they were in a very tight corner even as they spoke. James was silent for a moment before he responded.

"The gold does exist. I know for I have been there. I will never tell of its location for it is a place sacred to both Fiona and me. My daughter and I are here because it was my foolishness that revealed that a map existed. This map, and a diary, belonging to Esteban Santara I gave to Maria Cortez. You need know no more than that." He looked away for a moment, and his thoughts returned to that fateful day when his wife and son were killed. If he had not insisted in searching for the gold they would still be alive. The torment of the memory was etched on his face, before he shook his head angrily and continued.

"The gold is tainted with blood. It is cursed and has brought death and misery to all who have searched for it. What we must do now is to escape the hostiles following you, and evade the Sioux who would love to take our scalps. It is my intention to head back east. The search for the gold is over. We now need to focus our efforts on getting away safely." Ahern nodded his agreement. The sooner they moved the better, for the renegades trailing them would not be far behind.

From a nearby hillside Lone Wolf and Man Who Smiles had watched the meeting take place between the four Wasitchu and the stranger. The renegades had been closer behind the four riders than Rob had thought. This territory was well known to the Indians, who had split into two groups soon after setting off in pursuit. They had established the direction that the Wasitchu were travelling, and were therefore able to calculate their likely destination if they continued on the same route. The renegades had knowledge of a short cut that would enable them to head off the fleeing escapers.

There was a puzzled look on Lone Wolf's face. Who was this man who had called to the Wasitchu? Was he alone? There was something familiar about him, but he could not recall where they might have met. He was uneasy, for he disliked not knowing more about this person who had suddenly appeared from nowhere. Man Who Smiles was impatient and wanted to close in for an attack. There were four warriors with them and six should be enough to take care of these Wasitchu. He had rarely seen his companion so unsure of himself. He frowned in frustration, for many horses and scalps were a major enticement for any young brave who wished to enhance his reputation. There was even a woman in the party, and Lone Wolf liked his women. To Man Who Smiles' relief his leader finally decided what they would do. Under cover of darkness they would approach the camp and take up their positions, ready to launch an attack first thing in the morning. Their medicine was good and they had already taken horses, scalps and weapons from the Wasitchu. Tomorrow would see them completing the task of wiping out the remnants of these interlopers. He smiled, more confident that the additional stranger would not stop their efforts. Then there was the woman to enjoy later when it was over. He was looking forward to that, very much.

—⁓—

James confessed his feeling of unease to Fiona. There was something amiss and he stepped into the surrounding darkness to listen. Earlier he had spoken to a chastened Maria who had experienced enough horror and death to give her sleepless nights until the day she died. Her hunger for the gold had gone. Life was precious and she wanted to keep hers for a long time to come.

Some among the group were asleep while others remained awake. No words were spoken, but his senses told him that there was a stirring in the night. There is no place that is totally still, even the most remote and lonely corners have movement of a kind. Were his senses playing tricks with his mind he wondered? He did not believe so, for this sensation was a warning of trouble that was increasing with each moment that passed. James stood a while longer before turning towards his bedroll. He almost collided with Ahern, who was also wide awake and his face, dim in the morning gloom, reflected his concern.

"You can feel it too?" he whispered to James. "Something is not right and I have a feeling that the hostiles are not far away." He moved towards the place where Laidlaw was guarding the horses. As he approached he could smell them!

"Indians!" he screamed and turned sideways to avoid a thrust from a lance in the hands of a silent renegade. Rob caught his attacker's hair in one hand and pulled his head down to meet his rising knee. It collided with a satisfying thud that tossed the unconscious Indian backwards. Shots were fired and the screams and shouts mingled in a mad melee that erupted in a fusion of hatred, fear and bloodlust. It was Fiona who recognised that one of the attackers was Lone Wolf, the leader of those who had murdered her mother and her brother. She faced him and his eyes widened in surprise before he gave an evil smile. Now he remembered who the Wasitchu was he had seen earlier, and this woman was his daughter. They would pay for the disgrace that they had brought to his lodge.

"You will be mine this time my pretty one. I promise that you will suffer enough to beg me to end your life." He advanced, knife hand extended, a tomahawk in the other. "This is the axe I killed your mother with" he taunted. "I will use it to kill you once I have had my fill of you." He struck without warning and his knife blade caught her on the top of her arm. She clenched her teeth against the pain and she felt fear, for this man was dangerous. He came forward again, his body poised to strike at the first opening in her guard. In desperation she called out in Sioux.

"Strike father, kill him!" For a moment Lone Wolf hesitated, unsure if there was danger behind him. It was then that she struck, driving her knife into his body with all her strength. She stepped backwards and watched his face as he realized that he was dying.

"For my mother and my brother," she whispered and moving forward placed a pistol under his chin and pulled the trigger.

Within a few minutes it was all over. The hostiles had fled leaving six dead behind them. Sadly both Laidlaw and Carter had also perished in the fight.

They must leave this place now, for the musket shots would have been heard far afield and others would be coming to investigate. Their two dead companions were hastily buried in a small hollow that they filled with rocks. Some of the extra horses were turned loose before the remaining four riders, each with a spare horse in tow, rode away from the scene of death.

CHAPTER FIFTY NINE

It was a fine warm mid morning in Barcelona and Peter Lloyd had risen later than was his normal practice. A business meeting held the previous evening had prevented him from getting home before midnight, and he had enjoyed the luxury of a few extra hours in bed. The sounds of the daily hustle and bustle of the city filtered into the cool apartments where he and his wife resided. Consuella sat on a chair in the corner of the room, a smile on her lips as she watched her husband. He was behaving in a slightly guilty manner, like a school boy who had decided to play truant. As she began to tease her husband they were interrupted by a loud knocking on their front door. The voice of their manservant Manuel Jamon, and that of at least one other person could be heard in urgent discussion. This was followed by the sound of hurried footsteps, before an excited Manuel entered the room clutching a large envelope that was covered with seals.

"Sir," he blurted out, "It is a despatch for you delivered by two Royal Couriers of the King himself! They await your reply." Peter reached for the document and opened it, his mind in a daze. What could this possibly mean? He read aloud.

"His Royal Highness The King, Charles III of Spain, requests the company of his loyal subject, Senor Peter

Lloyd, to attend the ceremony of the Presentation of Credentials to the Royal Court, by Ambassador John Jay of the United States of America." There followed a stunned silence before Manuel reminded his master that the Royal Couriers awaited his answer. Peter paused only to kiss his wife before leaving the room and descending the stairs to where the two officers waited patiently. The senior of the two saluted smartly and introduced himself and his companion.

Peter had regained some of his composure on the way to join them, and offered some refreshment. The officers declined politely, for they had further tasks to complete before returning to Madrid. Peter thanked them for conveying the message to him from The King, and confirmed his acceptance with suitable humility. The duo saluted and took their leave. Peter returned upstairs to join Consuella.

"This is indeed a great honour for you Peter, you have every reason to feel proud."

"Indeed I am, although I remain unclear why this invitation has been extended, for I know naught of John Jay. It is a mystery to me." He scratched his head as he spoke and re-read the letter in full. "I note that I am to arrive early for the Ceremony in order that I can meet beforehand with The King's personal adviser, Philippe, Duc de Carano." Peter became increasingly worried as he sought to identify the implications behind the invitation. It was, he mused to himself, an order to attend rather than an invitation. He must put in an appearance and let the fingers of fate play their little games.

It was eight sleepless nights later that Peter was ushered into the private chambers of the Duc de Carano at the Royal Palace in Madrid. There were two men present in the room, and one rose and moved towards him, offering a handshake as he did so.

"Thank you very much for coming Senor Lloyd. I am Phillipe, El Duc de Carano, welcome to my humble quarters. This gentleman is Ambassador John Jay of the United States of America." The latter rose from his chair and exchanged a handshake. The men had sat down for no more than a few seconds before a servant appeared with three fine crystal glasses of chilled Madeira. Once they had a glass of wine to hand the Duc proposed a toast.

"Gentlemen, I propose a toast to The United States of America and to Spain. May they enjoy eternal friendship." There passed a few moments of small talk before John Jay spoke.

"If it helps ease any concerns you may have about me Senor Lloyd, I have been instructed to pass on to you and Senora Lloyd the very best wishes of General Washington. It appears that you and he had more than a few discussions when you were over there." He gently knocked the ash from a cheroot he was smoking before continuing. "Tell me, are you still in contact with that MP friend of yours in Westminster?" Alarm bells sounded in Peter's head. He needed to be careful. He knew that both men were watching him closely. This was no time to be evasive, but to speak honestly about his actions.

"Sir, as I explained to General Washington during our talks, my letters to my friend Edmunde Burke, an MP at Westminster, were to supply him, and others who wished for peace, with reasons why Britain and the Colonies should avoid war. There were no military secrets passed, only the application of common sense to show the wasted opportunities to both sides and, I confess, to the loss of potential trading opportunities between the Colonies and my adopted nation Spain." Peter sipped from his glass. "I also reminded the General that he was known to correspond regularly with relatives of his in Yorkshire. Would he too qualify to be suspected of being a spy?" he asked with a smile. Ambassador Jay responded with a laugh.

"Well said sir. The General warned me that you were more than capable of holding your own." The Duc intervened at this point, and laid his glass down before speaking.

"What I now say must remain in this room. I would inform you Ambassador that Senor Lloyd has proved to be a most valued friend to Spain. We too have received numerous informative reports during his time in the Colonies. There was nothing of military value, but rather proposals for trading partnerships between our two great nations. General Washington will doubtless become your first President once the war is finally at an end. Senor Lloyd is an honourable and trustworthy gentleman who has earned my complete trust. Who better to enable our two nations to have open and honest discussions regarding the forming of a strong trading alliance?" Ambassador Jay nodded his agreement.

"Mine is not the only American Ambassadorial appointment to Europe. I can tell you in confidence that France and The Nederlands will soon be receiving Ambassadors Silas Deane and Benjamin Franklin. These two nations, and of course Spain, declared war on the British when hostilities broke out. Your support will never be forgotten. There are exciting times ahead gentlemen. We can move forward as never before. Many barriers between nations can be broken down, if not completely then in part." He rose. "I must ready myself for the ceremony gentlemen. It has been a pleasure." He shook hands with both the Duc and Peter before taking his leave. The door had no sooner closed before the Duc spoke.

"Peter, may I call you Peter? I have a little news for you that you might find of interest. I received a letter many months ago from our mutual friend Pedro Palacio. He died before I could assist him. Spanish politics are ever variable and I was not in the position of strength I now enjoy. The court decision to nullify the inheritance of Senora Maria Cortez was a disgraceful one, but one that was supported by powerful friends of her son Hernando. That same young man has been less than discreet in his liaisons with the wife of a most influential and unforgiving nobleman. This gentleman has heard whispers of his wife's indiscretions and is more than a little annoyed." The Duc drained his glass before he continued.

"Two days ago I obtained the handwritten statement of a priest, a Father Tomas, who swears that he witnessed the consummation of the marriage between Don Philippe Cortez and Maria Cortez on their wedding night. The verbal and unsupported claims that she was pregnant by another man at that time are unproven and incidental. I have already lodged an appeal in the courts and am assured that it will be successful. You may wish to convey this news to your friend Senora Cortez who I believe is still in Boston." He smiled. "I am always available to help a friend whenever I can. Now I too must prepare for the ceremony." He shook hands with Peter and left.

The rest of the day flew passed in a blur of pomp and ceremony. Countless people shook his hand and seemed very keen to meet this man who was held in such high regard by so many. At last, however, Peter was able to take his leave and rode overnight in order that he could impart the Duc's good news to Consuella. He must waste no time in writing to Maria, for he had not heard from her in some time. He would also write to Andrew McDougall and Douglas McDonald asking of her whereabouts. Her fortunes had changed dramatically and she now had the world at her feet. She must be found and Peter prayed to a God that he tended to neglect except when in times of great need. Let her be safe and well he begged, but was God listening?

CHAPTER SIXTY

James lay on the edge of a knoll, eyes searching for any sign of pursuit. Nearby, Fiona was quietly preparing some food while Rob Ahern, who had stood the previous watch, was catching up on some sleep. Maria sat on her bedroll, Esteban's diary clutched tightly to her chest while she rocked gently to some tune that she hummed to herself. She was becoming a major concern to the others, for her mental state was deteriorating with each passing day. There were moments when she was perfectly lucid, but for the rest of the time she spoke in Spanish to an imaginary group of friends from a previous life. It appeared to the others that she was losing her mind.

James continued to scrutinise the surrounding area. A gentle east wind rippled the long grass in waves across the meadow, the movement orchestrated by an invisible hand. The morning sun provided the first warm kiss of the day and lay upon the scene like a lover's caress. Such beauty, and yet such great danger, existing side by side in the wilderness. James was in a pensive mood, and silently acknowledged that when a traveller ventures into lands such as this, everything appears larger and more vibrant when faced by the vast openness of the prairies and the breathtaking mountains. A man would have to be devoid of emotion not to feel the sense of freedom such views could generate within his soul.

"The food is ready father. I will keep lookout while you eat." Fiona's quiet voice interrupted his thoughts, and he nodded his agreement. Rob had also sat up at the mention of food, although what was on offer was poor fare indeed. The two men exchanged a few whispered words, for sound travelled over distance in this kind of terrain. Maria continued to hum to herself and disregarded the words from James encouraging her to eat. When they had finished their meagre meal Rob rose to check on the horses. They had a plentiful supply of wild buffalo grass growing nearby, and a small natural well provided a limited but fresh source of water.

The increasing heat from the sun above discouraged even the most aggressive insects from lingering too long. The fine tuning that warns the experienced traveller of minute changes to the sounds of the surrounding wildlife alerted James and Rob, even before Fiona spoke.

"We are in trouble. There are Indians gathering below." The braves, about thirty in number, were forming up in a line facing where the group of four lay. One warrior, clearly a chief, moved forward some twenty feet in front of the group. He reined in his pony, thrust his feather bedecked lance into the ground, then slid from his mount and sat down, cross legged, arms folded across his chest. Fiona spoke first.

"Father, it is Potaka of The People. You were unconscious when he saved our lives, but I am certain that it is him."

"He clearly wishes to talk. I will ride down and meet with him. Rob, you keep a bead on him. If there is any trickery be sure you send him to the land of his forebears." As he mounted up, he noticed that Fiona was also astride her pony. Before he could protest, she waved aside his objection to her joining the pow wow with Potaka.

"He knows me father and my presence shows peaceful intent. No warrior would knowingly take his daughter into danger." She kicked her pony into movement, leaving James no option but to follow.

They approached the Sioux chief at a trot and reined in some four yards from where he sat. Before dismounting, James addressed Potaka in fluent Sioux.

"It is good to see that my old hunting companion has prospered over the seasons. My heart is pleased."

The chief motioned for James to dismount and sit. This James did, while Fiona moved to position herself behind and to the left of her father. She kneeled, for no decent woman ever sat cross legged in the company of men. Potaka decided there had been enough pleasantries exchanged.

"The seasons have been kind to Shouts Plenty. Why have you come to the land of The People? Why did you seek out the yellow metal?" His face remained impassive as he awaited an answer.

"Many seasons ago when I left The People with my wife and child I did so because I feared for their safety. My visions of the threat from the Wasitchu were not welcomed by many. We travelled far to the land of our friends the Nez Pierce who met us with open arms. My son was born and there was much happiness in our hearts. My children were of mixed blood and, in the eyes of some, are regarded as being inferior. This thinking also exists amongst the Wasitchu." Potaka's eyes never left James, who took a deep breath and continued.

"It was always my intention to return to the world of the Wasitchu, for I believed that my wife and children would enjoy a better future than if they remained here. My beliefs have not changed since I spoke to The People about the multitudes of Wasitchu who will one day invade these lands. If the Indian tribes, even the Crow," he spat as he said their name, "are to survive then they must change their way of life." James paused, expecting a question, but the chief remained silent.

"I had persuaded my wife and two children that we should return to the place that I left to come to these lands. I had friends there who would help us to settle and learn how to live as they did. The yellow metal is highly valued amongst the Wasitchu, and I wanted to take some of it with us to enable us to barter for things we would need in our new life. The search for the yellow metal led us to the place where my wife and son were killed. My daughter Shining Star and I would also have perished had you not arrived in time to save us. My greed was the cause of the loss of my wife and son. My purpose in life now is to see my daughter properly provided for before I die." The pain on James' face was clear to see, and the honesty of his words touched Potaka, although he gave no sign of this.

"Your daughter is a woman full grown. I will take her as one of my wives and ensure that she never grows hungry, and produces many fine warriors." James was taken by surprise and frantically sought for a response that would not cause offence. It was Fiona who spoke.

"Chief Potaka does me a great honour and I am grateful. My heart however belongs to another who rides with us. He loves me and will marry me soon, although he doesn't know it yet," she added coyly. Potaka laughed at her words while James regarded his daughter with astonishment.

The chief studied James for a moment before he voiced his thoughts.

"Your concerns for Shining Star are clearly unjustified, for she has already arranged her own future." He continued, a deep thoughtful look on his face. "The seasons have come and gone since Shouts Plenty left the lodges of The People. The thinking of some amongst us has undergone a change and we have opened our minds to the words of Shouts Plenty before he left us. Stories have come to our world telling of the experiences of our distant brothers in the east. They tell of disease, lies and how the Wasitchu wishes to own land. This 'ownership' is foreign to our way of life. Many of the things you spoke of are being confirmed by the whispers we have heard. Our thinking is split. Some cannot accept that there are enough Wasitchu to defeat The People, who are fearsome warriors. Others like me wish to learn more of these people from one who knows them. I extend this invitation to you Shouts Plenty. Come and live in our lodges. I personally guarantee your safety."

"Potaka is a wise leader of his people. I thank you for your offer and I will think upon it. Before I decide however, I must return the woman who is with us to her people, for they do not know where she is and will be greatly concerned. Once this is done I will await my future son in law, who does not yet know he is marrying my daughter, to contact me and ask for my permission." He smiled at his daughter as he spoke the last few words. The pow wow was over. Potaka removed his head-dress and gave it to James.

"If you return wear this. It will protect you from attack, and you will be guided safely to my lodge" The chief mounted his pony and rode off without a backward glance. His warriors followed, and within a few moments only the fading sound of retreating hooves, and some minor dust stirred up by the horses, gave any sign of what had gone before.

CHAPTER SIXTY ONE

Cameron sat on a tiny bed, his only light generated by a small candle that barely penetrated the evening gloom. The months since his capture had dragged by with no sign of the promised exchange of prisoners taking place. He and ten other officers were being held in a partially destroyed farmhouse, and had been warned by the surly guards that any attempt to escape would result in every one of them being shot. Exercise was minimal and the food provided was barely enough to survive on.

Cameron rubbed his injured leg. It remained painful but was improving with time. He grimaced, for he was aware that his soldiering days were over. He was no longer able to move freely, and would require the use of a cane for the rest of his life. He sighed, close to despair. He had only received two letters in the ten months since his capture. The first was from his father Ewan in Scotland, urging him to return home to take over the role of Chieftain of the Clan McDonald. A bad fall from his horse had resulted in his father being paralysed from the neck downwards. Cameron's leadership was badly needed at home and he was urged to return as soon as possible.

The other correspondence he had received was from Anne, who had written a cheerful and loving letter, full of optimism that they would soon be together again. She had promised that she would write as often as possible, but no other letters reached him. He was deeply concerned that something terrible had happened to her, and the fear gnawed away at his soul like a rat at a bloated carcass. His black mood was interrupted by the sound of voices and approaching footsteps. There was the rattle of a lock being opened, and then the door swung inwards and the bright light from the guard's lantern flooded the room.

Cameron shielded his eyes from the glare and could make out the outline of a tall figure who had stepped into the small space available. His eyes adjusted to the light, and he was astounded to realise that his visitor was none other than General George Washington! Cameron struggled to get to his feet but was held down by a restraining hand.

"Sit Captain, your efforts to rise could well undo the fine work of my surgeons. It would be a pity, and inconvenient, if you were to die now." He pulled a battered wooden stool closer and sat down. No words were exchanged as the two men eyed each other in silence.

"The actions of you and your men caused me and my army considerable irritation during the months you were raiding our stores and supply lines. I should have you shot, but there is no doubt that your soldiers were skilled and resolute and well led." There was sadness in the General's eyes as he spoke and there was a further lengthy pause before he continued.

"You will be unaware that your wife's grandfather, my dear friend General Hugh Mercer, has died from wounds received in battle against the British. He was more than just a friend, for he was also one of my most capable generals. Although a surgeon to trade he had a keen military brain in his head and he used it well."

He rose as he spoke, pacing the tiny room in three strides. "I am subject to much ridicule by those who dislike my 'Attack and retreat' tactics. They would rather I march my men into the field to face a force that is well drilled in such methods of warfare. However, General Mercer always encouraged the use of evasive tactics, and to fight only at a time and place of our own choosing. He reminded me that a great Scottish warrior, Robert The Bruce, used these same tactics against the English to good effect." He paused to clear his throat before continuing." The British and their allies have suffered two crushing defeats recently, and I am confident that the conflict will soon be at an end." The lantern hissed in the small room and the flickering light betrayed the tears in the General's eyes.

"Tomorrow you and your fellow officers will be taken to Boston harbour and an exchange of prisoners will take place. Admiral Sir John McLean will be in attendance aboard his flagship 'The Albion' to convey those released back to England. I am pleased to inform you that your wife Anne is already aboard and will accompany you on the voyage. I wish you both a safe journey and a long and prosperous life together." Before Cameron could utter a word, the General had turned and left the room. The enormity of what he had been told began to sink in. He was going home and Anne would be with him! His heart lifted and he was overwhelmed with joy as he let his tears flow freely. Tomorrow his life would begin again!

—◊—

The journey to Boston began early the following morning and did not take long to complete. The location of the farmhouse where the prisoners had been held was less than twenty miles from the port area. The exchange of prisoners was a muted affair with the minimum of military rituals involved. Each of the British personnel being released had to sign a document stating that they had been well treated and that they would never again take up arms against the American Colonies. When this was completed the freed men were ushered aboard the waiting Flagship. 'The Albion' was being made ready to set sail within the hour. At the top of the gangway Cameron was taken to one side by the ship's first officer.

"Follow me please Captain, the Admiral has requested your company in his quarters." Cameron followed as asked and was ushered into the Admiral's spacious accommodation. It was gloomy inside after the bright sunshine on deck, and he took a few seconds for his eyes to adjust. A voice spoke softly. It was Anne!

"Hello my darling Cameron. I have prayed for this day," she stepped forward as she spoke and threw herself into his arms.

The Admiral had only listened outside his quarters long enough to confirm that the young couple were together again. It would be a lengthy voyage before 'The Albion' reached Liverpool. He smiled grimly, for he had already lost a war at sea, the further loss of his quarters for the duration of the crossing was of little consequence.

Chapter Sixty Two

The journey to the land of the Pawnee was a long and arduous one lasting six months, and the four travellers twice avoided ambush by their skill and a large slice of luck. Night camps were chosen with particular care. It was vital to find a suitable place to build a fire that could not be seen, and in a location where surrounding shrubbery would spread the smoke from the flames. There was the constant need to avoid any careless movement of riders and horses that would result in being skylined, and therefore more exposed to discovery by watching hostiles. Bodies and minds were stretched to breaking point. Lack of proper sleep took its toll and, at times, angry words were exchanged over petty issues.

Finally, as the first snowflakes of the coming winter fell upon them, 'Pawnee' Rob Ahern gestured towards a group of hills that lay ahead and to the right of the route they were travelling. He assured his companions that the Pawnee winter camp would be somewhere nearby. Even as he spoke a band of curious braves approached them on horseback at speed. The leader recognised Rob and there followed a great deal of friendly insults before the two groups rode towards the camp.

It was a great source of pride to the Pawnee that visitors were treated with courtesy. Within a short period of time Rob was accommodated with an uncle of his, whilst a lodge was provided for James, Fiona and Maria. A constant line of visitors brought food, pots, and blankets for the comfort of the visitors. James and Fiona made a point of thanking this generosity in sign language while trying to remember names, a task that proved to be almost impossible.

Rob dropped by carrying a haunch of deer, and in no time at all the four companions had enjoyed a hearty, hot and tasty meal cooked by Fiona. The talk then turned to what preparations were needed to enable them to be self sufficient throughout the coming winter months. Rob took charge of the planning at this point, and suggested to each in turn, excluding Maria, what they should do in regards to food, proper cold weather clothing, and provision of the care of their horses.

In the weeks that followed much progress was made, even to the extent that James became friends with a warrior, ages with himself, who had been badly injured by a bear. Aptly named Bear Claw, the injured man was more concerned for his daughter, White Dove, than his own circumstances. The pretty maiden felt unable to encourage courtship by a youthful warrior, Black Pony. Bear Claw was ashamed, for it was clear that his daughter loved the young brave, but would not consider marriage while her father was unable to provide for his wife and daughter due to his injury. James suggested a compromise solution that would help both fathers, and the courtship of their daughters.

"Bear Claw, let White Dove come to live in my lodge. She would help my daughter with her daily tasks and provide care for Maria who has been touched by the Gods. More importantly, both maidens would be able to receive suitors in my lodge, even when I am away, for each would watch over the other and proper etiquette maintained. It might also speed things up a bit." Both men were pleased with the plan.

"I would also undertake to provide food for your lodge throughout the months of the snow, as payment for White Dove's work in my lodge." Bear Claw was not naive and realised that the offer from James had been made in such a way as to save the warrior any embarrassment. He grunted his grateful agreement.

It was true that Maria was becoming more and more of a problem, for she required to be watched wherever she went. The Pawnee were no different from other tribes in that anyone who had been 'Touched by the Gods' was treated gently and with great tolerance. With the winter approaching it was important that Maria was not allowed to stray too far from the camp, for the cold months were a time of hunger for many of the dangerous beasts that roamed the surrounding area. It was a sad sight to watch Maria sitting clutching Esteban's diary, her shoulders hunched as she hummed a tuneless dirge and swayed from side to side.

The arrangements agreed between the two fathers proved to be as effective as planned. James was free to hunt for food throughout the winter months, and still had time to enjoy some male companionship with his friend Bear Claw. The various courtships between Fiona and Rob, and White Dove and Black Pony continued with enthusiasm, although James became impatient that the couples seemed no nearer to agreeing to marry than before. Bear Claw smiled at his friend and advised that these things took time. After all, the Pawnee warrior pointed out, he was almost able to walk and ride a pony again. This was a sign that things happened, even if we did not notice them at that moment.

The winter months came and went, as they had for as long as man could remember. A warm breeze entered into the fray, and some of the icicles hanging from the surrounding trees started to melt. The Chinook had arrived, the Indian name for the warm winds from the far mountains that heralded the coming of spring. Bear Claw surprised James by asking if he could sit in his friend James' lodge that morning. James was puzzled by the request but agreed. Shortly after Bear Claw's arrival James was aware that small groups of the villagers were gathering outside his tepee. James turned to Fiona and White Dove who were seated at the rear of the lodge. For the first time he noticed that both were decked out in their finest clothes.

"It is time my friend," chortled Bear Claw amused by James' surprise, "the young men will now come calling. Let us sit outside and watch the suitors squirm under the gaze of these two terrible fathers!"

The proceedings took place under the watchful eyes of young and old alike, who gathered to watch this important event unfold. A nervous Rob produced six ponies and as fine a buffalo robe that James had ever seen. He had been advised earlier by Bear Claw to ignore the first gifts offered, to show mild interest in the second gifts offered, and to put the young man out of his misery by accepting the third offer. The acceptance by James of the gifts presented by Rob met with a great delighted cry, and some impromtu singing, by the watching villagers. James sat back contented that the marriage between Fiona and Rob would finally take place. The joy in his daughter's face proved beyond doubt that his decision had been the correct one.

The next proposal of marriage between White Dove and Black Bear followed the same pattern as the previous one. The villagers were no less enthusiastic during the proceedings, for two in one day was a rare treat indeed!

Things moved on swiftly from that day, and the wedding arrangements were put into place with the ease and efficiency brought about by years of practice within the Pawnee community. James began to realise that he would see less of his daughter. Her heart belonged to a young man, a better man than he could possibly have hoped for. He should be happy for her, but privately conceded that he was aware that he was losing the last member of his family, although in much happier circumstances than the loss of his wife and son.

CHAPTER SIXTY THREE

The wedding ceremonies had taken place earlier in the day and the young couples had retired to their specially prepared lodges. It had been a long day, full of dancing, singing and various sporting events to enable the young men to show off their prowess at riding, wrestling, and other skills with the bow and arrow. James was tired but content. He had retreated to his tent, where Maria had been cared for by an elderly Indian woman during the festivities. He thanked the woman, who smiled and left.

The sound of singing continued into the night and James felt himself relax. As on most nights, his thoughts turned to his wife and the many happy times they had shared. He remembered the warmth of her body and the comfort of her arms, where he would lie both safe and content.

The warm breath upon his face stirred him from his sleep. The hot lips upon him awoke a desire within him that he had not felt in years. His hands touched her naked flesh once again and he held her tightly to him. His need for her rose into an all consuming desire, an inferno raging within his very soul. She was with him again! He would never let her go! She whispered in his ear as he prepared to take her.

"I love you Esteban." James recoiled in horror. What nightmare was this? The naked woman who lay beside him was Maria! With a cry of revulsion at his conduct he pushed her roughly to one side. He felt sick at what he had nearly allowed himself to do. Picking up his coat he staggered from the lodge and sought sanctuary amongst the stand of aspen that stood some way off from the village.

Maria was in torment, and her damaged mind could not grasp what had taken place. Esteban, her one true love had just rejected her in the cruellest of ways. She had wanted to give herself to him but he had pushed her to one side. He no longer loved her! She staggered from the lodge, still naked, carrying only Esteban's diary with her. Where was she to go now? Her tortured mind provided no answer. She stumbled on through the crisp snow and was halted only by some movement ahead. She was about to die but did not know it, for the creature facing her was a huge ravenous grizzly bear that had gone in search of food. Mercifully Maria did not feel the blow that killed her, and she fell to the frozen ground before the beast started to feast on her flesh. The diary had fallen from her hand, and the loose pages fluttered into the evening sky. As Maria ceased to live, so too did her lover's diary disintegrate into nothingness.

It was the following morning before what remained of Maria was discovered. James was beside himself with guilt and unable to come to terms with the events leading up to her death. He brooded for weeks afterwards, and Fiona could not get him to discuss his feelings with her. He spent many lonely hours on the hills, before he informed Fiona and Rob that he had decided to take up Potaka's offer and return to The People. Perhaps he could help them understand better how the Wasitchu regarded the Indian and their way of life. Anyway, he was determined to leave and made his preparations accordingly.

It was the morning of his departure and he solemnly shook Rob's hand. No words were exchanged between them. The hardest part came when he tried, but failed, to explain his need to get away to a distraught Fiona.

"My love for you will always be out there, in the wind and the whispers of the long grasses. Reach out for me and you will find me." He smiled and held her close before mounting up and riding off westwards. When he reached the last piece of high ground before he would disappear from view, he stopped his horse and waved once, and then he was gone.

Fiona let her tears fall unchecked as Rob put a comforting arm around her. Despite her father's words she knew he would never return. He was gone forever. She placed her head on her husband's shoulder and sighed deeply. Her father had taught her to always remember to look back over the way she had travelled, but never to forget that looking ahead was more fulfilling. She had a husband and a life together to look forward to now, although she knew in quieter moments she would look back and remember.

Epilogue

Bear Claw had ridden for over twelve sunsets before he found the place he was seeking. He looked down upon the neat ranch building, noting the care and attention that had been given for the provision of running water and sweet grasses for the horses. He had been told that Rob Ahern and his wife Fiona had settled here some years ago and were breeding top horses for the more discerning rider. As he drew nearer he saw some young colts racing around a fenced in area that was situated close to the house. They were very good animals, and the promise of speed and stamina was already showing in their juvenile frames. He called out as he neared the ranch, just to make sure that his presence was known to those inside. He was after all a bit long in the tooth to have his head shot off by some fool who had never seen a real live Indian before.

The front door opened and he recognised both Rob and Fiona instantly. Neither had changed much, although the young child that trotted along behind them would be a recent addition to the family. Rob greeted Bear Claw in fluent Pawnee. Fiona picked up her son while the visitor carefully dismounted. His injuries had healed reasonably well over the years, but there was still stiffness in his joints.

Once the formal pleasantries had been exchanged, Rob introduced his son, Barry James Ahern, to the

Pawnee warrior. The boy had been named after his two grandfathers.

"He is in his third year of life and is into all kinds of mischief." Rob hesitated for a moment. "Bear Claw, old friend, I sense that you are here for a purpose other than a social visit." In response the Indian produced a medicine belt and laid it on the ground. The markings showed the belt belonged to a warrior of The People. Fiona's eyes widened.

"That was my father's belt. The fact that you have it means he is dead." The Indian's silence confirmed this to be true.

"The belt came to me by various means. The Indian who brought it was of the Sioux nation and claimed to be on a sacred journey to return this belt to the daughter of a great warrior who was no longer of this world. This warrior gave his life to save a woman of The People, who was heavy with child and who was attacked by a mountain lion. The warrior killed the lion with his knife, but was badly injured. The day before he died the woman gave birth to a girl. The mother asked the warrior to name the child, for his sacrifice had given her life. He did so and then went to meet the Great Spirit in the sky."

Bear Claw carefully opened the belt that contained two pistols, a lock of Little Bird's hair and a small bracelet that a young Shining Star had made as a present for her father. There were also two tiny bootees that belonged to the child whose life he had saved.

The Pawnee politely refused numerous offers of hospitality and rose to leave, for he had far to travel and did not wish to linger. He mounted up, bade them farewell and turned to go.

"Wait Bear Claw," Fiona pleaded, "tell me, what is the child's name?" The warrior gave a knowing smile as his pony started off, and his reply could just be heard over the sound of his horse's hooves.

"She is named Shining Star," he called out, and then he was gone.

About the author

Leslie was born in Glasgow, the youngest of four children. After leaving school at fifteen he worked locally, before joining the Army in 1962.

During the next 26 years he served in a variety of locations and attained the rank of Major, before leaving to work for the Royal College of Surgeons of Edinburgh.

After 16 years at the College he and his wife retired to Crieff in Perthshire, where they are enjoying a full and busy retirement.

Esteban's Gold is Leslie's second novel.